UNDERSTANDING
COLSON WHITEHEAD

UNDERSTANDING CONTEMPORARY AMERICAN LITERATURE
Matthew J. Bruccoli, Founding Editor
Linda Wagner-Martin, Series Editor

Also of Interest

Understanding Chang-Rae Lee, Amanda M. Page
Understanding David Foster Wallace, Marshall Boswell
Understanding Gary Shteyngart, Geoff Hamilton
Understanding Karen Tei Yamashita, Jolie Scheffer
Understanding James Baldwin, Marc Dudley
Understanding Jonathan Lethem, Matthew Luter
Understanding Marge Piercy, Donna M. Bickford
Understanding Randall Kenan, James A. Crank
Understanding Stewart O'Nan, Heike Paul
Understanding William T. Vollmann, Işıl Özcan

UNDERSTANDING

COLSON
WHITEHEAD

Revised and Expanded Edition

Derek C. Maus

THE UNIVERSITY OF
SOUTH CAROLINA PRESS

© 2021 University of South Carolina

Published by the University of South Carolina Press
Columbia, South Carolina 29208

www.uscpress.com

Manufactured in the United States of America

30 29 28 27 26 25 24 23 22
10 9 8 7 6 5 4 3 2

Library of Congress Cataloging-in-Publication Data
can be found at http://catalog.loc.gov/.

ISBN 978-1-64336-173-4 (hardback)
ISBN 978-1-64336-174-1 (paperback)
ISBN 978-1-64336-175-8 (ebook)

For Gogol

CONTENTS

SERIES EDITOR'S PREFACE

The Understanding Contemporary American Literature series was founded by the estimable Matthew J. Bruccoli (1931–2008), who envisioned these volumes as guides or companions for students as well as good nonacademic readers, a legacy that will continue as new volumes are developed to fill in gaps among the nearly one hundred series volumes published to date and to embrace a host of new writers only now making their marks on our literature.

As Professor Bruccoli explained in his preface to the volumes he edited, because much influential contemporary literature makes special demands, "the word *understanding* in the titles was chosen deliberately. Many willing readers lack an adequate understanding of how contemporary literature works; that is, of what the author is attempting to express and the means by which it is conveyed." Aimed at fostering this understanding of good literature and good writers, the criticism and analysis in the series provide instruction in how to read certain contemporary writers—explicating their material, language, structures, themes, and perspectives—and facilitate a more profitable experience of the works under discussion.

In the twenty-first century Professor Bruccoli's prescience gives us an avenue to publish expert critiques of significant contemporary American writing. The series continues to map the literary landscape and to provide both instruction and enjoyment. Future volumes will seek to introduce new voices alongside canonized favorites, to chronicle the changing literature of our times, and to remain, as Professor Bruccoli conceived, contemporary in the best sense of the word.

Linda Wagner-Martin, Series Editor

CHAPTER 1

Understanding Colson Whitehead

Perhaps it should come as no surprise that the career of an author whose first novel focused on a power struggle between rival groups of elevator inspectors would develop in eccentric ways. As of 2020, Colson Whitehead has published seven idiosyncratic novels, a collection of nonfictional essays about his native New York, and a memoir about playing in the 2011 World Series of Poker. Over the course of the two-plus decades during which he has become one of the foremost figures in twenty-first-century American literature, he has deliberately avoided repeating either the forms or subjects of his books. Whitehead has always walked a fine line between avant-garde experimentalism and formulaic popular fiction, fusing aspects of each into hybrids that run the risk of underwhelming devotees of the former and overwhelming fans of the latter.

It would not, however, be accurate to say that Whitehead's work defies categorization; in fact, his relationship to literary categories—that is, genres and subgenres—is quite strong and explicit throughout his work, whether in the film-noir undertones of *The Intuitionist,* the zombie-apocalypse plot structure of *Zone One,* or the fusion of alternate history and slave narrative in *The Underground Railroad.* Whitehead intentionally flirts with genres and their conventions by first suggesting and subsequently frustrating the easy interpretations they appear to offer to both writers and readers. Whitehead discussed how his novel *Sag Harbor* exemplified his approach to literary genres in a 2013 interview with Nikesh Shukla: "That novel is my take on a traditionally realist genre, the coming of age novel. I was wearing realist drag in the same way that I have worn detective drag or horror drag in my other books" (102). The "wearing drag" metaphor drives home the point that Whitehead's works take on the superficial appearance of particular literary genres but stop short of conforming entirely with their storytelling formulas: "By avoiding certain expectations of plot and a certain kind of narrative satisfaction I'm doing my own kind of version of [a given genre]" (Shukla 102). He made it clear that playing with expectations not only defines his approach toward an individual work but also forms part of a conscious strategy to test his artistic limits from one book to the next:

> I think I just don't want to do the same thing over and over again, so on one level each book becomes an antidote to the one [that] came before. . . . And that allows me to just challenge myself: can I do a book that has less plot?; can I learn the rules of a horror novel, and adapt it to my own concerns about the world?; can I do a coming of age novel that doesn't remind me of all the stuff I hate about coming of age novels? So I'm trying to keep it fresh for me. I'm just trying to not bore myself. And if I can do a detective novel, and if I can do a horror novel, then why do it again? To keep the work challenging I have to keep moving. (Shukla 100)

An overview of Whitehead's life and career highlights some of the twists and turns to which his efforts to keep the work challenging and to keep moving have led.

Colson Whitehead was born Arch Colson Chipp Whitehead in New York City on November 6, 1969, the third of four children of Arch S. Whitehead and Mary Anne Woody Whitehead. His father had a lengthy career as an executive search and research consultant, founding his own consulting company—which his wife helped run—after being rebuffed by other agencies because of his race and despite his Dartmouth undergraduate education ("Obituaries"). As Howard Rambsy has noted, aspects of the elder Whitehead's biography recur in the father of Lila Mae Watson, the protagonist of Whitehead's first novel ("Four"). Whitehead lived in Manhattan throughout his youth and attended the esteemed Trinity School on the Upper West Side. Whitehead spent many of the summers of his childhood and adolescence in the predominantly African American section of Sag Harbor in the Hamptons area of eastern Long Island and would eventually mine this experience for his fourth novel. He has reminisced about his childhood in numerous interviews, emphasizing the ways his avid consumption of popular culture stimulated his artistic curiosity: 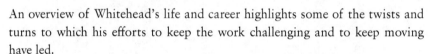 "I grew up watching B-movies, horror movies, science fiction movies, reading a lot of horror comics, Stephen King, H. P. Lovecraft, and it was those different influences that made me want to write in the first place. You know, if you're a writer, you can stay at home and think up weird crap, so it seemed like a good job when I was a kid" (Sky).

Whitehead attended Harvard University in Cambridge, Massachusetts, from 1987 until 1991, graduating with a degree in English literature. In a 2003 address at his alma mater, he recollected his career there as one in which he "turned his papers in late, sat in the back of his classes and 'didn't say anything'" (Bernstein). Nevertheless, he has also singled out particulars from his time in Cambridge as instrumental to his future career as a writer: "There weren't a lot of twentieth-century fiction classes, just the classics. So I spent a lot of time going to the library to look up Ishmael Reed and Thomas Pynchon. Harvard has a really cool drama program with the American Repertory Theatre, so I took a lot of postmodern drama classes. I got this absurdist theater training, which, you know, comes out periodically in different things" (Sherman 17).

Upon graduating, Whitehead returned to New York and began his formal writing career as a freelancer and occasional music, book, and television critic for the *Village Voice*. He described this formative period—during which he wrote the manuscript for "a satirical novel about the adult life of a 'Gary Coleman-like former sitcom star'" (Zalewski 8) that was rejected by twenty publishers—in a 2008 interview with Linda Selzer:

> I grew up in New York City and was a big fan of *The Village Voice*. In high school and college it was my dream to be one of these interdisciplinary critics they had there at the time, merging the so-called high and low, talking about Derrida one day and Grandmaster Flash the next. Ah, youth. I was pretty excited when I started working for the *Voice*'s book section and began writing for different parts of the paper. But I knew I wanted to write fiction eventually. Writing for an audience, getting my voice down, and supporting myself by my work gave me the confidence to start writing fiction. The freelance lifestyle gave me the time I needed. ("New" 395–96)

In 1996 he began work on the novel that would eventually become *The Intuitionist*, inspired by the odd combination of a televised news story about defective escalators and his reading of works by three prominent authors of detective fiction: "I read James Ellroy and Walter Mosley and Elmore Leonard. When I hit upon this idea of making a jokey detective novel about elevator inspectors, I was really drawing from this neo-noir tradition" (Kachka). Upon its publication in 1999, the novel garnered widespread critical accolades and was named a finalist for the Hemingway Foundation/PEN Award for debut fiction.

Whitehead followed up this initial success in 2001 with *John Henry Days*, a novel about a subject that had been percolating in his mind since elementary school, when he first became intrigued "by the idea of this black superhero. I hadn't seen that before" (Zalewski 8). Having encountered John Henry in myriad forms throughout his life, Whitehead said that he "was waiting until I got to a point where I thought I could do the story justice. I wanted to approach

John Henry as a man, not as some mythical figure born with a steel hammer in his hand" (Zalewski 8). The novel received the Anisfield-Wolf Book Award (which recognizes exemplary literary works dealing with racism and cultural diversity) in 2002 and was a finalist for the Pulitzer Prize, the National Book Critics Circle Award, and the *Los Angeles Times* Book Prize. As a result of the promise shown by his early work, Whitehead received both a Whiting Award in Fiction in 2000 and a MacArthur Fellowship (colloquially called a "Genius Grant") in 2002. These awards allowed him to focus on his literary writing exclusively, although he has continued to publish occasional essays on literature, sports, and pop culture in such venues as the *New York Times* and the *Grantland* website.

Whitehead ventured into nonfiction for his third book, *The Colossus of New York: A City in Thirteen Parts,* which was published in 2003. This work originated as an experiment with a series of "impressionistic portraits of key New York places and states of being" (Selzer, "New" 400). In the wake of the September 11, 2001, terrorist attacks, Whitehead adapted thirteen of these essays into a book as part of his personal effort "to figure out how to live in a place that had been so injured" (399). *Colossus of New York* again earned Whitehead substantial critical praise, even though its structural and intellectual complexity likely rebuffed many potential mainstream readers. Both of those trends continued as Whitehead returned to fiction in 2006 with *Apex Hides the Hurt.* Although somewhat less lauded than his previous efforts, his third novel tells the story of an anonymous "nomenclature consultant" (essentially a marketing specialist whose sole function is to think up the ideal names for new products) who has been hired to mediate a dispute among several parties involving the name of a small city. The book uses dark satirical comedy to examine the interconnections among history, race, and identity, as well as looking at the role language plays in forming and revising—for better or worse—those interconnected relationships.

Whitehead began markedly widening his audience with the publication of *Sag Harbor* in 2009. He has repeatedly noted that although his own family spent much of the summer in Sag Harbor during the time period (the mid-1980s) in which the book is set, its autobiographical aspect is only superficial: "I tend not to act or feel or talk in a way that would add anything worthwhile to an extended work of fiction. I tend not to do things that lend themselves to dramatic unity, aesthetic harmony, and narrative discharge. My leitmotifs are crappy. I need an editor or someone of artistic bent to shape my useless existence into something that would interest other people. Also, I am a real person" (Treisman). Nevertheless, the novel's critical and commercial success—it was the first of Whitehead's books to crack the *New York Times* best-seller list on its hard-cover release—suggests that he accomplished his goal of creating a broadly sympathetic cast of characters by fictionally repurposing his first- and second-hand experiences as a teenager in the age of Run-DMC and New Coke: "I was going to dive into all that grisly and gruesome adolescent muck and try not to gag—if I didn't, the reader wouldn't see their own horrible squirming existence in Benji's existence. Once I was up to my chin, it was easy to be truthful about other things—things I had experienced myself and could transform into something that would serve the story, and things I have witnessed in other people's lives" (Holt). The novel was a finalist for both the PEN/Faulkner Award for Fiction and the Hurston/Wright Legacy Award in 2009.

Using numerous elements of the well-established genre of zombie fiction, *Zone One* is perhaps Whitehead's most immediately recognizable foray into a popular storytelling formula. Unsurprisingly, he is deeply familiar with the genre's conventions: "I wrote *Zone One* because I wanted to fulfill my own curiosity—which goes back decades—about the creatures. . . . I became demonically attached to *Night of the Living Dead, Dawn of the Dead,* and *Day of the Dead,* the first George Romero trilogy. *Zone One* comes out of me trying to work through some of my ideas about why, for me personally, zombies are scary" (Fassler). Whitehead emphasized that he is not simply paying tribute to this pedigree but also altering it: "You take what you want from a genre, deform it, steal from it, pay homage, and at the same time, if you're doing it right, you are extending the possibilities of that genre, reinvigorating it. I wanted to be true to a Romero-style version of existential zombie dread, but of course the fun part of being a writer is making up shit" (Madrigal). Whitehead's summation of the place *Zone One* occupies in his body of work reiterates his comment about using genre as a form of "drag": "It's one of my books, not a zombie book. I've had the same publisher for six books, and they know it's not just about elevator inspectors, it's not just about zombies—it's about people, it's about culture. I'm lucky that they know that, no matter what the one-sentence description is, it's completely false" (Fassler). *Zone One* proved to be Whitehead's most commercially successful book to date, debuting at number sixteen on the *New York Times* best-seller list in November 2011; like *Sag Harbor* it was a finalist for the Hurston/Wright Legacy Award.

The end of Whitehead's first marriage served as the emotional backdrop to his next book. *The Noble Hustle: Poker, Beef Jerky, and Death* grew out of a commission from the now-defunct *Grantland.com* website, which subsequently also sent him as a correspondent to the 2012 London Summer Olympics. *Grantland* paid Whitehead's entry fee into the 2011 World Series of Poker (WSOP) tournament; in return, he produced a four-article series titled "Occasional Dispatches from the Republic of Anhedonia," which recounted his preparation for and participation in the WSOP amidst the stresses resulting from his divorce and the concurrent onset of single parenthood. Upon the republication of an expanded version of these essays as a book in 2014, the critical response was comparatively lukewarm, exemplified by Dwight Garner's opinion that "nothing much is at stake" and that Whitehead might even be "half embarrassed to be writing it" despite being "such a gifted writer . . . that he nearly pulls this all off" (C23). As of 2020 it remains the only one of Whitehead's books not to be discussed at length in any published critical work (a condition this volume will not remedy).

Whitehead's reemergence from this difficult stretch is extraordinary. Not only did he remarry and become a father again (he has a daughter with his first wife and a son with his second wife), but the runaway success of his next two books raised him into the highest echelon of contemporary literary authors.

Whitehead indicated in numerous interviews that—as was true of *John Henry Days*—the central conceit of *The Underground Railroad* had long been forming in his mind: "I had the idea sixteen years ago and didn't feel ready. I came up with the premise of exploring that childhood notion that the underground railroad is an actual subway. I kept putting it off. I didn't want to tackle the enormity of slavery. I didn't feel emotionally ready and I didn't feel mature enough as a person. As a writer, it seemed very daunting. Every couple years, I'd go back to my notes and think, 'Am I ready?' and the answer was always, 'No.' But finally, about two years ago, it seemed I was afraid of doing this book and it was time to confront why and just take the plunge" (Mochama 143). Although he cites several historians—and their books—on the novel's acknowledgments page, Whitehead has repeatedly noted that first-hand testimonies collected by the Federal Writers' Project during the Great Depression proved invaluable to his preparatory research: "[T]he main thing was just reading the words of former slaves themselves. There are the big famous slave narratives by Frederick Douglass and Harriet Jacobs, but in order to get people back to work, the government in the 1930s hired writers to interview former slaves. We're talking 80-year-old and 90-year-old people who had been in bondage when they were kids and teenagers, and that provided a real variety of slave experiences for me to draw upon" (Harrison 110–11). The novel was originally slated for publication in September 2016. However, when Oprah Winfrey selected it for the relaunch of her popular book club, its release was moved forward by a month. This change also allowed it to appear on President Barack Obama's "summer reading list" for 2016 (Garunay). Furthermore, the book's hastened publication was accompanied by a 16,000-word broadsheet excerpt in the Sunday, August 7, 2016, edition of the *New York Times*. Buoyed by this massive publicity, the novel immediately became a bestseller and remained one well into the following year. *The Underground Railroad* earned Whitehead the Pulitzer Prize, the National Book Award, the Andrew Carnegie Medal, and the Arthur C. Clarke Award. Oscar-winning director Barry Jenkins signed on to direct a miniseries based on the novel that is slated to air on Amazon's online streaming service in 2021.

After more than a year of international publicity tours for *The Underground Railroad,* Whitehead turned to his next project, one that moved him still further from genre-fiction. *The Nickel Boys* is primarily a work of historical fiction set during the Jim Crow era. It depicts the horrendous abuse perpetrated on the young men confined in the Nickel Academy, a fictionalized version of the notorious Arthur G. Dozier School for Boys in the Florida Panhandle. As Whitehead explained in an interview, the novel also speaks to how the prevailing attitudes of local and national authorities engendered decades of willful disregard toward the school's institutionalized (and frequently lethal) cruelty, particularly toward its Black students: "It is a story . . . about how powerful people get away with abusing the powerless and are never called to account. . . . In the Dozier School, you had the actual abusers . . . but you also have a system wherein all those in positions of power looked the other way. The Florida government didn't follow through with an investigation, they didn't fire the corrupt superintendent or the corrupt director. Instead, they let them stay in their jobs even though people were getting killed or disappeared" (O'Hagan).

As had been the case with *The Underground Railroad,* the publication of *The Nickel Boys* was accompanied by fanfare that confirmed Whitehead's status as "one of the greatest American writers alive" (Jackson 48). Whitehead was featured as "America's Storyteller" on the cover of the July 8, 2019, issue of *TIME* magazine, and fellow novelist Mitchell S. Jackson's lengthy profile included both an overview of Whitehead's career and a far-reaching interview. Although Jackson rightly noted that "[e]xplorations of race and history have been a through line from his early work," he also maintained that "Whitehead's two most recent novels stand apart in that they most directly satisfy a mandate set out by W.E.B. Du Bois, co-founder of the NAACP, for black writers to create work in service of justice" (48). Whitehead won the Pulitzer Prize again for *The Nickel Boys,* making him only the fourth novelist ever to have won it twice and the first to have done so with consecutive books. It also won the Kirkus Prize for fiction and was nominated and/or a finalist for several other major literary awards. In 2020, he became the youngest-ever recipient—at the age of fifty—of the Library of Congress Prize for American Fiction, a lifetime achievement award honoring both virtuosity and inventiveness.

Whitehead indicated in a July 2019 interview that he had begun working on "a crime story set in the '60s, and it isn't as bleak, as it deals with class as opposed to race. Class in America is a ruthless machinery that can be as terrible as the institutional monstrosities I'm describing in the last two novels. That's there, but the jokes are there too. . . . Writing about the '60s in New York is exciting" (Arjini). On July 15, 2020, he announced on his Twitter feed—@colsonwhitehead—that this novel will be titled *Harlem Shuffle,* and it will be published in the fall of 2021.

Whitehead and Historiographic Metafiction

Unifying Whitehead's output is challenging for a number of reasons: the diversity of his subjects, settings, narrative voices, and styles; his sweeping command of both popular culture and literary history; and his oft-stated resistance to overarching concepts (i.e., the very things that might serve as unifying principles). In a 2009 essay titled "Picking a Genre," Whitehead offers a mildly satirical commentary on the supposed categorical choices that a contemporary novelist faces. He not only critiques aspects of the publishing industry but also gently mocks previous critical attempts at defining his work:

> I recently published a novel, and now it's time to get back to work. If you're anything like me, figuring out what to write next can be a real hassle. A flashy and experimental brain-bender, or a pointillist examination of the dissolution of a typical American family? Generation-spanning doorstopper or claustrophobic psychological sketch? Buncha novellas with a minor character in common? To make things easier, I modified my dartboard a few years ago. Now, when I'm overwhelmed by the untold stories out there, I head down to the basement, throw a dart and see where it lands. Try it for yourself! (23)

Some of the options on his presumably imaginary dartboard are self-effacingly comic—for example, "Simply add -ist to any oddball or unlikely root word, and run with it. You'd be surprised"—but there are also numerous outward-facing barbs.

For example, Whitehead remarks that the encyclopedic novel suits the "postmodern, or postmodern-curious" because of "the beauty of the postmodern —it's not what it is, it's what you say it is." Likewise he invites "Africans in America" to explore the "Southern Novel of Black Misery" (with clichéd titles such as "I'll Love You Till the Gravy Runs Out and Then I'm Gonna Lick Out the Skillet" and "Sore Bunions on a Dusty Road"). He defines the contours of this genre as follows: "Slip on your sepia-tinted goggles and investigate the legacy of slavery that still reverberates to this day, the legacy of Reconstruction that still reverberates to this day, and crackers" ("Picking" 23). Although its satire is generally mild, the piece nevertheless provides abundant insight into the sources and nature of Whitehead's resistance to labeling.

Whitehead has repeatedly stated that "literary theory is great for discussing literature, but hasn't been much help in writing the stuff" (Selzer, "New" 398). Although he bristles at "being pigeon-holed, ghettoized, held in a different category [from] other authors" (Shukla 99), I believe that there is nevertheless value in examining his works through a pair of critical concepts—historiographic metafiction and the postsoul aesthetic—which both allow for (or possibly even demand) great diversity of expression while still meaningfully clustering groups of authors and their works according to common artistic and rhetorical techniques in the first instance and a particular generational zeitgeist in the second. Each concept places Whitehead's books in a broader interpretive context without constraining their potential meanings. Also, both are critical discourses that are not so arcane as to require a highly specialized vocabulary—beyond the names of the terms themselves—or an advanced degree in literary analysis to understand. Finally each honors and even seeks meaning in the various forms of indeterminacy that Whitehead consciously builds into his texts. Numerous scholars have applied one or the other of these approaches to individual works by Whitehead—for example, Michael Bérubé states that *The Intuitionist* "skirt[s] the edge of preposterousness while crafting yet one more elaboration on . . . 'historiographic metafiction'" (164), while Jesse S. Cohn analyzes *Apex Hides the Hurt* in terms of the Oedipal symbolism of its "postsoul condition" (20)—but none have yet combined them, much less used that combination to consider Whitehead's entire output. Fusing the interpretive "lenses" of historiographic metafiction and the postsoul aesthetic emphasizes a recurrent feature of Whitehead's prose: parodic and also generally satirical commentary on the processes by which contemporary Americans—especially, but far from exclusively, African Americans—construct, maintain, and reinforce various aspects of both their individual and collective identities.

In her groundbreaking study *A Poetics of Postmodernism* (1988), Linda Hutcheon coined the term "historiographic metafiction," isolating a distinctive quality she found in an extensive subset of contemporary fiction. Her terminology derives from the fact that the works she examines are simultaneously historiographic (meaning that they look critically at the ways in which histories have been and are written) and metafictional (meaning that they openly call attention to their own status as constructed works of fiction): "Such novels both install and then blur the line between fiction and history. This kind of generic blurring has been a feature of literature since the classical epic and the Bible . . . but the simultaneous and overt assertion and crossing of boundaries is more postmodern" (113). Hutcheon observes that works of historiographic metafiction break down the presumed distinction between an inherently objective, factual rendering (history) and a playful, "made-up" version (fiction); instead, both are explained as alternate ways to "re-write or to re-present the past" (110). She also contends that historiographic metafictions expose their own "constructed, imposed nature of . . . meaning" (112) to draw attention to how and why "history itself depends on conventions of narrative, language, and ideology [and not just raw, objective facts] in order to present an account of 'what really happened'" (Mazurek, qtd. in Hutcheon 112). Such an approach invites deeper scrutiny of the processes through which particular historical "truths" have become fundamental assumptions within a culture or society. Hutcheon argues—and, based on his public comments, it seems likely Whitehead would agree—that such scrutiny is not always a hostile or revolutionary act. Instead, it reminds the reader that such guiding historical narratives are neither produced nor perpetuated by accident, but rather through selective processes that depend on factors such as political power, socioeconomic privilege, and relative access to education, among others.

Madelyn Jablon and Darryl Dickson-Carr expand the applicability of Hutcheon's concept by contextualizing Whitehead's use of parody and satire, respectively, within both American and African American literary lineages. Jablon's *Black Metafiction: Self-Consciousness in African American Literature* (1997) combines critical discussions of metafiction with a range of contemporary arguments about the African American literary tradition's distinctiveness. Jablon performs a complex balancing act, articulating a critical methodology that acknowledges and values the characteristics of African American literary expression while employing a critical terminology—that is, metafiction—that was initially formulated with almost no reference to either African or African American cultural traditions. For example, she noted that Black metafictionists transcend the inherent narcissism of the almost exclusively White group of authors studied by previous scholars of metafiction. They do so by making a racially distinct sense of literary ancestry an integral part of their self-consciousness: "These writers seem to advise that it is better to find out who you are by looking into the eyes of others than into the eyes in the mirror. Better yet, find out who you are by looking at the people you came from and listening to their stories. The black metafictionist refuses to be trapped by the gaze. The narcissism that serves as a cornerstone in Linda Hutcheon's theory fails to explain self-consciousness in black texts. . . . Black metafiction constructs its own reading of self-consciousness" (54). This self-consciousness is important not only because it provides a retrospective cultural basis for identity (in other words, knowing "the people you came from") but also because it offers a forward-looking impulse for aesthetic, personal, and societal transformation. Whitehead has repeatedly suggested that both processes are of great importance to him: "I feel like I'm trying to face black literature, I'm trying to extend the canon of black literature and I'm a black writer doing this" ("Eavesdropping" 5).

Jablon argues that this impulse to revisit the past while also refreshing the present (and thereby the prospects for the future) is what is distinctive about the use of parody—a literary technique that uses intentional imitation of existing forms, mostly, but not exclusively, for comic effect—by Black metafictionists such as Whitehead: "Rather than view it as a desperate effort to keep a dying art form alive, many black metafictionists view parody as a pause in the continual metamorphosis of a work. . . . While white metafictionists are preoccupied with the novel's obsolescence at 'the end of the road,' black metafictionists envision mutating forms and limitless possibility" (30–31). In this way Black metafiction does not just reveal how and why a text (and its author) exists as it does in a given moment but also places that revelation into a longer (and ongoing) cultural–textual history that is significantly—but no longer exclusively—influenced by race.

Dickson-Carr's *African American Satire: The Sacredly Profane Novel* (2001) adds to the discussion by accentuating the presence of satire—a moral or ethical critique accomplished by pointing out the folly, absurdity, or duplicity of a person, idea, or behavior—in the African American literary tradition. Satire often overlaps with parody as a way of conveying a particular meaning within a literary text, but the terms are not synonymous, despite often being used so incorrectly. Dickson-Carr provides an indispensable history of satire's role in African American expressions of dissent:

> It is when African American satire utilizes the broad rhetorical trope of irony that it has the distinct advantage of being an excellent tool for those wishing to speak the otherwise unspeakable; it is the primary tool of the iconoclast. In African American literature the voice of the satirist is often sorely needed (though not always heeded) to provide the critiques of his or her community that might otherwise be elided. These critiques are especially useful when we consider the adverse conditions under which African Americans live now. Satire can expose the fallacies within popularly accepted schools of thought to push African Americans forward to improve their liminal, physical, and economic conditions. (18)

This critical approach helps explain how Whitehead's use of genre "drag" entails not only a formal parody of literary conventions he feels are overly limiting or hackneyed but also a pointed ethical criticism of simplistic, outdated, or otherwise damaging notions that are reinforced through such conventional thinking and writing (i.e., "the fallacies within popularly accepted schools of thought").

Distinguishing between modal and generic forms of satire is crucial in considering Whitehead's body of work. Generic conceptions of satire treat it as a specific literary form, akin to the coming-of-age novel, the Petrarchan sonnet, or the fairy tale. For example, a work in the European fairy-tale genre is recognizable because of familiar tropes: a youthful protagonist leaving home for an unknown place, abductions and rescues, transformations of characters from animals to humans. Tropes are literary devices of plot, characterization, setting, or storytelling technique that reliably convey particular connotations beyond just their literal meaning; for example, starting a story with "Once upon a time" leads to a series of associative expectations about its subsequent development and meaning—among others, that it will end with "and they lived happily ever after"—for anyone even dimly familiar with fairy tales. Until recently, satires were primarily characterized by the use of specific conventions, usually ones that appeared in works by classical models such as the Greek playwright Aristophanes or the Roman poet Horace. For example, satires frequently unmask—literally or figuratively—a duplicitous character (as in Molière's *Tartuffe* or Gogol's *The Government Inspector*) or reveal the flaws in an idea by depicting its application on a broad scale (as in the various societies depicted in Jonathan Swift's *Gulliver's Travels*). Within such a generic definition, a work is recognizable as a satire primarily due to its distinctive building blocks.

When defined instead in modal terms, satire functions not as a genre of its own but rather as a "passenger" that comments ironically on conventional elements of the "vehicle" of another recognizable genre. Internet memes that alter the original meaning of an image with superimposed text that mocks either the original image or some other related target are a familiar twenty-first-century example of modal satire. Literary examples include Mark Twain's novel, *A Connecticut Yankee in King Arthur's Court* (1889), a parodic imitation of the Arthurian romance genre, which much of Twain's readership would have known well. It satirizes not only the importation of the genre's inherent chivalric values into Twain's present but also the hypercapitalist values of the late nineteenth-century United States that Hank Morgan, the novel's protagonist, retroactively introduces into Camelot. Modal satire functions like adjectives in English grammar, modifying an existing thing that otherwise has a different meaning (e.g., a "mad dog" is importantly distinct from a "dog").

Numerous commentators have classified specific works by Whitehead—most often, *Apex Hides the Hurt* (cf. Jackson 48)—as generic satires.

Whitehead himself seems to have had such a genre-based definition in mind when he insisted that *The Underground Railroad* "[i]s not a satire," despite close correspondences with an eighteenth-century model: "Once I thought about making each state its own place with its own set of rules, the first analogy for me was *Gulliver's Travels*. I'm not a *Gulliver's Travels* fanatic, but . . . I think it's a good structure" (Harrison 114). Nevertheless, other scholars have illustrated how a modal understanding—essentially, interpreting a work (or a portion thereof) as "satirical" rather than as "a satire"—is more useful than a generic one in considering Whitehead's output. For example, Steven Weisenburger's modal approach helps explain Whitehead's transformative play with genre conventions as one tactic within a broader strategy of metafictional satirical subversion: "[S]atire is stuck with the very simulacra of the knowledge it so distrusts—stories. This is why the satirist often turns metafictionist and parodist, seeking out 'intramural' and self-referring ways of striking at the aesthetic rules hemming us in." He adds that this mode transcends or perhaps even contradicts earlier definitions of satire: "[D]egenerative satire is realist narration backlit by fantastic outrage. . . . [W]hat I call satire is not simply 'the ridiculing of human vices and follies in order to correct them,' as countless textbooks and critical studies would have us understand" (5–6).

Although the book in which Weisenburger formulated this concept focused predominantly on White American postmodernist authors from the 1960s and 1970s, his definition of "degenerative" modal satire meshes well with the aforementioned ideas of Jablon and Dickson-Carr as well as more recent scholarship by Ramón Saldívar and Yogita Goyal. Weisenburger isolates a "problem facing any African-American satirist" while analyzing works by Chester Himes, Charles Wright, and Ishmael Reed: "[H]ow to put across a contrary 'knowledge' [when it] . . . can only be written in the language of hegemonic culture [that] . . . already encodes every quality of oppression the writer might oppose[?]" (156). In discussing *The Intuitionist* as "a novel that falls into a mixed set of genres . . . part urban thriller, part alternate history, part fantasy meditation on race, technology, and the imagination, all filtered through the visionary metaphor of 'elevation'" (7–8), Saldívar echoes Weisenburger's synthesis of realism and fantastic outrage in arguing that Whitehead's novel expresses

> something of a completely different order of comedy. . . . Decidedly not postmodern parody, satire, or play, then, but the double-edged sharpness of the racial joke drives the narrative. . . . Whitehead's joke is double-edged because it is the kind of joke that turns you on your head even as you laugh at its implied violence because you can never be certain that perhaps

laughter is exactly the wrong response to the joke. In fact, it is probably more accurate to say that *The Intuitionist* takes us through the tragic arc of the racialized joke to the limits of postmodern satire and parody, into a new kind of realism. (11–12)

Goyal explicitly cites Weisenburger (112) in surveying a set of contemporary works by African American novelists that depict "the historical scene of slavery in the mode of satire" (13–14). Analyzing *The Underground Railroad* alongside Mat Johnson's *Pym* (2011) and Paul Beatty's *The Sellout* (2015), Goyal contends that Whitehead intertwines meticulously realistic historical fiction with "a speculative register" as part of a "deliberately fantastical strategy [that] challenges the conceit of the rational apprehension of slavery today as well as a visceral identification with the slave ancestor" (132). She concludes that "Whitehead mines the speculative power of racial allegory to disturb . . . both fable and history, thus joining (and extending) the efforts of Johnson and Beatty to corrode any comfortable revival of slavery today" (140).

Even though most of his works direct some satirical criticism toward the status quo they depict, Whitehead's scrutiny has rarely, if ever, resulted in a specific prescription for change. He adamantly maintained that even *The Nickel Boys,* perhaps his least abstracted commentary on American society, "isn't a didactic directive. . . . Hopefully the readers can come to their own conclusions about what I'm laying out there" (Arjini). Whitehead's novels end with ambiguous or even incomplete resolutions that confound readers who are searching for concrete instructions about what to think or how to act, another trait that Hutcheon identified as particular to postmodernism in general and historiographic metafiction in particular: "Postmodernist discourses . . . need the very myths and conventions they contest and reduce; they do not necessarily come to terms with either order or disorder, but question both in terms of each other. The myths and conventions exist for a reason, and postmodernism investigates that reason. The postmodern impulse is not to seek any total vision. It merely questions. If it *finds* such a vision, it questions how, in fact, it *made* it" (48, italics in original). Weisenburger's "degenerative" satirical mode is similar in not only critiquing discernible external targets, but also "function[ing] to subvert hierarchies of value and to reflect suspiciously on all ways of making meaning, including its own" (3).

When Selzer asked Whitehead whether the ending of *Apex Hides the Hurt* "suggests . . . that [the protagonist] becomes more hopeful about the ability of words to push through the hype and uncover the hurt," his playfully noncommittal answer parallels Hutcheon's assertion about not coming to terms with either order or disorder: "That sounds almost hopeful. There's probably evidence to back up that hope. Also evidence that undercuts it. In my own life, I try to hope that the world will improve. That various things will get better. Whether or not I put that in my books is a different matter" ("New" 399). William Ramsey further illuminates Whitehead's approach:

> [He] plays ironically and wittily with contemporary constructions of truth. Choosing not to counter a totalizing master narrative with an alternative, black micronarrative, he exposes all history as suspicious text. . . . Whitehead's irony does have a vitally progressive potential—namely its radical tendency toward openness, not fixity. In the following passage he describes John Henry at work with other railroad men, while dismissing any historical myth we might attach to the scene: "Behind him the other workers are bent over the track, small and human compared to the black titan in the foreground. Building the country mile by mile. This is the forging of a nation. This is some real hokey shit" [*John Henry Days* 40]. Captivity to all "hokey" or false narratives is what Whitehead determinedly resists. (783)

Whitehead's body of work becomes a quilt-like commentary on the various fragments of the past that have been preserved as "historical myth[s]" for the present. The contexts and plots for this project range from the abstractly universal (the allegorical rivalry between factions of elevator inspectors in *The Intuitionist*), through the national (the constant [re]contextualization and [re]appropriation of the story of one Black man's resistance in *John Henry Days;* the lasting reverberations of slavery and other forms of institutionalized racial discrimination in *The Underground Railroad* and *The Nickel Boys*), and down to the local (the dispute over the renaming of a town in *Apex Hides the Hurt;* the seeming collective consciousness of New Yorkers in *The Colossus of New York;* the tenuous identity of the Black upper-middle class in *Sag Harbor;* and the attempts to restore Manhattan to some semblance of its previous state in *Zone One*).

According to Hutcheon, historiographic metafiction's "theoretical self-awareness of history and fiction as human constructs . . . is made the grounds for its rethinking and reworking of the forms and contents of the past" (5). In almost all of his books—*The Noble Hustle* being perhaps the only exception—Whitehead has reproduced innumerable "forms and contents of the past" to survey their origins and to determine whether they need to be reaffirmed, revised, or abandoned. Whitehead, like historiographic metafictionists generally, is "willing to draw upon any signifying practices [he] can find operative in a society. [He wants] to challenge those discourses and yet to use them, even to milk them for all they are worth" (Hutcheon 133). Whitehead "is an especially versatile and productive cultural cataloguer" (Ramsby, *Bad* 100), filling his novels with scraps and fragments—in some cases real and in others parodic imitations—of all manner of cultural artifacts, including song lyrics, advertising slogans, philosophical tracts, journalistic accounts, local histories, oral histories, letters, television programs, folktales, museum exhibits, newsletters, emails, runaway slave bulletins, online message-board postings, overheard conversations, and civic ceremonies. All of these fictionalized artifacts reverberate with received notions; exposing the ways in which such "stories" are established, transmitted, maintained, and manipulated remains a constant in Whitehead's writing from *The Intuitionist* through *The Nickel Boys*.

Whitehead and the Postsoul Condition

Most of Whitehead's major characters occupy an uncomfortable space between belonging to and being outcasts from the societies in which they live. As such, they themselves become another kind of cultural artifact through their awareness of, comments on, and frequent resistance to the roles they are expected to play, generally (though not exclusively) in terms of the intersectional categories of gender, class, and race. Many of Whitehead's protagonists are noteworthy for their relationship to "the postsoul condition," a concept developed through a lengthy dialogue about individual and collective identity within African American intellectual culture.

In *Soul Babies: Black Popular Culture and the Post-Soul Aesthetic* (2002), Mark Anthony Neal argues that there is a significant generational difference in worldview between African Americans who came of age before and during the massive cultural upheaval in American society of the 1960s and those who succeeded them. Neal claims that African Americans "born after the early successes of the traditional civil rights movement are in fact divorced from the nostalgia associated with those successes and thus positioned to critically engage the movement's legacy from a state of objectivity that the traditional civil rights leadership is both unwilling and incapable of doing" (103). This legacy (and the concurrent nostalgia for it) has often been culturally linked with the word "soul" in a manner that supposedly encapsulates the entirety of Black experience, not just in terms of social and political movements but also in terms of artistic representations of those movements' values. Nelson George, who coined the term "post-soul" in his book, *Buppies, B-Boys, Baps and Bohos: Notes on Post-Soul Black Culture* (1992), discusses how his conception of the word influenced the effort to rename a popular music chart:

> At *Billboard* magazine in 1982, I pushed to update the title of the "Soul" chart. Prince wasn't soul, nor was Kurtis Blow, or Run-D.M.C. The direction of black music, one of the truest reflectors of our culture, had changed

profoundly, as it always does. After much discussion, the chart was renamed "Black," which outraged many white retailers and black musicmakers. Too ethnic. Too limiting. Too damn black. Where "soul" was once universally accepted, the new era had yielded no new all-purpose catchphrase for the black mood. . . . This diversity said a lot about the new African American mentality desegregation has spawned. (1)

Although *Billboard* ultimately chose the name "Rhythm and Blues"—a bland phrase that George called an "anachronistic evasion" (1)—George develops his observations of the new mentality that was expanding the parameters of behaviors and ideas associated with African American identity in popular culture. He arrives at the concept of a postsoul Black identity for himself and other members of his generation (which includes Whitehead): "We are some combustible compound. . . . All of us have seen African American culture evolve . . . from gospel-and-blues rooted with a distinctly country-accented optimism to assimilated-yet-segregated citified consciousness flavored with nihilism, Afrocentrism, and consumerism. The soul world lingers on, but for the current generation it seems as anachronistic as the idea of a National Association for the Advancement of *Colored* People and as technologically primitive as a crackly old Motown 45" (7, italics in original). This passage evinces an intergenerational tension that Daniel White Hodge has diagnosed as follows: "The Civil Rights generation tends to see the post-soul person as immoral, disrespectful, irreverent, and 'secular.' The post-soul person tends to view the Civil Rights generation person as old school, out of touch, hierarchical and extremely judgmental" (62).

Several of Whitehead's books have explicitly featured some version of this intergenerational conflict, most prominently *Sag Harbor* and *John Henry Days*. Benji and his adolescent friends experience summers in Sag Harbor very differently from his parents' generation because of their somewhat incompatible experiences of race and racism, whereas J. Sutter struggles to determine whether the frequently retold and repurposed story of John Henry still holds any value for him. The protagonists of both *The Intuitionist* and *Apex Hides the Hurt* are also embroiled in conflicts that echo the postsoul condition, albeit in more abstract and implicit ways. *The Intuitionist*'s Lila Mae Watson is a trailblazer both because of her race and her gender, but she is also the inheritor and author–reviser of a suppressed philosophical knowledge with profound implications for the future. Likewise, the protagonist of *Apex Hides the Hurt* has been living without much opportunity for self-definition before receiving his unusual commission from the town of Winthrop. For example, he originally gets his job as a nomenclature consultant not because of any particular affinity for it but because, like his employer, he is an alumnus of the prestigious Quincy College. His personal identity crisis is concurrent with his investigation into the town he has been hired to rename, including the complex racial dimension of its history. Even though Whitehead's two most recent novels mostly take place well before the concept of "postsoul" existed, they nevertheless undermine the ways in which present-day cultural memories—including civil rights-era revisions thereof—of slavery and Jim Crow segregation maintain what Salamishah Tillet calls the "civic estrangement" of African Americans: "Because racial exclusion had become part and parcel of African American political identity since slavery, it cannot simply be willed or wished away. This protracted experience of disillusionment, mourning, and yearning is in fact the basis of African American civic estrangement. Its lingering is not just a haunting of the past but is also a reminder of the present-day racial inequalities that keep African American citizens in an indeterminate, unassimilable state as a racialized 'Other'" (9).

Several critics have asserted that the contemporary struggle for African American self-definition contains great potential for artistic renewal and reinvigoration. In an influential and controversial 1989 essay, Trey Ellis outlined what he called the "New Black Aesthetic" (NBA) that pervaded artistic works by members of the post–civil rights generation. Ellis found great comfort in observing that he was "not the only black person who sees the black aesthetic as much more than just Africa and jazz. Finally finding a large body of the like-minded armors me with the nearly undampenable enthusiasm of the born again. And my friends and I . . . have inherited an open-ended New Black Aesthetic from a few Seventies pioneers that shamelessly borrows and reassembles across both race and class lines" (234). According to Ellis, the unavoidable irony of the NBA is that it arises out of the successes of the very generations against whom it rebels: "There is now such a strong and vast body of great black work that the corny or mediocre doesn't need to be coddled. NBA artists aren't afraid to flout publicly the official, positivist black party line. . . . Like any new movement of artists and like most people in their mid-twenties, part of the process of stamping our own adult identities includes rebelling against our parents, cautioning ourselves against their pitfalls" (236–37). Whitehead described his own perception of this generational interplay in a 2001 interview. When asked about whether the fact that "blackness is reinterpreted generationally" imparts any "weight of reinterpretation" (i.e., a sense of responsibility to stay within certain boundaries), Whitehead's response strongly resonates with Ellis, Neal, and George: "Coming out of the post-Black Arts movement, and having blackness being reaffirmed in literature and drama, I think the young black writers of my generation have the freedom to do what we want" (Sherman 17).

Bertram D. Ashe coined the term "blaxploration" in 2007 to describe the process through which postsoul writers shaped their authorial voices: "These artists and texts trouble blackness, they worry blackness; they stir it up, touch it, feel it out, and hold it up for examination in ways that depart significantly from previous—and necessary—preoccupations with struggling for political freedom, or with an attempt to establish and sustain a coherent black identity" (614). Paul Taylor indirectly links the notions of historiographic metafiction and the postsoul aesthetic by noting the latter's ironic representation of subject matter previously considered sacrosanct: "Where soul culture insisted on the seriousness of authenticity and positive images, post-soul culture revels in the contingency and diversity of blackness, and subjects the canon of positive images to subversion and parody—and appropriation" (631). Whether expressed as Ellis's "borrowing and reassembling" or Ashe's "blaxploration" or Taylor's "parody and appropriation," these descriptions all denote a cultural attitude shared among a generation of African American artists that includes Whitehead. This attitude underpins their reworking of existing cultural artifacts in ways that correspond closely to Hutcheon's theorization of historiographic metafiction.

In fact, if one expands Taylor's definition here to include "the contingency and diversity" of ways in which people classify themselves and each other in general (race is certainly an important issue for Whitehead, but it is far from his only concern) then it effectively encapsulates the overarching project of Whitehead's first nine books. In his choice of *forms* Whitehead parodies and appropriates the conventions of literary genres as a means of subverting the formulaic conclusions to which they have been reduced. At the same time, Whitehead's choice of subjects parodically appropriates various forms of "conventional wisdom" present in American culture as a means of subverting the unexamined, ignored, or malevolent aspects thereof.

Whitehead has hinted at this parallel structure in describing his multifaceted reaction to the zombie movies to which *Zone One* harks back: "The blaxploitation movies I saw as a kid provided one example for a black hero, and *Night of the Living Dead* gave me another one. Black guy on the run from hordes of insane white people who want to tear him limb from limb? What's more American than that? It's like T.G.I. Friday's, and Pez. The movies stuck with me" ("When Zombies Attack!").

CHAPTER 2

The Intuitionist

Even before Whitehead's debut novel *The Intuitionist* was published early in 1999, advance reviewers were already heaping praise on him, often comparing his prose to that of major figures in twentieth-century fiction. Sybil Steinberg insisted that Whitehead "has a completely original story to tell, and he tells it well" (56) while Donna Seaman wrote that the novel "can claim a literary lineage that includes [George] Orwell, [Ralph] Ellison, [Kurt] Vonnegut, and [Thomas] Pynchon, yet it is resoundingly original" (651). These reviews set the general tone for the book's almost entirely positive reception but also initiated the somewhat paradoxical context into which his works have consistently been placed since. Be they professional reviewers writing in mainstream venues, literary critics writing in academic journals, or avid readers commenting on literary blogs, interpreters of Whitehead's work have seemingly been pulled in two directions at once: they fervently assert the unmistakable novelty of his style and subject matter, while also pointing out the equally unmistakable trail of cultural touchstones that he incorporates into his work. Although there is neither shame nor malice in writing literature that is influenced—even *heavily* influenced—by earlier models, Whitehead's work is distinctive in stimulating what appear to be oxymoronic reactions (after all, can a book "claim a literary lineage" and still be "resoundingly original"?).

Whitehead's first two books—*The Intuitionist* and *John Henry Days*—are both deliberate provocations intended to unsettle the interrelated acts of reading and writing in both literal and symbolic ways. Both books superficially entice readers with a range of familiar literary conventions and cultural commonplaces; however, both of them also then gradually, inexorably veer away from those conventions, thereby detaching themselves from any predictable associations that arise from their use. Whether in the form of the recognizable style and plot elements of "hardboiled" detective fiction and/or film noir that appear in Lila Mae Watson's decidedly idiosyncratic story in *The Intuitionist*, or in the form of the fourteen contradictory accounts of John Henry's story (twelve of which are reprinted from actual historical sources and two of which are Whitehead's own creation) that appear in the prologue of *John Henry Days*, Whitehead baits his reader into a false sense of familiarity. He then uses its eventual disappearance to kindle a more judicious and intricate questioning of both his subjects and the words through which he presents them.

As previously noted, such an approach is consistent with both the literary technique of historiographic metafiction and the cultural mindset of the post-soul aesthetic. *The Intuitionist* and *John Henry Days* represent Whitehead's first two forays into postsoul historiographic metafiction. In his analysis of *Apex Hides the Hurt*, Cohn specifies how Whitehead's work in general can be deeply linked to a "literary lineage" while also meaningfully departing from it:

> If the concept of "soul" in African American culture traditionally meant a precious racial "essence" . . . the failure to manifest "soul" would seem to imply unreality, fakery, crossing over and selling out, betraying the culture and history of sacrifice (the "hurt") that created it.
>
> While definitions of post-soul, at least those posited by those who have staked their own generational sense of identity on it, have tended to suspend such judgments of value, . . . it seems to me that Whitehead's writings betray a sense of anxiety over the source of cultural value, of guilty indebtedness to the past. (20–21)

Cohn concludes that Whitehead's writing suggests that "questions of African American literary and cultural ancestry continue nonetheless to be fraught with Oedipal anxieties, haunted by debts to shadowy cultural fathers and to the names they have bequeathed" (21). Whitehead's practices of wearing genre drag and his elaborate reconstructions and deconstructions of the various pathways by which the past is remembered by the present are both manifestations of the anxiety Cohn mentions. *The Intuitionist* and *John Henry Days* present readers with characters who suffer from similar forms of cultural anxiety—a psychological state that results from the inability to resolve feelings of uncertainty or dread—and offer elaborate diagnoses for how the worlds in which they live have fostered those anxieties. Although both novels end with glimpses of futures in which those anxieties are lessened or even entirely relieved, neither provides an outright solution, suggesting that such "indebtedness to the past" is not easily discharged. Whitehead's first novel grows out of not "find[ing] history very reliable" (Sherman 15), a process that is expanded and extended in *John Henry Days,* a considerable portion of which Whitehead wrote prior to the publication of *The Intuitionist.*

The Set-up: How Whitehead Makes the Reader Comfortable

The opening sentence of Whitehead's first novel is hard to outdo in its ability to pique a reader's curiosity: "It's a new elevator, freshly pressed to the rails, and it's not built to fall this fast" (*Intuitionist* 1). Whitehead introduces his protagonist Lila Mae Watson as she approaches a nondescript building in which she is to conduct a routine inspection of an elevator, but he prefaces the description of her mundane errand with this single dramatic sentence that portends something sinister. Within a few pages, the reader learns what this something is: "One of the elevators in the Fanny Briggs [Building's] stack went into total freefall. . . . The Mayor was showing the place to some guys from the French embassy so they could see how great the city works and whatnot. He presses the call button and boom! The cab crashes down. Luckily there was no one on it" (35). Upon hearing about this incident, Lila Mae (who had inspected the doomed elevator a few days earlier) incredulously responds, "That's impossible. Total freefall is a physical impossibility" (35) and sets out—as befits her status as one of the "detective-philosophers of vertical transport" (55)—to solve the mystery of whether the elevator's failure was a deliberate act of sabotage and, if so, by whom and for what reason.

These are but a few of the many touches Whitehead uses in the opening sections of *The Intuitionist* to establish a mood of dread, danger, and intrigue reminiscent of such quintessential film-noir movies of the 1940s and '50s as *The Maltese Falcon* (1941), *The Big Sleep* (1946), *Out of the Past* (1948), *The Killers* (1949), *The Third Man* (1949), *Sunset Boulevard* (1950), *Kiss Me Deadly* (1955), and *Touch of Evil* (1958). These films were heavily influenced by the so-called hardboiled brand of crime fiction that flourished from the early 1930s through the 1950s. Dashiell Hammett, Mickey Spillane, and Raymond Chandler each became best-selling authors during this period, writing lurid, usually mass-produced paperback novels about downtrodden "private eyes." Their ambiguous heroes usually work on the fringes of the legal system to enforce an intensely moralistic—if at times also idiosyncratic—code of justice in the place of corrupt and untrustworthy authorities. Humphrey Bogart's acting career took off in large part by playing the lead characters in the film adaptations of such novels (Hammett's Sam Spade in *The Maltese Falcon* and Chandler's Philip Marlowe in *The Big Sleep*).

Starting with the book's opening sentence and continuing throughout its expository first section—entitled "Down," in contrast to "Up," the concluding section—Whitehead consistently uses tropes borrowed from these two inter-related forms of storytelling to set the tone for Lila Mae's tale of mystery and discovery. Given the frequency with which distinctive elements of film noir and hardboiled detective fiction appear in the novel's early stages, it is not surprising that critics have emphasized them in their interpretations. Michael Bérubé, for example, states that *The Intuitionist* is, among other things, a "wry postmodern *noir* in the by-now-familiar mode of Thomas Pynchon, Don DeLillo, and Paul Auster" (163), and Jeffrey Allen Tucker adds that "it marries an evident enthusiasm for detective fiction with a willingness to poke fun at that same genre. *The Intuitionist* wears its identity as detective fiction, or affectionate parody thereof, on its sleeve" (152). Tucker's metaphor echoes Whitehead's comment that likened writing in a particular genre to wearing drag; to use Tucker's parlance, *The Intuitionist*'s "identity" as detective fiction only superficially indicates its underlying intentions, much as a shirt's sleeves offer only partial information about the arms beneath. Allison Russell added another wrinkle by noting that Whitehead intentionally misdirects readers even within the broad category of detective fiction: "Any character named Watson in a detective novel will tempt readers to think of another Watson, the well-known chronicler of Sherlock Holmes's adventures, but Whitehead's parody of detective fiction targets the American hard-boiled variety rather than the tamer English version" (50).

Michele Elam suggests that Whitehead's recombination of recognizable pieces from various sources is significant because it reveals *The Intuitionist* as not only a detective novel but also a "passing" novel. Such works—exemplified by James Weldon Johnson's *Autobiography of an Ex-Colored Man* (1912) and Nella Larsen's *Passing* (1929)—feature characters whose outward physical characteristics are indeterminate enough to allow them to be perceived (i.e., to "pass" without notice) as White when they would otherwise be legally and/or socially defined as Black. Elam argues that *The Intuitionist* is "a passing novel in both form and content" and claims that its most significant acts of passing use superficial participation in formulaic, relatively simple literary genres to mask more open-ended literary aims:

> *The Intuitionist* passes as a dystopic naturalist novel, replete with gro-tesque one-dimensional characters who seem socially and genetically over-determined, only to transmogrify into a realist novel with characters of psychological depth, qualified agency, and unpredictable futures. It passes as detective fiction—opening with a catastrophic accident that we are initially led to believe is the result of worldly political intrigue and sabotage. In fact, we discover . . . a glimpse into a postlapsarian world in which the social

and racial order will suddenly and utterly collapse. The detective novel's epistemological requirement—that the world can be known—dissolves into science fiction's conceit—that the world can be imagined." (762–63)

By intentionally suggesting that *The Intuitionist* is heading in a predictable direction and then radically altering that course, "Whitehead's novel asks readers to consider not only the ways in which words, generic preconceptions, social texts, cultural narratives, and shared signifiers may get you where you want to go, but also the degree to which they may direct you to where you *can* go" (Selzer, "Instruments," italics in original). It becomes an examination of both the benefits and the limitations of "reading" one's world in unchallenging ways.

Lila Mae is an unlikely hero for a novel that takes place "in a kind of detective novel Gotham that is like an essential city, not necessarily New York" (Naimon) and at a time that both "is and is not the 1940s or 1950s" (Bérubé 169). Whitehead's elusive setting prevents readers from being able to interpret the novel exclusively as a commentary on a particular bygone age. The society Lila Mae inhabits is run almost entirely by men and marked by pervasive racial discrimination; Bérubé points out that "African-Americans are referred to as 'colored' throughout the book" (169). Nevertheless, Whitehead's narrator also states that "the times are changing" inasmuch as "an increasingly vocal colored population [is] not above staging tiresome demonstrations for the lower tabloids, or throwing tomatoes and rotten cabbages during otherwise perfectly orchestrated speeches" (*Intuitionist* 12). As the first African American woman inspector in the Department of Elevator Inspectors, Lila Mae faces a distinctive variety of loneliness and isolation: "the difficulty of all colored 'firsts' is well documented or at the very least easily imaginable" (25). Whitehead alludes here to the well-known stories of such African American groundbreakers as Thurgood Marshall and Jackie Robinson, adding yet another layer of association with existing genres and their tropes. Her "one friend in the Department" (20) is himself lumped together with "perennial outsiders like Lila Mae" because of both his Jewishness and his specialization of inspecting escalators, "the lowliest conveyance on the totem pole" (21). Her isolation is further compounded by her adherence to Intuitionism, the smaller and more mystical of two rival philosophical factions among her nominal peers in the Elevator Guild. As the narrator wryly observes, Lila Mae is "three times cursed" (20) due to her sex, her race, and her philosophy.

Lila Mae has been quietly ambitious since her early childhood, seeking to succeed in the very line of work that was denied to her father, Marvin, decades earlier because of his race:

He has worked here for twenty years, driving the control lever into its seven slots, opening and closing the doors to the floors. Studied engineering at the colored college downstate. . . . In magazines he'd read about the new field of elevator inspection, and it seemed like a good opportunity for a man like him, an industrious fellow like himself. The secretary handed him a package when he walked in the door. He returned it to her thin white hands and informed her he was here for an interview. When he stood before the man's desk, the professor glanced up from his papers for only a moment, the time in which it takes to say, "We don't accept colored gentlemen," not meeting Marvin's eyes and returning quickly to his paperwork. (161)

In Whitehead's fictionalized parallel America, elevator inspection is a profession that demands a rigorous combination of academic and practical preparation along the lines of law or medicine. Lila Mae accomplishes what her father "had never been able to do" in being admitted into the prestigious Institute for Vertical Transport, although she is compelled to live in a "converted janitor's closet above the newly renovated gymnasium" while there because the Institute "did not have living space for colored students" (43).

At the Institute, Lila Mae continues what had already been a lifetime of relatively solitary and diligent study: "As she had when she was in elementary school, she sat in the final row of her classes and did not speak unless there was no other option." Because of the Institute's policy of only admitting one "colored" student at a time to "prevent overlap and any possible fulminations or insurrections that might arise from that overlap," she is largely anonymous on campus; some of Lila Mae's professors even call her by the name of her male predecessor "even though it would have been difficult to say there was any resemblance" (44) beyond their skin color. Furthermore, although she eagerly absorbs all manner of specialized knowledge regarding the history of elevators during her first year, she also "discovered she was often ignorant of much routine information her fellow students possessed" (45), a condition that seems to result equally from her segregated status on campus and her own inclination toward seclusion. All in all, she remains practically unnoticed at the Institute, a racially defined state of diminished existence that links her with the protagonist of Ralph Ellison's *Invisible Man* (1952), to which *The Intuitionist* has frequently been compared.

Late one night, Lila Mae is inflicted with insomnia due to a headache caused by reading under the "single naked [light] bulb" in her cramped room (45). This detail symbolically encapsulates the obstacles to Lila Mae's "enlightenment" represented by the deliberately inferior conditions she faces on campus as a Black student (the kind deemed unconstitutional by the Supreme Court's *Brown v. Board of Education* ruling in 1954). It also establishes an inverse relationship to the protagonist of *Invisible Man,* whose basement apartment is lit by 1,369 light bulbs powered with stolen electricity (Ellison 6). As she looks out across the darkened campus, she sees another light on in a top-floor room in the adjacent library, which is named Fulton Hall after James Fulton, an eminent yet also somewhat mysterious theoretician of elevator science and the founder of Intuitionism. She notices the same light several more times, eventually also spotting an unidentified male figure "moving through the stacks . . . with a cane." Although she never personally meets this man, she feels a deep kinship with him: "She saw him about a dozen times in all, and always felt as if they were the last people on earth." The figure turns out to be Fulton himself— a fact Lila Mae never learns—and when she sees him on what happens to be the last night of his life, he "waved at her, slowly, communicating all he knew and what she already understood about the darkness" (Whitehead, *Intuitionist* 46). This last word at first refers equally to the darkness of the elevator shafts she is studying at the Institute and the darkness of the nights in which these two otherwise solitary figures commune. However, it turns out to have a third meaning related to Fulton's race that becomes central to both Lila Mae's life and the novel's resolution. As Lila Mae learns during her investigation of the unexplained elevator crash, Fulton has been "passing" as White for the better part of his life, and his rebellious, visionary philosophy of Intuitionism begins resonating for her not just in the context of the elevator inspectors' rivalry but also in terms of race relations.

Fulton's moment of "communicating all he knew" across the quad corresponds to Lila Mae's transformation from a dutiful student of Empiricism (the prevailing—and dominant—philosophy both at the Institute and among the working inspectors) to an adherent of Fulton's Intuitionism. Isiah Lavender III succinctly defines the differences between the two approaches: "Intuitionists rely on contemplation, instinct, and gut feeling to observe, remedy, and repair elevators. . . . In contrast, Empiricists depend on the cold hard facts of physical measurement to rigorously check the structural and mechanical details of the elevators" (192). Lila Mae first encounters Fulton's unfinished masterpiece, *Theoretical Elevators,* during the same semester in which she repeatedly sees the man across the quad. Upon graduating from the Institute, she is a dyed-in-the-wool devotee of its methods, which the reader first encounters during a routine elevator inspection in the book's opening chapter: "She leans against the dorsal wall and listens. . . . Lila Mae can feel the idling in her back. . . . She can almost see them now. This elevator's vibrations are resolving themselves in her mind as an aquablue cone. . . . You don't pick the shapes and their behavior.

Everyone has their own set of genies. Depends how your brain works. Lila Mae has always had a thing for geometric forms" (Whitehead, *Intuitionist* 6). In addition to depicting Lila Mae's practical applications of Intuitionism, Whitehead intersperses excerpts from Fulton's book throughout the novel. In doing so, he epitomizes the literary "passing" process that Michele Elam mentions, juxtaposing a rational search for insights into the mysterious elevator crash with a fantastical meditation about whether "the next elevator [is] a bubble or . . . shaped like a sea shell, journeying both outward and into itself" (37).

Intuitionism is constantly denigrated by such Empiricists as Frank Chancre, the head of the Elevator Guild, and the power struggle between these two ways of conducting the business of elevator inspection permeates the book. In fact, the main action of the novel takes place during a campaign for the Guild's presidency between Chancre and an Intuitionist opponent named Orville Lever. Lila Mae theorizes that Chancre orchestrated the Fanny Briggs elevator crash to discredit her, since she was the last inspector to visit the building prior to the accident, seeking thereby to discredit Intuitionism—and perhaps also "coloreds" and women—by association. During a press conference, Chancre disdainfully notes Lila Mae's affiliation in highlighting the implications of her possible failure to notice the flaw in the elevator: "Yes, the inspector of the Fanny Briggs building, a Miss Lila Mae Watson, is an Intuitionist. I'm real reluctant to turn this terrible affair into a political matter, but I'm sure most of you are well aware that my opponent in the election for Guild Chair is also an Intuitionist." When asked if he still considers Intuitionism to be "heretical and downright voodoo" (the latter word is also uttered sneeringly by a building superintendent to whom Lila Mae issues a ticket), Chancre responds with language strongly reminiscent of the historical defenses of "traditional" ways of life—for example, "Jim Crow" racial segregation laws—that were dependent on inequality: "Some people ask me how I made this Department the crown jewel, the very pearl of city services. I tell them that sometimes the old ways are the best ways. Why hold truck with the uppity and newfangled when Empiricism has always been the steering light of reason? Just like it was in our fathers' day, and our fathers' fathers'. Today's incident is just the kind of unfortunate mishap that can happen when you kowtow to the latest fashions from overseas" (27). Chancre's use of the term "uppity"—a loaded word historically applied to African Americans who refused to remain subservient and reserved—as well as his patriarchal and nativist invocation of "our" history marks Empiricism as a mindset that will always endeavor to keep Intuitionism and any other disempowered group within "the nomenclature of dark exotica, the sinister foreign" (57–58). Chancre's views also presage the slave catcher Ridgeway's conception of the similarly discriminatory "American Imperative" (222) in *The*

Underground Railroad, though within the respective chronologies of the two novels it is Chancre's philosophy that would be foretold by Ridgeway's.

Lila Mae begins her private investigation as the principal suspect in the formal inquiry into the Briggs Building crash. As in much of hardboiled detective fiction, the system of official authority is thoroughly corrupt. Chancre is uninterested in the truth behind the accident except as a means of influencing the election and simultaneously currying favor with the two major elevator manufacturers, whose products the Guild's inspectors are supposed to evaluate objectively for safety. Moreover, Lila Mae resembles other hardboiled detectives in that she is unjustly implicated—in other words, "framed"—by that same corrupt system. A prime example of such a hardboiled detective hero is Ezekiel "Easy" Rawlins, the central figure in fifteen (as of 2021) books by Walter Mosley set mainly in the predominantly African American neighborhood of Watts in Los Angeles from the late 1940s through the late 1960s. Rawlins is constantly harassed by the Los Angeles Police Department (the institutionalized racism of which was exposed by the Rodney King case in the early 1990s, as Mosley began the series), as well as by the FBI and other law-enforcement agencies. This treatment stems partly from being an African American in a deeply racist society, but it is also a retaliation for his sleuthing, which frequently threatens to expose the pervasive corruption in the ruling system.

The hardboiled detective becomes a kind of champion for those excluded from various forms of social and political influence as well as a potentially empowering role model. As Mosley noted in conversation with Whitehead: "I had written four Easy Rawlins novels before I realized that one of the subjects of my books is black male heroes. I mean, I just never thought of it before. . . . But one day, I realized, Oh, I'm writing about black male heroes. And then it helped me reinterpret the previous work, and it also sent me in a new direction on future work. Even outnumbered, stick to your guns" ("Eavesdropping" 10). Lila Mae is outnumbered in practically every aspect of her identity but sticks to her guns in resisting the intimidation by Chancre, the elevator manufacturers, an organized crime figure named Johnny Shush, and others as she tries to learn why the Briggs Building elevator failed.

The Complication: How Whitehead Starts to Break with Expectations

In the course of her investigation, Lila Mae also learns more about her intellectual mentor, James Fulton. She returns home one evening to find her apartment being ransacked by two thuggish men identified only as Jim and John, who menacingly claim to be "the watchdogs of the Elevator Inspectors Department." As Lila Mae demands proper identification from them, she is interrupted by a Mr. Reed, who claims to be Orville Lever's secretary. Reed quickly convinces Jim and John to leave, but his intervention does not soothe Lila Mae: "She feels dizzy but hides it well. She doesn't know Mr. Reed from Adam. So far he's just another white man with an attitude, never mind his keen sense of timing." When Reed suggests that the accident at the Briggs Building "has some very disturbing repercussions," Lila Mae responds that she doesn't "need looking after." However, after Reed suggests that she was "set up" to take the fall for the elevator accident (Whitehead, *Intuitionist* 41), she agrees to accompany him to the safe haven of the Intuitionist House, a sort of social club for Fulton's—and later Lever's—followers. She remains skeptical, noting that she "doesn't know why he's bothered to intercede in her Fanny Briggs mess, but knows she'll find out soon." The tone of ominous premonition from the novel's opening sentence returns in her observation that "the grim mist of master-plan comes out of [Reed's] pores and pollutes the air in the garden" (60).

After sheltering Lila Mae at the Intuitionist House, Reed provides her with additional context for Chancre's oblique implication of her culpability in the Fanny Briggs incident. Reed refers cryptically to the fact that Chancre is "talking about the black box," and Lila Mae instantly recalls this philosophical concept from the Institute: "The infamous design problem from her school days: What does the perfect elevator look like, the one that will deliver us from the cities we suffer now, these stunted shacks? We don't know because we can't see inside it, it's something we cannot imagine, like the shape of angels' teeth. It's a black box" (61). Unlike the suffering that Lila Mae and all other "colored 'firsts'" have endured, this story is explicitly *not* "easily imaginable," and this passage marks the novel's initial departure from the formulas of detective fiction.

Although numerous detective stories revolve around the search for exotic and valuable objects, both Whitehead's description and naming in this case importantly set the black box apart from such icons of hardboiled fiction as the statuary bird that gave *The Maltese Falcon* its name. Not only is the black box purely hypothetical, a seeming paradox that requires "separat[ing] the elevator from elevatorness" (62), but it also alludes to another literary precedent, Thomas Pynchon's epic 1973 novel *Gravity's Rainbow*, which Whitehead first read "as I started to write and to learn what I could and couldn't do" (Sherman 20). The elaborate plot of Pynchon's novel revolves around the frenzied quest by a diverse assortment of competing forces for a mysterious object known only as the *schwarzgerät* (literally, the "black device") in the ruined landscape of Germany immediately after World War II. As an impromptu detective caught amid influential forces she does not fully comprehend, Lila Mae is—as reviewers and critics have noted (Russell 48–49; Bérubé 168)—also strongly reminiscent of Oedipa Maas, the protagonist of Pynchon's earlier novel, *The Crying of Lot 49* (1966). Whitehead's story shares with both of these novels by Pynchon a steadfast resistance to the notion that stories should end with prescriptive resolutions; given that *The Crying of Lot 49*, *Gravity's Rainbow,* and *The Intuitionist* are all stories about seekers, the unwillingness of their authors to validate those acts of seeking unreservedly becomes a significant linkage, as noted below.

Even as Lila Mae offers a series of reasons why the black box is impossible "from an engineering standpoint" (Whitehead, *Intuitionist* 62), Reed informs her that Fulton seems to have devised a plan for it in the year before he died, which happens to be the same year in which Lila Mae unknowingly saw him pacing from across the Institute quad:

> Two weeks ago . . . Lever received a packet in the mail. It contained torn-out journal entries dating back a few years, and they were notes on a black box. . . . It was Fulton's handwriting. They were obviously ripped out of his final journals, the ones we've never been able to find. Obviously we were very interested. We made a few inquiries and discovered that a reporter from *Lift* had received portions of it, too. Chancre as well. . . . The diary shows that he was working on an elevator, and that he was constructing it on Intuitionist principles. From what we can tell from his notes, he finished it. There's a blueprint out there somewhere. (61–62)

As an advisor to the Intuitionist candidate for the leadership of the Guild, Reed unsurprisingly emphasizes the political implications of Fulton's apparent breakthrough: "The most famous elevator theoretician of the century has constructed the black box, and he's done it on Intuitionist principles. What does that do to Empiricism? . . . Now Chancre's up for reelection. . . . Not only do you lose the election, but everything else, too. Your faith. You have to embrace the enemy you've fought tooth and nail for twenty years" (63). Lila Mae quickly understands that Chancre and his cronies are amply motivated to find the black box before their rivals; only by suppressing this new development that promises a new order—a "second elevation" (61) as Fulton quasi-religiously calls it—can they maintain their power. Lila Mae commits herself to the pursuit, simply and fatefully telling Reed, "I want to find the black box" (65). Whitehead stated in a 2001 interview that "[e]veryone in *The Intuitionist* has all sorts of hopes and aspirations tied into the perfect elevator" (Sherman 14) and Lila Mae proves to be no exception, although her motivation differs greatly from the economic and political intrigues in which she becomes enmeshed.

At Reed's suggestion, Lila Mae returns to the Institute for Vertical Transport to speak with Marie Claire Rogers, Fulton's longtime live-in maid and, as Lila Mae later learns, the source for the journal pages containing fragmentary

evidence of the black box's existence. Mrs. Rogers has stymied all previous inquiries into Fulton and the journals, and she initially sees Lila Mae's presence
merely as a callous ploy by "them other men [who have] been coming around
here in their city suits all full of themselves" to use someone who "belongs to
the same club" (i.e., another African American woman) to extract what they
want. Although Mrs. Rogers remains tight-lipped, she also cryptically hints
that Fulton is "not the man you think he is" (Whitehead, *Intuitionist* 94). Lila
Mae finds out later that the light-skinned Fulton has been passing for White
since his adolescence to avoid the racial discrimination that dominates both the
country and the elevator inspectors' microcosm.

Fulton's incentive for passing becomes apparent in two scenes immediately
preceding the disclosure of his personal "darkness." First, Lila Mae meets
with Chancre, who hints that she will be tortured or possibly even killed if
she doesn't give him the blueprint for the black box. He punctuates his threat
simply by reminding her that "no one cares about a nigger" (116). Second, the
narrator recounts an apparently forgotten incident from Lila Mae's childhood.
Just as she would later do with Fulton—"the father of her faith" (84)—she had
encountered her father, Marvin, late at night during a bout of insomnia. He
surprised her in the dark while she was getting a drink of water, and Lila Mae
noticed that he had "been sitting in the dark with a glass of his whiskey" (119)
at a table strewn with elevator catalogues, from which he gruffly asked her to
read. Six-year-old Lila Mae predictably struggled with the complex mechanical
language, at which point her father took over, paraphrasing the more difficult
concepts as he "read every word on the page to her." Sending her back to bed,
he admonished her to "listen to [her] teacher and learn what she tells [you]"
(120). Despite the fact that his own education had not granted him full access
to the world of elevators that clearly still fascinated (and pained) him, he nevertheless believed that Lila Mae might be able to succeed where he could not.

As Lavender points out, the name of the novel's elusive prize contains
strong racial overtones: "It is no mistake that Fulton's theoretical elevator design is named 'the black box.' It symbolizes the plight of the black race. Blacks
can ride up and down, but they are forever boxed in, enclosed, trapped by the
racist ideals of an unchanging society, ensnared in a horizontal environment.
The black box realizes America's vertical race hierarchy. The novel's black characters are restricted to horizontal movement by overt racism, politics, and mob
activity" (193). As the basis for a radical reconstruction of a city dominated by
Chancre, Shush, and their ilk. Fulton's invention *seems* to promise release from
these restrictions. If Fulton's prophetic words are true, the "second elevation"
would make possible "another world beyond this one" (Whitehead, *Intuitionist* 134) in which those such as Lila Mae and Fulton must neither obscure nor

otherwise restrict their identity. However, just as Marvin Watson's frustrated ambitions suggest that education by itself does not offer a pathway out of racial discrimination, the novel's ambiguous resolution questions such a utopian interpretation, thereby complicating the metaphor of "racial uplift" that underlies the image of the elevator.

In broad terms, "racial uplift" is an ideology originating with such prominent African American thinkers as W. E. B. Du Bois, Booker T. Washington, and Alain Locke. In his 1903 essay "The Talented Tenth," Du Bois insisted that the solution to anti-Black racism was higher education:

> The Negro race, like all races, is going to be saved by its exceptional men. The problem of education, then, among Negroes must first of all deal with the Talented Tenth [the limited number of African Americans with access to higher education]; it is the problem of developing the Best of this race that they may guide the Mass away from the contamination and death of the Worst, in their own and other races. . . . How then shall the leaders of a struggling people be trained and the hands of the risen few strengthened? There can be but one answer: The best and most capable of their youth must be schooled in the colleges and universities of the land. (188)

Du Bois's idea expanded on the slavery-era proverb "each one teach one," which originally referred to slaves who overcame the systematic denial of education to become literate and thus had both an opportunity and an obligation to extend the potential power of that knowledge by teaching other slaves how to read. Proponents of "uplift ideology" believed that the successes of comparatively privileged African Americans would diminish and eventually eliminate racial prejudice by demonstrating that African Americans had equal capabilities when given equal opportunities. In essence, racist White Americans would be forced to change their views by the sheer volume of evidence that contradicted their prejudicial perspective. Both Marvin and Lila Mae Watson are products of uplift ideology. Even though they both still harbor significant—and understandable, given their experiences—doubts about the benevolence of White people, they also believe that industrious application of the knowledge gained through education is the antidote to the pervasive racism they face.

Selzer points out that Whitehead questions the relatively uncomplicated logic of the cultural uplift narrative—exemplified by Du Bois's insistence that "[t]here can be but one answer"—while chipping away at the formulaic thinking engendered by literary conventions:

> On the one hand, uplift, elevators, and other tropes of transcendence in *The Intuitionist* reflect powerful human yearnings for a form of life that is free

of the debilitating effects of racism (and sexism). . . . On the other hand, several elements in the novel imply that Lila Mae's quest for uplift through technological perfection may foster solipsistic fantasies of self-reliance that can obscure the importance of communal relationships, valorize techno-logical progress over human welfare, defer social action to a utopian world of technological perfection that is not yet realized—and is perhaps not realizable. ("Instruments" 682)

Selzer dissects Lila Mae's complicated relationships to both Fulton and Fanny Briggs, one of Lila Mae's role models since the third grade and the namesake of the building in which the fateful elevator crash occurred. "As a slave woman who taught herself to read . . . Fanny Briggs provides what appears to be an originary model of black uplift through education and self-reliance" (685). The fact that Marvin Watson explicitly helped teach his daughter to read us-ing elevator catalogues further links Briggs's story of self-empowering literacy with the elevator accident. As Selzer points out, the building's name is sig-nificant not because it is evidence of real progress toward recognizing African American achievement, but rather because it shows how a cynically insincere *performance* of such recognition actually prevents the very kind of collective betterment that uplift promises. She notes that the Mayor originally named the building after Briggs to quell unrest among the "increasingly vocal colored population" and that the move was "shrewd" rather than ethically principled: "It only makes sense to name the new municipal building after one of their heroes." Explicitly marked as *their* (not *our*) hero, Briggs thus becomes a token, grudgingly acknowledged because "the Mayor is not stupid" in his approach to seeking "few complaints, and fewer tomatoes" (Whitehead, *Intuitionist* 12). Selzer sums up Briggs's "complexly ambivalent" legacy in the story as follows: "On the one hand, Briggs represents a potentially subversive black agency. By learning literacy . . . Briggs recalls the transgressive possibilities of black educa-tional empowerment. On the other, the uses to which her paradigm of uplift is put suggest the degree to which uplift ideology may be effectively appropriated to [exclude] communal contributions to personal and racial progress" ("Instru-ments" 685–86).

The Ambiguous Ending: Is the "Black Box" Really the Hope for the Future?

This ambivalence extends to the resolution of the novel, especially as both the process and results of Lila's Mae's investigations become so muddled that she feels "mistrust [is] now as useless as trust" (Whitehead, *Intuitionist* 227). For example, Lila Mae believes that she has discovered the secret of Fulton's racial identity through a young African American man named Natchez, a servant to

Orville Lever. Natchez also claims to be Fulton's nephew and gains Lila Mae's confidence—and her somewhat awkward romantic affection—by telling her that he considers Fulton's "black box" writings to be rightly his as a familial heirloom. As it turns out, Natchez resembles Fulton in not being the man who Lila Mae thinks he is; his real name is Raymond Coombs, and he is a junior executive with one of the elevator manufacturers. In an echo of Mrs. Rogers's initial suspicions about Lila Mae, Coombs's blackness is used as a deception— "perhaps she will trust one of her tribe, his story of correcting the injustices done to her race" (230)—by his employers to investigate the appearance of Lila Mae's name in Fulton's notebook. Coombs quickly loses interest in Lila Mae after this detail turns out to be an irrelevant coincidence. Whether it is Fulton's words, the elevator accident, or Fanny Briggs's legacy, the primary—if not sole—value of truth in the novel is its capacity to be turned into leverage for the powers that be.

This point is reinforced by the fact that, despite Lila Mae's ardent belief— expressed as late as the book's next-to-last sentence—that she is "never wrong" (9, 255), all of her theories about what happened to the Briggs elevator prove incorrect. Rather than being an intrepid detective working tirelessly to uncover the real truth, Lila Mae is just a pawn in a much larger game whose rules she barely understands. Coombs makes this clear to her after he reveals his true identity: "At first we really did think that Chancre had sabotaged Number Eleven . . . but our spies informed us that he was as surprised as we were. Luckily, you were fixated on the idea, with our encouragement" (249). Coombs also calls Lila Mae out on her hostility toward the only other "colored" inspector in the department, a somewhat curmudgeonly man named Pompey whom Lila Mae not only suspects of being involved with the Briggs Building accident but whose fawning obedience makes him a "shuffling embarrassment" (197) in her eyes. Coombs chides Lila Mae for her egotism in not recognizing that Pompey, too, had "an exceedingly hard time of things" (25) as a racial groundbreaker: "Let one colored in and you're integrated. Let two in, you got a race war as they try to kiss up to whitey" (249). Finally, Coombs tears down a core tenet of uplift ideology by denying the relevance of Fulton's racial passing, insinuating that the black box's potential to generate wealth and power trump any possible social significance of Fulton's blackness: "Colored people think two of our presidents were colored. We make noises about it, but nothing ever comes of it. The rank and file in the industry won't believe, and those who know care more about his last inventions. His color doesn't matter at that level. The level of commerce. They can put Fulton into one of those colored history calendars if they want—it doesn't change the fact that there's money to be made from his invention" (250). Taken as a whole, Coombs's comments imply that Lila Mae's attitudes about race—according to him, she is simultaneously too trusting in Natchez's apparent authenticity, too dismissive of Pompey's shared struggles, and too invested in Fulton's ultimately insignificant blackness—make her vulnerable to con men such as himself (and, by extension, other powerful men such as Chancre, Lever, Johnny Shush, and Coombs's employers).

With only a handful of pages remaining in the novel, Whitehead has *seemingly* abandoned the idea that the black box or any other metaphor of uplifting unity offers much hope to his book's African American characters, leading Selzer to observe that "when Lila Mae arrives in the city she identifies herself with larger forces of social uplift—economic, national, social, and especially, technological. But the uplift narrative she uses to define herself as the 'first black female elevator inspector' may prevent her from appreciating the full ramifications of her own position three years later as a lonely, isolated professional woman living in a small apartment" ("Instruments" 686–87). Selzer concludes that Whitehead is ultimately "exploring the troubling contradictions that lie at the heart of uplift ideology, especially those that pit a seemingly laudatory self-reliance against more collective forms of community life" (687).

The novel does not end with Lila Mae utterly defeated by the powerful forces around her, though. Its final two sections offer some hope that things may eventually improve. Moreover, the particular kind of hope they offer is distinctly a feature of the novel's status as a work of postsoul historiographic metafiction, relying as it does on a conscious act of self-empowerment through the renovation of an existing text. In the penultimate chapter, Fulton walks around in the library attic, remarking to himself that the world "will not be ready before his time runs out" (Whitehead, *Intuitionist* 253) to receive his nearly completed theory of the perfect elevator. Fulton worries about its fate after his death: "He thought it through as far as he can see. It will be up to someone else to execute the plan. Maybe the wrong person will come. They'll think the time is right when the time is actually not right, and that would be terrible. . . . He would definitely prefer if whoever comes for it has a good sense of timing" (252). As "he writes the elevator," he recalls asking the Dean about "the young colored girl who always walks fast with her head down to the cement," and being told that "her name was Lila Mae Watson and that she was a credit to her race." Mirroring Lila Mae's actions from earlier in the book, he looks across the quad and sees her through her window, enjoying a fleeting moment of sympathy before returning to his work: "She looks so frail and slight through the window. He wishes she had better sense. But he cannot concern himself with her. The elevator needs tending." The narrator notes that Fulton "has written *Lila Mae Watson is the one* in the margin of his notebook" but also nullifies any grand intentions that might adhere to this remark: "That's the name of the only other person awake at this hour of the night." Fulton returns to his work without again mentioning Lila Mae, only remarking that "he has given Marie Claire her instructions and trusts her to carry them out" (253, italics in original).

Mrs. Rogers follows his instructions dutifully, sending out tantalizing fragments of Fulton's notes on the black box to various recipients with a stake in its development. She keeps the full "sacred scrolls" in a dumbwaiter—"a primitive hand elevator containing all the principles of verticality"—from which she eventually retrieves them to give to Lila Mae (242). The book's final scene shows Lila Mae, having resigned her position as an elevator inspector, working alone in a small room to finish an optimistic third volume—"as opposed to the arid, academic voice of Volume One and the aimless mystic voice of Volume Two" (254)—of *Theoretical Elevators*. She is neither simply transcribing Fulton's notes nor making up her own theories; rather, she is "filling in the interstitial parts that Fulton didn't have time to finish up. She knows his handwriting. The most important parts are there. They just need a little something to make them hang together. Seamlessly" (254). She is working according to instructions from Fulton's notes, but "she is permitted to alter them according to circumstances," thereby creating a new hybrid narrative that grafts her own understanding onto a mimicry of Fulton's voice. Essentially, she has abandoned the literal drag of being an elevator inspector—Mrs. Rogers observes at their first meeting that Lila Mae is "wearing a man's suit like you a man" (94)—and dons the metaphorical drag of Fulton's authorial persona to find a valid means of expressing herself.

She has also sent the remainder of Fulton's work to the other recipients, allowing them to build a version of the black box that "should hold them for a while" until they "realize it is not perfect" (255). Only then will she decide whether "it is the right time" to give them the perfect elevator on which she is working. Whitehead never describes this perfect elevator, and Selzer rightly notes that Lila Mae's "earlier mistakes in judgment" ("Instruments" 697) call into question her confidence that "she will make the necessary adjustments" (Whitehead, *Intuitionist* 255). However, Whitehead's own comments suggest that he sees Lila Mae's active role as a creator—rather than just a passive reader or consumer—of texts and ideas to be "optimistic and open-ended" (Sherman 23). Madhu Dubey interprets this conclusion positively as well, stating that Lila Mae "becomes the custodian of Fulton's dream, as she finds and devotes herself to decoding his manuscript. . . . Recognizing that no text can be definitive in its grasp of a changing and open-ended reality, Lila Mae resolves to revise and update Fulton's text" (*Signs* 2). Dubey furthermore claims that the novel is a "project of corrective reading" (238). Lila Mae and Mrs. Rogers articulate the need for such a project when discussing Fulton's intentions in formulating the philosophy that became Intuitionism. As Mrs. Rogers tells Lila Mae, "They had all their rules and regulations. They had all this long list of things to check in elevators and what made an elevator work and all, and he'd come to hate that. He told me—these are his words—'They were all slaves to what they could see.' But there was a truth behind that they couldn't see for the life of them." To this Lila Mae adds, "They looked at the skin of things" (Whitehead, *Intuitionist* 239). Like Fulton, Whitehead implores his readers to look deeper into the narrative he offers them, past the tropes of detective fiction, the echoes of other writers' works, and the accepted cultural truths about race and gender, and to become more like Lila Mae at the end of the story. By recognizing the limitations of her prior worldview, Lila Mae has once again "learned how to read, like a slave does, one forbidden word at a time" (230). In doing so, she is becoming a new kind of Fanny Briggs, one who can wisely interpret and revise received knowledge, thereby "mak[ing] it more responsive to the need of future cities" (Dubey, *Signs* 2). With Whitehead's unnamed city symbolizing the United States of the relatively recent past, the future cities to which Dubey refers similarly represent the range of hopeful, albeit far from inevitable, positive consequences of reexamining the damaging cultural narratives that sustain racism, sexism, and other forms of unjust discrimination.

CHAPTER 3

John Henry Days

Whitehead weaves a complex narrative web across the sixty-two chapters of *John Henry Days* (2001). Loosely centered around a fictionalized retelling of an actual event—the weekend-long celebration of a commemorative John Henry postage stamp in the neighboring towns of Talcott and Hinton, West Virginia, in July 1996—the novel ranges widely in time, space, and style of narration to move beyond a simple assessment of John Henry's historical legacy. Whitehead intertwines a multitude of stories directly and indirectly related to John Henry with the story of a jaded freelance journalist named J. Sutter, who is sent to West Virginia to cover the stamp-release festivities for a "new travel website" (*John Henry* 19) in the early days of the Internet boom. As Whitehead himself put it, "there are chapters that serve to further the story of what happened during the John Henry Days stamp festival weekend, and then there are chapters which serve to further the advancement of different notions of John Henry, what John Henry-ness is to different people" (Sherman 18). In telling these assorted stories, Whitehead unleashes a torrent of artifacts related to John Henry—song lyrics, folktales, sociological narratives, snippets of archival research, antique statues, postage stamps, T-shirts, and so on—to examine the far-reaching implications of how and why his legend has been repackaged for different audiences and to assess its significance at the turn of the millennium.

In part because of its expansive scope, *John Henry Days* was again compared to some giants of English-language fiction. James Wood called it "an African American version" of Don DeLillo's 1997 novel *Underworld* (30) while fellow novelist Jonathan Franzen's appraisal noted that "like its great-uncle *Ulysses* and its great-grandfather *Moby-Dick, John Henry Days* has encyclopedic aspirations" (8). Like repeated references to Ellison and Pynchon in reviews of *The Intuitionist,* these comparisons to Melville, Joyce, and DeLillo generally intended to praise Whitehead's talent, although Wood also asserted that Whitehead "lacks the composure of DeLillo's often distinguished prose." Whether intended as commendation or denigration, such linkages risk limiting potential interpretations of Whitehead's work by overstating its relationship with literary ancestors. Most reviewers stopped short of seeing the intentional allusions to and correspondences with other works and writers in *John Henry Days* as a springboard for Whitehead's own innovative reexaminations and redirections, preferring instead to identify his technique simply as stylistic accumulation and/or homage without much added value.

Wood, for example, damned Whitehead with faint praise while deeming him vastly inferior to the nineteenth-century Russian writer Nikolai Gogol:

> Gogol wrote great prose, and Whitehead writes what might best be called interesting prose—extraordinarily uneven, and sometimes barely comprehensible. . . . Whitehead's models may be various: perhaps the freaked allegorist Thomas Pynchon is somewhere behind this, perhaps DeLillo and David Foster Wallace and Dave Eggers, perhaps the fogged yearnings of rock journalism and the parish poetry of the semi-literate theorists at *The Village Voice* . . . perhaps the mad fluency and the near-modernist pulse of e-mail. Whatever the influences, Whitehead's prose seems decidedly a contemporary instance, a prose of the virtual age that is often merely virtual: imprecise, swaggering when it should be controlled, fruitlessly dense, grossly abundant.

Even while praising the book as "daring, nervy, knowing, and smart," Wood's review negatively compared *John Henry Days* to DeLillo's novel: "Like *Underworld*, it is a bristle of bricolage; but unlike that book, it gives off, despite its bulk, a curious fear of longevity, of entanglement. Its mode is generally filmic—the rapidity of cutting seems more important than the depth of scenes, as if Whitehead were continually saying to himself, "Keep it moving, keep it moving!" (30). Whitehead might agree with this last speculation, given his stated belief that "to keep the work challenging [he has] to keep moving" (Shukla 100). However, he would surely refute Wood's condescending assessment that his "bristle of bricolage" results from an unwillingness to become "entangl[ed]" with his characters or his subject matter—a strange claim in a review that also complained about there being "barely a page in the book that does not mention John Henry" (30). If anything, Whitehead's comments suggest that the entire 389-page novel (still his longest to date) is a complex attempt "to explore the *idea* of John Henry, to attack it from different angles, different ways people interact with the myth" ("Post Office" 35, italics in original). Rather than being either a mishmash of random fragments or an "exhaustive" collection of "interludes that read, at times, like the work of somebody getting $2 a word" (Franzen 9), Whitehead has constructed an interlocking narrative that considers various facets of a complex unifying theme: "John Henry becomes a way to talk about different things and different things become a way to talk about John Henry. It goes back and forth. . . . My ideal reader sees how both play and interact" ("Post Office" 35). *John Henry Days* is a historiographic metamyth that depicts the appropriation, alteration, dilution, and possible rejuvenation of the John Henry legend over the course of two centuries.

Whitehead's comments about his ideal reader's reaction suggest an interpretation that allows for—and even encourages—an *initial* categorization as an encyclopedic narrative or as a bricolage. However, it also requires an additional kaleidoscopic perspective that transcends the boundaries of what either of those two approaches offers individually. Considering how the chapters focused on the John Henry story, the chapters focused on J. Sutter, and the chapters about various characters in other times and places "play and interact" involves looking not *just* at the constituent parts or *just* at the resulting whole, but also at how and why the parts are juxtaposed to make up the whole. This is an inherently metafictional mode of reading.

Edward Mendelson already moves in this direction by defining an encyclopedic fiction as an "attempt to render the full range of knowledge and beliefs of a national culture, while identifying the ideological perspectives from which that culture shapes and interprets its knowledge" (1269). Whitehead is not necessarily trying to relate the John Henry story to *all* of American culture (the "full range of knowledge and beliefs") during the late nineteenth and twentieth centuries. However, his manifold vignettes highlight some of the more durable and pervasive aspects of the American value system—such as White racial superiority, free-market capitalism, technological utopianism, and the so-called Protestant work ethic—that the John Henry myth has been used either to reinforce or to challenge. These episodes are particularly sensitive to how those values have shaped the lives of African Americans. Whitehead enfolds this encyclopedic montage of American history since the Civil War within the fictional biography of J. Sutter, a man who shares a host of biographical characteristics with both his author and the entire postsoul generation. The near-constant interplay between the sociological/historical dimension of the highly mutable John Henry story and the personal/generational dimension of J. Sutter's experiences extends the novel's meaning beyond the "big picture" implications of the encyclopedic fiction label.

The term "bricolage" is also useful in critically examining *John Henry Days,* especially in explaining the significance of the novel's labyrinthine structure. Margaret A. Rose defines bricolage as a predominantly postmodern artistic technique that is closely related to the broader and more familiar term "pastiche." Both words describe the collection and reassembling of "different texts or objects in a work of art" and once carried negative connotations indicating "the work of a tinkerer or amateur." However, Rose notes that many contemporary critics have "defined bricolage as denoting a meaningful assemblage of parts in contrast to the meaninglessness attributed by [literary critic Fredric] Jameson to pastiche" (225). As a critical term, pastiche has generally been used derisively, implying mere imitation of surface forms, whereas bricolage involves an artistic transformation of the appropriated "bits and pieces" into something new. *John Henry Days* is far from meaningless and the episodes Whitehead includes are never arbitrary or tangential, as becomes clear by considering them as postsoul historiographic metafiction. Selzer argues that "Whitehead's evocation of new media formats, satiric juxtaposition of generic elements, and artistic play with previous intellectual and artistic traditions also invite comparison to the sampling and mixing techniques of hip hop music." She applies the term "New Eclecticism" to Whitehead's "reworking of literary traditions" ("New" 393), drawing inspiration from Hutcheon's conception of historiographic metafiction as a "rethinking and reworking of the forms and contents of the past" (Hutcheon 5).

Rather than using the legendary "steel-drivin' man" John Henry either to add an African American spin to *Underworld*'s criticism of consumerism's shallow wastefulness or to assess "the interior crisis of manhood in present-day America" (Franzen 8), Whitehead turns him into the vehicle for a new historiographic metafiction. As he told interviewer Suzan Sherman, he uses "different moments in history to accentuate how issues of race and class have been dealt with" (Sherman 17) because of his grave misgivings about the received understanding of such moments: "The end of slavery is not a happy ending; it is not the complete triumph as it's presented in children's schoolbooks. The John Henry myth is so ambiguous. He challenges the mechanical steam drill that will replace him to a race; he drills faster and farther and wins, and then he dies from the exertion. So is that a triumph? Is it a defeat? Is it a triumph for the individual, a triumph for the machine, a necessary sacrifice that the community needs? I was trying to emphasize that kind of ambiguity" (15–16).

Whitehead recalled feeling this sense of ambiguity as far back as his first encounter with John Henry in elementary school: "he was the first black superhero I knew. I grew up in the early '70s, and one day—I think it was in third or fourth grade—the teacher said 'We're going to see a movie,' and it was a half-hour cartoon about John Henry. It was really moving. It was a black family in a cartoon; they were dynamic. John Henry is a superhero and he's fighting a machine" ("Eavesdropping" 4). He fictionalizes this memory in the novel, thereby emphasizing his unresolved sense of confusion about the significance of John Henry's fate: "J. was sure Mrs. Goodwin had led a discussion about the lessons of John Henry's story and its ambiguous ending, but he doesn't remember it now. Mrs. Goodwin, why did he die at the end? Mrs. Goodwin, if he beat the steam engine, why did he have to die? Did he win or lose?" (Whitehead, *John Henry* 142).

Instead of artificially resolving this ambiguity by throwing the weight of both his research and his fictional musings behind a particular interpretation of the John Henry story, Whitehead leaves the ending of his second novel even more open-ended than the first. He has even claimed that he "still [has] no idea what the hell the John Henry story means" after writing the novel ("Post Office" 36), which strongly hints that the book's intention is not to answer the questions surrounding John Henry's identity but rather to rethink how, why, and by whom such questions are asked and answered in the first place. Whitehead's massive catalogue of both the cultural products and cultural producers of the John Henry legend exemplifies what Hutcheon calls "postmodern intertextuality," a pivotal feature of historiographic metafiction: it "is a formal manifestation of both a desire to close a gap between present and past of the reader and a desire to rewrite the past in a new context. It is not a modernist desire to order the present through the past or to make the present look spare in contrast to the richness of the past. It is not an attempt to void or avoid history. Instead, it directly confronts the past of literature. . . . It uses and abuses those intertextual echoes, inscribing their powerful allusions and then subverting that power through irony" (Hutcheon 122). Such intertextuality likewise permeates Whitehead's return to historical fiction in *The Underground Railroad* and *The Nickel Boys.*

Any definitive ordering of the past/present relationship in the novel is undermined by two related factors: the aforementioned sense of ambiguity surrounding the John Henry story and Whitehead's constant metafictional commentary about the difficulties—or perhaps impossibility—of creating *any* meaningful story, especially when the "pick and shovel men of the information age" voluntarily "choose [their] own numbing drudgery" (Sherman 13, 17). The novel contains so many dissonant versions of the John Henry story that no harmonious synthesis is possible; as Whitehead noted in explaining his general distrust of history, "It's hard to keep up with everyone's version of the truth; they cancel each other out" (Sherman 15). His approach reflects what the Russian philosopher and literary critic Mikhail Bakhtin termed a "polyphonic" narrative. Stories told in a polyphonic manner not only incorporate multiple characters' voices—as the word's etymology suggests—but also lack a conclusive judgment on the part of either the narrator or the author regarding which, if any, of those voices should be considered authoritative.

Whitehead establishes the polyphonic tone of *John Henry Days* in the prologue, which consists of fourteen testimonies concerning John Henry and/ or the songs and stories about him. The testimonies about his physical person contain claims that are irreconcilable with one another. Some place him in Alabama in the 1880s, while others have him in West Virginia in the early 1870s. Some claim he died in his contest with the steam drill, whereas others claim that he was hanged for murder, even as another set denies his existence altogether. The testimonies about the songs all essentially echo the last excerpt: "It is scattered all over the states and some places on the outside. I have heard any number of verses cribbed bodily from some other song or improvised to suit the occasion" (Whitehead, *John Henry* 6). Although there is no mention of these testimonies' origins in the prologue, the novel's copyright page indicates that all but two of them are taken from actual scholarly works about the John Henry legend. It is significant that Whitehead makes no distinction whatsoever within the novel itself between the two that he has created and the twelve that he has reproduced from other real-life sources, thereby emphasizing the questionable—at best—factuality of any of them. Whitehead later uses a similar technique in *The Underground Railroad,* which incorporates four real—albeit slightly edited—runaway slave bulletins before including a wholly fictionalized one about the novel's protagonist, Cora. In *John Henry Days,* he prefaces the novel's fictionalized cacophony of voices with an equally irreconcilable mini-archive of (mostly) historical texts, thereby forcing his reader to mirror his protagonist's transformation from a passive, at times downright blasé receiver of information into a more inquisitive and receptive interpreter.

The World According to Puff

Even a cursory summary of the novel's serpentine plot is an elaborate task. Although Franzen's claim that "there is very little story to speak of beyond the pageant, the scripted performance, of the eponymous event [the John Henry Days celebration]" (8) is mostly accurate, Whitehead also leaves a trail of verbal breadcrumbs scattered throughout his wide-ranging story that enable its parts to cohere in ways not evident from a broad overview of the plot. J. Sutter is a young African American writer from New York City who has become one of a group—cryptically identified throughout the novel simply as "the List"—of "die-hard junketeers" (Whitehead, *John Henry* 29) willingly performing an endless string of freelance jobs. The chief attractions of these assignments seem to be the "passes at the hors d'oeuvres table" and the "promotional items by the bushel" that are provided to the obliging scribes in attendance (19). Sutter makes his living writing content—"Not stories, not articles, but content" (21)—that occasionally appears in reputable publications. More often, though, he works for in-flight magazines, start-up websites, and other "new media" venues. The "degraded standards" of his fellowship of journalists are indicated by the grotesque topics about which they write, including "Ronald McDonald's rap record" and "the plastic surgeon who specialized in Hollywood kindergartens" (20). In short, his life is wholly enmeshed in a material, superficial, and fleeting culture. From the book's opening scene, in which he chases a tumbling receipt around an airport terminal in order to fraudulently submit it to his employers for reimbursement of expenses, Sutter is presented as little more than a simultaneous consumer and purveyor of intellectually insubstantial kitsch. Even he and his fellow junketeers deride their own work as "puff" and "pop."

Sutter is hired to attend the John Henry Days festival in West Virginia by an as-yet unlaunched travel website. This represents his first foray into writing for a medium he considers "welfare for the middle class" and a realm in which "several hitherto unemployable acquaintances . . . were now picking up steady paychecks" (19). Whitehead's 2001 essay "I Worked at an Ill-Conceived Internet Start-Up and All I Got Was This Lousy Idea for a Novel" recounts his first-hand experience of a similar situation:

> In the summer of 1997, I found myself with a day job after a long time of not having a day job. . . . The debts had piled up, though, and to make things worse, my wife and I moved from Brooklyn to San Francisco, and well, moving costs money, so I needed some cash. Within two weeks of our arrival, I had a gig working for an internet company . . . .
>
> I worked there for six months, and it was a typical web job, with a job description that changed every week according to the latest industry buzz-word. My particular thing was writing forty word blurbs for upcoming web-chats, TV Guide-style. "Cuckoo for your cockatoo? Crazy for your crayfish? Come on down to Frida's Pet Chat every Thursday at 8 p.m. EST! Only on MyPet.Com!" That kind of stuff. It paid the bills. There was only about an hour of work to do everyday, so I spent the rest of the time web-surfing.

Whitehead used that opportunity to find bounteous information related to John Henry, until (as he self-deprecatingly claimed) he had everything he needed "except for characters, plot and sentences, but who cares about that?"

Although both works describe a grim and uninspiring working environment for a professional writer, Sutter's fictional experience is less pragmatically rooted than Whitehead's real-life one. Checking into a motel in Talcott, a fellow junketeer named Dave Brown asks Sutter if he is, as rumored, "going for the record." Whitehead leaves the explanation of this "record" unstated for the moment, as Sutter replies that he is on a three-month-long "jag" that started with an absurd "all-night party in FAO Schwarz" at which the "new Barbie [that] came with a Range Rover and vaginal cleft" was introduced. His only notable recollection of that event is that he "and Monica the Publicist groped each other while miniature robot tanks circled their feet" (Whitehead, *John Henry* 29). Brown replies that "if you've been junketeering that long, you've got a good start on the record," leading Sutter to assert that he "doesn't want to be another Bobby Figgis." Whitehead again does not explain this comment's significance, leaving the reader to understand only that Sutter's main motivation is to achieve a record-length "streak" of consecutive days with "puff" assignments (presumably all as vapid as the Barbie one) while simultaneously avoiding some unstated, yet clearly undesirable fate.

Bobby Figgis's story is revealed fourteen chapters later, only after Whitehead has already veered away from both the present day and West Virginia several times. As it turns out, his is a cautionary tale of what happens to skilled and conscientious writers who succumb to the lure of mindless hackwork. Figgis "began his career as a stock watcher for *The Wall Street Journal*" and "had always had ambitions and now that he had jumped through the hoops his parents had held for him, he was going to pursue them." Any sense of substance behind those ambitions quickly vanishes, though, and he goes from writing "small articles about fluctuations in the market that were praised by his superiors" to working "freelance to cover the world of the new Wall Street warriors." Writing this latter kind of piece depends solely on his having "a stock set of adjectives and [knowing] the bouncers at several trendy downtown nightclubs." Nevertheless, he retains a shred of integrity even after he is put on "the List" because he "still had this thing about paying his dues . . . and he found it hard to shake." Figgis becomes a minor celebrity with "entree to the best parties in the city" and marries a stockbroker who "looked good on his arm." This frivolous existence continues until the night he rashly bets a fellow List-member "that he could do an event every day for a year" (109–10). Although Figgis endures the early months of this wager with little noticeable effect—other than becoming a sensation among his peers for "set[ting] a record for the longest bout of junketeering anyone could remember"—his life and his personality begin to deteriorate due to long-term exposure to "puff." Even when told that he "could stop his odyssey short of the agreed-upon year with honor," he continues, attending a video game convention with "no end of monsters," at which he finally falls apart. He returns home, fails to file a story on the convention, and eventually ceases writing altogether. He is removed from the List and is "never seen again," having been utterly "devoured by pop" (111). Even though Brown agrees that "nobody wants to be another Bobby Figgis" (30), the steady decline of his own career—he once interviewed Robert F. Kennedy's assassin Sirhan Sirhan and also wrote about witnessing the murder of a Black man by a group of Hell's Angels working security for the 1969 Altamont music-festival—suggests that he and his peers are following a similar path.

Sutter intends to spend the entire weekend among the other junketeers, believing their shared contempt will insulate him from what he considers a redneck carnival in a backwater Appalachian hamlet. Afraid that his cab driver is going to "boil him up in a pot [as a] ritual sacrifice [that] helps the crops grow" (21), he spends his first few hours in West Virginia mentally separating himself from a rural landscape that leaves him alternately "confused" (20) and underwhelmed: "Forget the South. The South will kill you. He has arrived at a different America he does not live in. . . . J. waits for his driver to pull up in a red pickup with a bunch of chickens in the back spitting feathers" (14–15). Having had a few hours to "shoot the shit and catch up" (49) at their motel, the junketeers arrive together at a social event marking the start of the weekend-long celebration. They install themselves at a table from which they can mock the shabbiness and artificiality of the proceedings: "Is he supposed to take this place seriously? The walls of the rustic hotel and restaurant are obviously some factory concoction, J. sees that from yards away, the ridges and pocks identical from stone to stone. A hipster kid with more hooks in his face than some ancient, uncatchable fish, strutting down Soho in seventies' bell-bottoms, has more period authenticity than this place. What is he doing here?" (56). Despite the place's undeniable tackiness, Whitehead undermines any sympathy the reader might feel toward the junketeers' sneering attitude by narrating the entire chapter in a parodically excessive style. The narrator describes the junke-teers' behavior—stuffing themselves with free food and alcohol while laughing at both the locals and the John Henry enthusiasts—in language better suited for an Arthurian epic featuring chivalrous knights and noble quests. Sutter is described as an "inveigler of invites and slayer of crudités," and the chapter concludes with an intentionally overblown paragraph in which Sutter's acquisi-tion of a free prime rib dinner sounds like a religious epiphany: "The red light at the head of the buffet table signifies one thing and one thing only: prime rib. . . . In the airport he had glimpsed it in a vision and now it has come to pass. . . . This vision is the sublime distillation of all the buffets he's known, the one and true spirit summoned by caterly prayer. He waits for them to wheel out dinner, he waits to be fulfilled" (59–60). The mock-heroic tone of this chapter's narra-tion metafictionally calls attention to itself by its very inappropriateness. The junketeers' behavior is far from the idealized virtue exemplified by epic heroes such as John Henry, and Sutter's rapturous thoughts about a plate of beef suggest that his capacity for fulfillment has become entirely material, instead of spiritual or philosophical. From a symbolic standpoint, such a condition prevents him from ever being able to derive any meaning from John Henry's story, given that the fundamental question of its hero's material existence is seemingly unanswerable. Instead of seeking the Holy Grail or Nirvana, the junketeers have been reduced—apparently with their wholehearted consent— to chasing after "puff," making them no better than the hokey, superficial culture they scorn. When Sutter nearly chokes to death on a piece of the same prime rib he had earlier valorized, it is the first suggestion that Sutter could be convinced to renounce his devotion to conspicuous consumption.

Not long after he arrives in Talcott, Sutter is drawn—despite his desire to remain aloof—into contact with a series of people somehow associated with John Henry. These characters include Pamela Street, the daughter of a recently deceased proprietor of a John Henry museum in Sutter's native Brooklyn; Alphonse Miggs, a high-strung collector of railroad-themed stamps and a man with a violent secret life; and Benny and Josie Scott, the owners of the Talcott Motor Lodge, at which all of the junketeers are staying. The early chapters focusing on the Scotts particularly reinforce Sutter's observation that the tacky artifice all around him is "intended to service the legions of tourists who will flock here now for John Henry Days" (56), thus revitalizing the economically downtrodden area. The celebration becomes just the most recent example of a long line of instances in which John Henry's story is appropriated to serve intentions that include artistic self-expression, racial uplift, personal financial gain, and more.

John Henry: The Hero with at Least Fourteen Faces

Immediately after the scene in which Sutter chokes at the buffet, Whitehead begins interspersing brief snippets of two other storylines, thereby broadening his narrative beyond the thoughts and biographies of Sutter and the other festivalgoers. The novel's second section opens with the first of six chapters that focus directly on John Henry, albeit a much less superhuman version of him. Scattered throughout the book, these chapters recount some of the canonical details of John Henry's life working on the Big Bend Tunnel near Talcott and Hinton in the days leading up to the duel with the steam drill. Another set of chapters—which I will hereafter call the "flashbacks"—gives fleeting glimpses into seven other lives that have intersected with John Henry's tale since the 1870s. Whitehead revisits this technique in *The Underground Railroad*, in which Cora's experiences in particular states alternate with brief biographical sketches of various characters who are directly or indirectly pertinent to her

story. Some of the characters—for example, Guy B. Johnson and Paul Robeson
—thus depicted in *John Henry Days* are fictionalized versions of actual people,
whereas others are entirely invented. The chapters that depict John Henry himself not only introduce his story to those readers who have never encountered
it but also provide a baseline for noting the changes in all the subsequent retell-
ings and reappropriations.

The series of flashback digressions from the main storyline begins with the
story of an itinerant musician riding the rails at some point in the late 1800s.
In a chapter barely two pages long, this unnamed man transforms the oral tale
of John Henry into a song, admitting that his version both retells the story
and reframes it to suit his own purposes: "He wasn't there at Big Bend. This is
his own John Henry, who he figures is a man like himself. And if the man who
taught him the song has his own John Henry, let him. The next man will have
his. Someone else will change his verses and today's John Henry will be gone,
or secret in altered lines like memory" (103). Each of the subsequent flashbacks
depict the modifications an individual has made to the story in laying some
claim to John Henry's legacy. While looking at the statue of John Henry in
Talcott in the novel's main storyline, Pamela Street similarly muses, "All the
people who have heard the song on radio or had the story read to them from a
children's book, they all have their own John Henry" (262). As Allison Russell
suggests, *John Henry Days* "explores the resonance of a folk-hero story as it
changes and adapts through various media to sustain those who need to hear
its message" (60), although the nature of that need varies dramatically from
character to character.

The second flashback—four chapters after the first—depicts the owner of
the Chesapeake and Ohio railroad, for which John Henry worked in one of the
most widespread versions of his story. Taking an opium-fueled nighttime ride
in his luxurious private railcar, he thinks of the Big Bend Tunnel on which John
Henry and his fellow workers toiled. He can only conceive of it as a technological marvel and an economic asset, a typical perspective for a beneficiary of
the largely unfettered capitalism of the Second Industrial Revolution (roughly
1840–1870): "It took us almost three years to blast through it. We could have
gone around, but that would have added precious time to the journey, and time
is everything. Arduous work, of course, but with these new steam drills, the
work of excavation is much more rapid and efficient. God made the mountains
and man made the steam drill" (Whitehead, *John Henry* 121–22). Given the
unlikelihood that he ever personally swung a hammer or risked being crushed
by a cave-in, the man's appropriation John Henry's story for himself by repeatedly using the first person plural is abhorrent, especially in light of the hubristic
final sentence. Although the steam drill may have helped complete the tunnel, it

was the toil of malnourished and underpaid workers such as John Henry that accomplished most of the "work of excavation" that he proudly remembers while riding in a stupor that Whitehead attributes equally to his opium ingestion and to his dehumanized worldview.

Another six chapters pass until Whitehead follows University of North Carolina folklorist Guy Benton Johnson on a research trip to West Virginia. The real-life Johnson extensively studied John Henry in the late 1920s at the same time as a rival named Louis W. Chappell. Whitehead actually draws the twelve recollections of John Henry in the prologue that are not his own invention from published scholarship by Johnson and Chappell. In an important fictional change to this academic rivalry, however, Whitehead makes Johnson an African American, thereby introducing an inherent racial aspect to the two scholars' competition to "preserve the body of Negro folklore against the march of time" (160). Chappell and other White researchers have "taken the tale of John Henry to be God's truth" because it provided "confirmation of [their] ideas about the bestial aspects of the Negro" (160–61), whereas Johnson is concerned more with the story's cultural effects than with the authenticity of John Henry's existence: "For Guy, the question of whether the John Henry legend rests on a factual basis is, after all, not of much significance. No matter which way it is answered the fact is that the legend itself is a reality, a living functioning thing in the folk life of the Negro" (161). This attitude resembles Whitehead's own stated views about John Henry (which, in turn, may help explain his modification of Johnson's race). It also wholly inverts the junketeers' philosophy; whereas Johnson recognizes the story's value regardless of John Henry's material existence, the junketeers impart an almost sanctified air of importance to wholly material, artificial, and often useless objects. Nevertheless, despite Johnson's repeated insistence that "the veracity of the man's existence has no bearing on his mission here" (163), he also catches himself "continu[ing] to hope that each new informant will give him the affirmative, irrefutable proof" (161). This internal dilemma symbolically reflects the post-soul condition. John Henry represents a fluid sense of identity for Johnson that can build on connections to the past, while remaining a "living, functioning thing"; at the same time, John Henry offers a fixed example of African American heroism that can serve an affirmative or uplifting function for others engaged in unfair competitions (such as Johnson himself).

Whitehead turns next to the story of a Lithuanian-Jewish émigré songwriter who has "pruned his surname . . . to a simple Rose" because "this is America, this is the twentieth century" and "a guy's got to get ahead" (202). Jake Rose struggles to find subject matter to sell on "Tin Pan Alley," the name given to the small district on West Twenty-Eighth Street between Fifth and

Sixth Avenues in Manhattan that housed a number of music publishing busi-
nesses in the late 1800s and early 1900s. Having an opportunity "to get ahead"
in this context requires effacing his old identity as much as possible in order to
assimilate into mainstream America and strike it rich as an artist. Rose's story
at once exemplifies the stereotypical "American Dream" story and undermines
it; not only is Rose forced to alter his ethnic identity just to have a chance at success, but game remains rigged against him even after doing so. Like John Henry
in most of the traditional ballads, Jake has a wife and family who he is trying
to support, but Tin Pan Alley is a brutal environment that strongly evokes the
junketeers' milieu in its disregard of either substance or artistic merit: "Most
of them [songwriters] are hacks anyway, rhyming *sandwiches* with *languages*
and *Doherty* with *majority,* the dumbest stuff, trying to copy whatever song
made it big last week" (198). Rose sits amid the din of his tenement—described
as being "like living in a bum's tin cup" (197)—trying to compose a version of
the John Henry song. He imagines it as an antidote, albeit a backward-looking
one, to the "pop" of his day: "Least with this John Henry song, if he can remember it, he's trying to do something unexpected, bring back a ballad after
all this hopped-up ragtime stuff everybody's doing today" (199). What Rose is
attempting is far from an original work of artistic expression, but John Henry's
story resonates powerfully with him, in part because he heard the song while
bleeding in the snow after being mugged: "It was only when Jake finally mar-
shaled himself out of the blizzard and Ruth cleaned his face and he was falling
into bed like it was a chute that he was able to think, that was a pretty good
song" (205). As Frank de Caro suggests, "the song may express for him—and
presumably to those others he seeks to market it to—some of the pain of the
struggles of Americans as they labor to get by and get on in life" (10). But a
"pretty good song" is no guarantee in this world, as Rose knows well: "Stephen
Foster got paid ten dollars for 'Oh! Susanna' and made millions for his publisher and died broke of drink at a Bowery flophouse" (Whitehead, *John Henry*
204). Rose's story ends with his John Henry-like closing observation that his
song "isn't going to be a million-seller" but that in the twentieth century "you
got to make your own luck" (205). This statement simultaneously affirms his
perseverance and ruefully acknowledges that he is still "the littlest cog in the
machine" (203).

Five chapters later, Whitehead jumps ahead to 1940, showing the famed
African American actor and singer Paul Robeson preparing for the final perfor-
mance of "a real stinker" of a Broadway musical version of John Henry's story.
Roark Bradford, the real-life author of both the play and the novel on which it
was based, is described as citing the following expertise for writing about John
Henry: "He had a Negro for a nurse and a Negro for playmates when he was

growing up. He has seen them at work in the fields, in the levee camps, and on the river. He knows them in their homes, in church, at their picnics and their funerals." The narrator sarcastically comments that these are "very impressive credentials indeed. Especially that bit about the picnics. He might as well have a Ph.D. in Negroes" (226). He then proceeds to relate some of Bradford's ear-bending and horribly stereotyped depictions of John Henry and other African Americans. Like the folkloric research described in Johnson's chapter, this version of John Henry largely reconfirms existing racist notions of blackness, and the fact that Bradford's book "flew off the shelves" (227) testifies that the textual image of African Americans has been powerfully distorted by White writers.

As perhaps the most significant African American performer of the first half of the twentieth century, Robeson represents both a personal and professional contradiction to Bradford's minstrel-show. Robeson's career initially flourished through "performing bills mixing black spirituals with secular songs" (228). Once he began traveling outside the United States, though, Robeson discovered a political consciousness in folk music that was based more on class than race: "He said 'I have found that where forces have been the same, whether people weave, build, pick cotton, or dig in the mines, they understand the common language of work, suffering and protest.' The Negro sharecropper, the Welsh miner, the Slavic farmer. He said 'Folk music is as much a creation of a mass of people as a language. One person throws in a phrase. Then another—and when, as a singer, I walk from among the people, onto the platform, to sing back to the people the songs they have created, I can feel a great unity'" (229). Whitehead frames the scene of Robeson preparing to play John Henry onstage with these remarks, showing that even though "the dialogue is terrible, the characters racist, [and] the situation appalling," Robeson still believes he can transform the performance into something worthwhile because "out of this folktale, even if diverted down ruined streams, flows the truth of men and women" (229). The narrator suggests that this transformation fails to happen, both because of the wretchedness of the play and because of the country's hostility toward Robeson's Marxism. The narrator looks into Robeson's future, which includes being investigated by J. Edgar Hoover, being blacklisted from performing, having his passport revoked, moving to England, and finally returning to the United States "as a plate of scrambled eggs" (230–31) after a decade of mental and physical illness. Robeson is mocked in the newspapers upon returning, but he is also defended by a letter writer who fondly remembers the noble, doomed performance of John Henry for which Robeson is preparing throughout the chapter. The choice of verb in the chapter's final line—"He is John Henry tonight" (231)—suggests that Robeson has become a kind of John

Henry figure in his own right: he is steadfast and principled, but also martyred, possibly in vain, for his cause.

The final two flashback vignettes occur in rapid succession in the novel's fourth section. The first features a Mississippi blues guitarist identified only as Moses, who is visiting Chicago for a week. Back home his routine consists of playing blues songs mostly for the purpose of seduction, albeit generally of "the ugliest woman in the room" since "they were grateful and eager to please . . . [and] never had a man who was liable to cut him or send him running out the bedroom window with his drawers around his ankles" (250–51). Feeling "full of luck," he decides to "change his repertoire" and play the "one or two songs he's written that describe the devilment he'll get into tonight" for the beautiful women in the audience at Rudy's in Chicago. As Moses is flirting with a woman after his set, he is interrupted by a White man named Andrew Goodman who wants to record him. Although Moses distrusts Goodman's motives, he needs the money desperately, having already gambled away his night's earnings before leaving the club's premises. Goodman offers Moses forty dollars per side of a record and asks him to recreate the songs he played at Rudy's. Moses obliges, but Goodman's constant direction irritates him: "Goodman signals Moses to play. Goodman keeps telling the man his business. He'll nod at different parts in the songs, a quick jab, but he does it at parts that Moses doesn't think are important. Things Goodman hears in what he's doing that Moses doesn't even realize." Goodman corrects Moses's performance repeatedly, "waving his notes from the show last night at the man whose show it is no longer." Moses bristles at this, saying that his artistry is inherently flexible and interpretive—"I like to mix it up. Sometimes do this, and then some other time I'll do that" (256)—and even insists that an unplanned mistake often "makes a song better like it let off weight and now it can sail higher" (257). Moses is convinced that Goodman is unhappy with his performance and leaves the studio without asking about his pay.

After another show at Rudy's, Moses goes home afterwards with a young woman named Mabel, who like Moses is a transplant from the segregated South. Perhaps coincidentally, her name anticipates another would-be emigrant—albeit under vastly different circumstances—from the South in The Underground Railroad. Mabel tells Moses about leaving South Carolina because of the scant opportunities to make a living there. They sleep together, after which Moses finds himself reinvigorated for the recording process: "He felt he had to bounce back from the afternoon's session. What is it: this could be his one chance. . . . He was reaching for something all night and then he switched 'Long Time Blues' with 'John Henry' and that was what did it, he changed his mind, he didn't know why, half a second before he chased the first chord out he knew that he had hit it." Like the characters in the previous flashbacks, Moses feels a kinship with John Henry arising from the parameters of his own life: "He wasn't competing with himself, he wanted to beat the machine. The box on the second floor of Goodman's, the diamond needle cutting his frame into beeswax" (259). Like Jake Rose and Paul Robeson, Moses is an artist trying both to make a living and to find fulfillment; all three share the unhappy fate of doing so while imperiled by socioeconomic forces well beyond their control (a "machine" that is sometimes literal and sometimes figurative).

Moses's version of the John Henry song shows that his notion of satisfaction is moving towards the junketeers' materialism: "Most John Henry songs . . . tend to talk about the race and the man's death. He sang a version like that a few times but it never sounded right to him. The words 'nothing but a man' set him thinking on it: Moses felt the natural thing would be to sing about what the man felt waking up in his bed on the day of the race. Knowing what he had to do and knowing that it was his last sunrise. Last breakfast, last everything. Moses could relate to that, he figured most everyone could feel what that was like" (260). Nevertheless, Moses still recognizes that the John Henry song can also transcend the purely physical realm: "He plays it second-to-last in a show, to make them think about the night that is passing and almost over, what they have shared and in closing, that loss" (260). In doing so, he has "shut up the voices at the back of the room with their talk of wages and women, undone the low hands of lovers and forced them to the beat" (261). As Whitehead tends to do in these flashbacks, the chapter's last sentence punctuates but does not resolve the tension that has been building throughout it. Here, the tension exists between the artistic and commercial values of the song, with the latter's tempting nature having been made evident through Moses's envious glances at the boxes of records in Goodman's shop. When Goodman asks Moses to play the John Henry song, the narrator states simply that Moses "doesn't do requests but he agrees to Goodman's request and he does what he does for money: sings" (261).

The final flashback features Sutter's aunt Jennifer as a young girl in the late 1940s on "Strivers Row" (the punctuation of which is a subject of ongoing dispute), an exclusive Harlem neighborhood of relatively well-to-do African Americans who personify the "uplift ideology." The chapter opens with Jennifer "conscripted into serving duty" (a phrase with unmistakable echoes of slavery) for a meeting of the "Sepia Ladies Club," a social group to which her mother belongs. As Jennifer bustles back and forth with trays of food and drink, she overhears the women gossiping about various goings-on in the neighborhood:

Mrs. Barden (who has been attempting to join the Sepia Ladies Club for some time now but does not understand that she has to earn her place and that bragging about her Creole blood is not going to do the trick) and her husband moved into the corner brownstone on 138th Street and have fixed it up all nice . . . with lace curtains ordered from an English catalogue, but maybe she should be less worried about their nice lace and spend more time thinking about her young Angelique talking to the no-good shiftless Negroes who work at Hope's Garage, spend less time bragging about how her grandfather went to Harvard and the award he won for his speech about freedom in Haiti and more time thinking about their daughter's carrying-on. (269)

The Sepia Ladies Club exudes a quintessentially "bourgie" attitude criticized by numerous African American writers. For example, Wallace Thurman's *The Blacker the Berry* (1929) satirized ingroup discrimination against darker-skinned African Americans, suggesting it was a self-loathing attempt to assimilate into mainstream American life by eradicating one's blackness as much as possible. In Thurman's novel this process not only involves a literal eradication of blackness—its protagonist, Emma Lou Morgan, tries to bleach her skin and straighten her hair to look more White—but also features a metaphorical version of passing predicated on not behaving in an "uncivilized" manner that might reflect poorly on the race as a whole. Despite its positive intentions, uplift ideology also frequently imposed a strident and inflexible set of expectations regarding proper and improper behavior.

Such a constricting mindset pervades Jennifer's world; she is forbidden from chewing gum because her father, a doctor, insists that "eating gum will give her big lips" and that "it is very important for her to keep her mouth shut when not talking or forking food into her mouth, or else she will get big lips like so many of their race" (272). Strivers Row is bourgie to the core and John Henry has no place there, his heroic sacrifices notwithstanding. Jennifer quickly realizes this after whimsically deciding to spend a dime that her mother gave her to buy candy on a copy of the sheet music for Jake Rose's version of "The Ballad of John Henry" that is moldering at the back of a store. Jennifer has been taking piano lessons to satisfy her parents' expectations. They "bought the baby grand for Jennifer alone, it seems, for the day she would take her place in the scheme," and her mother informs Jennifer at the outset of her lessons with Mr. Fuller, the "best [piano instructor] in all of Harlem," that "it's never too early for a girl to get herself cultured" (276). This last word takes on an ominous connotation when Jennifer notes that "there's a notion forming in [her] head, not yet articulated but understood: if it's in another language, it must be culture"

(277). The other inhabitants of Strivers Row indoctrinate Jennifer to feel alien-
ated from everything non-European, thereby jeopardizing anything beyond an
elitist caricature of Black identity. When Jennifer plays Rose's version of the
John Henry song—ironically, a White man's interpretation of a Black man's
life—it sparks a repressed feeling: "There is something in this song that does
not exist in the music that Mr. Fuller brings, it quickens inside her. It doesn't
go to church and cusses, wears what it wants." As she plays on, the words and
music elicit a powerful identification with John Henry's situation: "She's in a
heat right now. She sings lyrics that tell a story of a man born with a hammer
in his hand and a mountain that will be the death of him: you think you push
but you are being pushed" (278).

She is so engrossed in the song that she fails to notice the arrival of her
mother, who begins screaming at her: "Do you think your father works ten
hours a day walking up and down the neighborhood treating sick people so that
he can come home and listen to his little girl play gutter music?" (278). While
her mother comdemns the music of "good-for-nothing niggers who don't care
about making a better life for themselves [and] who don't want to take their
place in America," Jennifer reflects to herself that "she hadn't thought she was
doing anything wrong, but apparently the sheet music was part of a larger
transgression that she had never considered" (279). As Whitehead noted in
an interview, Jennifer's mother is not simply expressing an aesthetic value
judgment by "forbid[ding] any street Negroness in the house," but she is also
"erasing the black contribution to pop music" (Sherman 18), thus manipulating
the conception of history she imparts to her offspring. As the chapter ends, Jennifer's mother reinforces the inherent uplift philosophy of "bourgie" Harlem
by asking "Do you know what striving means?" Jennifer's internal monologue
indicates her understanding that it means playing songs that are "just more nice
things to have in the house," objects without any emotional or cultural connection, much like the "puff" that the junketeers extol through their writing. When
Jennifer does respond verbally, the narrator explicitly notes that she "recites"
her answer like the musical pieces she plays with Mr. Fuller: "It means we will
do our best." As she resumes practicing her assigned piece, Jennifer thinks to
herself that the John Henry song "wasn't candy but it sure was sweet," suggesting that the taste of freedom from her parents' confining expectations will
linger on (Whitehead, John Henry 280).

Rejecting behavioral obligations tied to race is a major aspect of the post-
soul aesthetic, but the fact that Jennifer's rebelliousness is—like Jake Rose's—
stimulated by her sympathy with an artifact of an older and more complicated
past also reaffirms the idea that postsoul identity does not mandate wholesale
abandonment of what has come before. Considered as a whole, the flashback

chapters model a dynamic conception of history in which both stories and identities remain mutable. Whitehead does not suggest that all the transformations of John Henry's story are equally valuable in aesthetic or ethical terms; for example, he scorns Bradford's racist adaptation even as he commends Robeson's class-conscious portrayal of John Henry. Furthermore, John Henry's heroism becomes relevant for characters in ways that go beyond simple racial, economic, or gender associations, suggesting that the ambiguity Whitehead feels about him does not prevent—and may in fact encourage—diverse reinterpretations of the legend's significance.

Finding a Meaningful Place for John Henry in the Present

If, as Wood claims, the novel is a chiefly a satire of J. Sutter and his fellow journalists as "knights of negative faith" (30), then one should note that their would-be champion, Sutter, frequently laments his own inability to tell a better story. Departing for his weekend in West Virginia, he wonders about the potential audience for the piece he has been assigned to write: "Who in the world would possibly care about this event? What magazine employed copy editors who could bear to touch a comma of such a piece, what newspaper had a readership that consisted entirely of drooling and defenseless shut-ins? . . . J. just wanted to know if the world had progressed to a point where such a thing was possible" (Whitehead, *John Henry* 20). The culture of puff has not developed in a vacuum, however, and even if the characters featured in the flashbacks are not as roundly ridiculed as the junketeers in West Virginia, they are all situated on a technological continuum that starts with "oral ballad transmission, and then sheet music, the advent of vinyl, and then the late 20th century where we have all different technological formats for expression" (Sherman 13), which allows Whitehead to examine how each of those developments contributed to the contemporary moment of the John Henry Days festival.

For example, Jake Rose is presented as a hardworking family man, but the world of tenements, music halls, and cutthroat competition for copyrights in which he produces his ballad already shows signs of creative debasement reminiscent of "the List." Likewise, Robeson's portrayal of John Henry represents his effort to leave behind the "Stepin Fetchit comics and savages with leopard skin and spear" of his early career; Robeson seeks a role that "represents the experience of the common man" (Whitehead, *John Henry* 229). However, the play moves the action to the city of New Orleans—indelibly linked to the North American slave-trade—and depicts John Henry dying after a contest with a mechanical winch used for loading cotton bales onto ships. This transplantation essentially turns John Henry into a tragic slave, rather than the universal folk hero that Robeson hopes to embody. Whitehead's own retelling in the novel even suggests that the duel with the steam drill was intended as much to conceal John Henry's fatalistic fear of death as to inspire his fellow railroad workers. Whitehead performs creative acts of historiographic metafiction by "challenging" conventional expressions of cultural values as he "use[s] them, even . . . milk[s] them for all they are worth" (Hutcheon 133) to make new art that expresses a different set of values.

The two characters at the core of the contemporary timeframe are both initially disconnected from any inspirational potential the John Henry legend might contain. However, the novel's turning point involves both Sutter and Pamela sensing a more profound dimension of their lives while standing inside the Big Bend Tunnel: "Step in here and you leave it all behind, the bills, the hustle, the Record, all that is receipts bleaching back there under the sun. What if this was your work? To best the mountain. Come to work every day, two, three years of work, into this death and murk, each day your progress measured by the extent to which you extend the darkness" (Whitehead, *John Henry* 321). Sutter feels that the mountain literally and figuratively "defeats the frequencies that are the currency of his life" and removes him from time: "E-mail and pagers, cell phones, step in here and fall away from the information age." He also suggests that a renewed sense of purpose takes the place of those blocked signals: "The daily battles that have lost meaning are clearly drawn again, the opponents and objectives named and understood. The true differences between you and them" (322). Sutter and Pamela have both been unable or unwilling to feel such "lost meaning," and its restoration represents whatever sense of hope for a better future the novel can impart to its readers.

Whereas Sutter came to West Virginia explicitly intending to remain detached from the festival, Pamela Street has been in a personal state of limbo since her father's death several months earlier: "Pamela temped aimlessly, a migrant worker harvesting words per minute. The agency called her early in the morning if they had anything for her; otherwise, she watched television in her pajamas and contemplated the bills from the storage facility, which distilled her hatred for John Henry into a convenient monthly statement" (45). This "hatred" is a response to her father's dedication to curating a makeshift and largely ignored Brooklyn museum devoted to John Henry, the contents of which she feels obliged to dispose of after his death. At the age of six, she felt the first stirrings of this emotion as a "sibling rivalry" after her father used "her favorite red blanket" to swaddle a ceramic John Henry figurine (114). Pamela came to loathe her father's obsessive accumulation of John Henry memorabilia, including "original sheet music of ballads, railroad hammers, spikes and bits, playbills from the Broadway production, statues of the man and speculative paintings" (45); she calls these objects his "planets" and resents "their

interminable trajectories through her space" (348). Pamela comes to West
Virginia to relieve herself of "this burden" (46), a process that involves selling
all her father's material relics and, more symbolically, also entails scattering his
ashes in a place he found meaningful.

Although Sutter and Pamela share a cab into Hinton on the festival's first
night, they do not actually interact until the next day. Whitehead's clever
word-choice emphasizes that their growing attraction to each other over the
course of the weekend is simultaneously rooted in the development of a greater
appreciation for John Henry and in their need for more profound lives. Each
of them is initially locked into simplified, predictable, and limiting ways of
interacting with the world that Whitehead describes in terms related to reading
and writing. For example, when J. and Pamela meet by chance in a restaurant,
they immediately define each other through the lens of their unsatisfying past
romantic exploits. The narrator ends each of their lengthy recapitulations with
a parenthetical aside that indicts them as products of unstrenuous thinking:
"(It takes her about four seconds to concoct this narrative)" and "(It takes
him about five seconds to concoct this narrative)" (186, 189). As Sutter nevertheless continues to flirt, he muses, "She's a thin broth, but let's say there's a
story here" (189), expressing mild interest but also uncharitably lumping her
in with his junketeering pursuit of "puff." Later, as he recalls his on-again, off-
again relationship with "Monica the publicist" (221) from the aforementioned
Barbie event, he can only imagine their lives within the cliché-ridden context
of a formulaic wartime romance: "He was a soldier in the French village, he
brought her clothes and stockings, real treasures in these times of scarcity. She
was a nurse tending the wounds of our boys, she taught him that it is enough
to make it alive to the end of the day, that it was okay for a man to cry" (225).
Neither anecdote suggests that Sutter is emotionally attuned to the "connection afforded by a story worth telling" (Russell 59).

Pamela's emotional starting-point is little better. Her temporary job at a
"content-driven interactive information provider" (Whitehead, *John Henry*
287) consists solely of writing thirty-five-word summaries of other websites,
essentially the same job Whitehead had during the early stages of writing *John
Henry Days*. In overly euphemistic language typical of the "information age,"
she is told that her mind-numbing job "is ontology," the branch of philosophy
that seeks to define the nature of things and to categorize them accordingly.
The company is working on a search engine called "The Tool" that pales in
comparison with another tool, namely John Henry's powerful steel-driving
hammer. The Tool is designed to tell unsophisticated users what they should
value while navigating the vast amount of information on the Internet. The
intentions of this behavior-controlling function are implicitly questioned by

being juxtaposed against the imposition of bourgie values on Strivers Row two chapters earlier. Pamela's work life is also lonely and dehumanized; employees in "the Box" (the nickname given to the room in which she works) sit at workstations that are simultaneously cramped and isolating: "No one talked in the Box. If you wanted to borrow your neighbor's stapler, you sent them an e-mail and waited. They sent you back an e-mail in the positive or negative. Only then did you reach over to the next workstation for the stapler or whatever" (288–89). As arduous and dangerous as John Henry's work is, it does at least produce something (the railroad, the tunnel). It also requires the active cooperation of multiple workers, a point made clear when John Henry accidentally crushes the hand of a "shaker" (the person who holds the spike that the hammer-swinger drives) who momentarily loses his concentration. "The Tool" has more in common with the steam drill, and Pamela's work on it distances her from sympathy with John Henry's plight.

In fact, most of the characters' work environments frustrate their efforts to counteract the purposelessness of the stories that dominate their lives. In a flashback to the early 1980s, Sutter remembers interning with a publication called the *Downtown News*. In contrast to Whitehead's generally positive recollections of working at the *Village Voice*, Sutter dourly notes that "every day in that place reduced his notions" (169). While recalling an editorial meeting about the death of Eleanor Bumpurs, a sixty-nine-year-old pensioner shot by New York City police in 1984 while being evicted from her home, he describes the idealism he once felt about journalism: "These were real stories. He had been raised in a cocoon, programmed for achievement, but there was a whole city out there that was unruly and didn't give a shit about plans. . . . J. felt a part of the Bumpurs piece" (175). This sense of connection to something larger than himself fades quickly as the meeting devolves into a brainstorming session for sensationalistic headlines reminiscent of supermarket tabloids.

Likewise, the anonymous author of fictionalized excerpt from a stamp-collectors' newsletter alludes to "the sad events of July 14 . . . at the unveiling of the **John Henry** stamp," remarking that "[e]veryone knows a stamp with a 'story' tends to bring out the worst traits in the philatelic community" (214, boldface in original). This is one of several hints in the book that a shooting —possibly of J. Sutter himself—happens on the festival's final day. The narrator not only neglects to identify the "two dead and one wounded" (370), but also notes that the story of the shooting is "bumped from the front pages" by a "puff" piece about the death of a "beloved star of stage and screen, whom most people believed had died years before" (366). Whitehead forces his readers to notice the influence of both morbid curiosity and short attention span on the news-cycle. Near the novel's conclusion, the narrator describes Pamela's father going through his daily routine of preparing a lecture for the visitors he hopes will come to his museum: "The speech slept in his mouth. He had composed the speech over many years, for each new item required a deep caption to situate it in the collection. . . . In some ways it was less of a speech and more of a story" (382). He imagines the transformation incited through attentive "reading" of John Henry's story (i.e., seeing the objects and hearing the stories): "Beautiful children with round faces and wide eyes who were hearing of the legendary steeldriver for the first time and learning possibility, teenagers slouching and cracking jokes to hide what they see in the man but cannot admit, adults, men and women pushed here for so many reasons, getting reacquainted with the story they first heard as children and now connecting it to every one of their hard mornings . . . all of them a family he had lost at last returned to him" (383). Sadly, he dies before this hypothetical reunion can take place and it seems unlikely to occur in the carnival-like atmosphere—exemplified by the tacky green foam-rubber hammer that the mayor of Hinton gives Pamela as recognition of the donation of her father's collection—of the John Henry Days.

These instances all suggest that establishing meaningful connections via stories of any kind is inherently difficult because of the constantly shifting values and perspectives of their potential producers and audiences. However, such difficulty can seemingly be lessened by essentially the same factors, since the same story can create different forms of idiosyncratic value for different individuals, even if they cannot communicate (or perhaps choose not to communicate) that value to one another. This potential paradox—in which a lack of definitive meaning stimulates a multitude of meanings—helps explain Whitehead's withholding of a conventional resolution to any of the novel's major plots and subplots.

Whitehead deliberately builds parallels between Sutter and John Henry only to confound the reader by leaving both of their stories incomplete. The novel's pervasive ambiguity abides despite several insinuations of an impending resolution. In a chapter with the same unusual formatting as the prologue, Sutter accompanies Pamela as she reconciles herself with her dead father by burying his ashes in a secluded field where "legend had it [that] John Henry was buried" (376). As they scour the countryside for John Henry's grave, Pamela's unwitting allusion to the first flashback chapter emphasizes the John Henry story's innate subjectivity:

> She said there are many versions of the song, as many versions as there are people who sing it. . . . You could split the song into so-called official versions [and the] songs of the people, entirely different, the mis-sung versions,

belted out by people who misremembered the lyrics and supplied their own haphazard verses. Like when you sing in the shower, she told him, and if you can't remember the right words, you make up your own to fill in the gaps. Her father used to say that what you put in those gaps was you—what you inserted said a lot about you, what you grabbed from your personal dictionary and stuck in there was you. You mix it up, cut a verse or two and stick to the verses that you like or remember or mean something to you. Then you've assembled your own John Henry. (373)

They find several headstones but nothing that indicates the presence of John Henry's remains. Pamela decides to bury the urn with her father's ashes there anyway, concluding that the "truth" of the situation does not dictate her gesture's significance: "Her father might have preferred that his ashes were scattered, she didn't know, it just made sense to her once they got up there to bury it. She walked out into the middle of the field and without an overlong consideration of where the perfect place would be she stopped and said, Here" (376–77). In essence, Pamela has abandoned the pursuit of definitive truth that shackled both Lila Mae and Guy Johnson. Instead, she fuses the received myth with her perceived reality to write a metaphorical story that satisfies her need for psychological closure.

In the final pages, Sutter stands in his motel's parking lot debating whether to return to New York with Pamela on an earlier flight. She had previously asked whether he "got his story" (387) and his thoughts while formulating his answer seem to foreshadow an imminent epiphany: "He had put on paper some of the things she had said the day before but now he thought what happened today was the real story. It is not the kind of thing he usually writes. It is not puff. It is not for the website. He does not know who would take it. The dirt [in which they buried Pamela's father] had not given him any receipts to be reimbursed. He does not even know if it is a story. He only knows it is worth telling" (387). Whitehead keeps this story from his reader too. Not only does he refuse to answer any of the questions that young Sutter asked his grade-school teacher about John Henry, but he also leaves unresolved the mystery of who is killed on the last day of the festival, the question of whether Sutter succeeds in breaking the record for junketeering, and the question of whether Sutter and Pamela leave together and start a meaningful relationship. Just as Whitehead's retelling of the John Henry myth ends not with his death but rather with him "walk[ing] down the road with his hammer in his hand" toward the showdown with the steam drill, Sutter's story (and thus the novel) ends with the cryptic line "When they came down the mountain, she asked. What's the J. stand for? He told her" (389). By mischievously teasing them with this ending, Whitehead requires his readers to insert their own subjective speculations regarding Sutter's response, thereby preempting any claims to a conclusive interpretation. By insisting that his novel has at least as much uncertainty built into it as John Henry's story does, Whitehead challenges his readers with one final gesture of historiographic metafiction. Whitehead confounds the genre expectations of historical fiction by refusing either to tie up the story's loose ends or to provide a conventional happy ending. Nevertheless, he suggests that even though it remains unknowable whether Sutter goes back to New York with Pamela or whether he is shot by Alphonse Miggs the next day, this story *has* been worth telling, just as the John Henry story was valuable to all the characters through whose hands it passed.

CHAPTER 4

Apex Hides the Hurt

Each of the protagonists in Whitehead's first three novels is some sort of writer. Lila Mae Watson emulates Fanny Briggs and learns to compose her own identity beyond external constraints. By the end of *The Intuitionist* she has also become an odd kind of ghostwriter, completing Fulton's visionary work on elevators. J. Sutter, on the other hand, needs to develop *more* affinity with others as he interprets the world around him, and the John Henry myth eventually helps him (re)discover a sense of meaningful storytelling. Whitehead has said that he "thought of both J. and Lila Mae as writers; Lila Mae writing *The Last Elevator* and having a room of her own, being apart from the world in order to create, and J. having his existential dilemma about writing and if it's worthwhile" (Sherman 23).

Whitehead's third protagonist significantly evokes both of his predecessors in numerous ways. Whereas Sutter contributes to the dissemination of popular culture and consumer goods by writing his puff pieces in *John Henry Days,* the "appropriately nameless" (Gates 12) protagonist of 2006's *Apex Hides the Hurt* is a writer even more directly implicated in the interrelated worlds of marketing and commerce. His job as a "nomenclature consultant" represents the most fundamental aspect of the advertising process, as plainly described in the novel's opening line: "He came up with the names" (Whitehead, *Apex* 3). As such he is the most minimalist of writers; his creations usually consist of one word, perhaps two or three in extraordinary circumstances. Unlike the Madison Avenue copywriters, designers, and visual artists, whose elaborate marketing campaigns were made familiar by the popular television show *Mad Men,* the protagonist's sole responsibility is discerning the name that best fits his clients' products or services. His creative process is nearly as mystical as Lila Mae's Intuitionist approach to elevator inspection: "Much of the work went on in the subconscious level. He was making connections between things without thinking and then, *bam* on the subway scratching a nose, or *bam* while stubbing a toe on the curb. Floating in neon before him was the name" (4). Also like Lila Mae, who insists that her metaphysical assessments of elevators are "never wrong" (Whitehead, *Intuitionist* 9), the protagonist claims professional infallibility: "When the products flopped, he told himself it was because of the marketing people. It was the stupid public. The crap-ass thing itself. Never the name because what he did was perfect" (Whitehead, *Apex* 4). He in fact does seem nearly perfect, having quickly risen to the pinnacle of his profession before being derailed by a "misfortune" (6). As is Whitehead's hallmark, the nature of this adversity remains cloaked in mystery for half the novel. The protagonist sees himself as a conduit between the as-yet insignificant thing and the name that will make it desirable to consumers by imparting precisely the appropriate meaning.

Apex Hides the Hurt continues fictionally exploring themes that Whitehead introduced in *The Intuitionist* and developed in *John Henry Days*. Like those earlier novels, *Apex Hides the Hurt* scrutinizes language and its functions in contemporary American society. Whitehead is especially interested in this novel in how names relate to the people, things, and places they identify: "What do names mean? What does it mean for a city to evolve over time? And how do we ascribe meaning to places with the faulty tool of language, which is already a mediated meaning?" (Chamberlin 61). Combining the intensely personal allegory of *The Intuitionist* with the mosaic-like polyphony of *John Henry Days*, *Apex Hides the Hurt* is an extended deliberation about the relationship between things (called "signifiers" in semiotic discourse) and their meanings ("signifieds") in the commerce-driven United States of the early 2000s. Such a subject raises certain questions about authority and motivation: Who has the means and opportunity to influence both the denotative (i.e., the most explicit and widely accepted) and connotative (more indirect and implicit) meanings of words? How and for what reasons has such influence been exerted, and what effect has it had on societies that use these words? What alternate meanings have been excluded or suppressed, and can they be recovered or rehabilitated? Like Umberto Eco, John Barth, Angela Carter, and Paul Auster, Whitehead uses historiographic metafiction to tell a vibrant story while also training his audience to become more semiotically proficient readers of both their words and their worlds.

Although the initial reviews of *Apex Hides the Hurt* were predominantly positive, they also expressed a notable degree of dissatisfaction with Whitehead's return to fiction five years after *John Henry Days*. Whitehead's receipt of a MacArthur Fellowship in 2002 significantly raised the already-high expectations for his next novel. The occasionally grudging appreciation of *Apex Hides the Hurt* suggests that Whitehead only partially satisfied reviewers who longed for a reprise of "the epic scope of *John Henry Days*" (Kirkus 15). For example, Anna Shapiro wrote that "readers not looking for direct emotional access to the characters may find it gratifying to solve the intellectual puzzle set here." The anonymous reviewer for *Publisher's Weekly* similarly complained that Whitehead presents his readers with an important "problem" regarding the relationship between history and language but then "doesn't give the problem enough room . . . to develop, and none of his characters is rich enough to give it weight."

Other reviewers seem to have recognized that although *Apex Hides the Hurt* has some thematic connections to Whitehead's earlier work, it also marks a conscious departure in form. It neither borrows from character-driven genres such as detective fiction like *The Intuitionist* did, nor does it have the encyclopedic inclinations of *John Henry Days*. Both David Gates and Saul Austerlitz recognized that Whitehead intentionally strips down his prose in *Apex Hides the Hurt*. Gates noted the novel's "parablelike" aspect and the effect of its metafictional intentions on its form: "Whitehead communicates his critique of language by way of language—which is the only imaginable delivery system. The old-time modernists used to think that honesty and precision in language, what Pound called 'direct treatment of the "thing" whether objective or subjective,' could Make It New, or as Eliot put it, 'purify the dialect of the tribe.' But like Shakespeare's fools, and like many writers of his own generation, Whitehead stakes what hope he has on indirection" (12). Austerlitz likewise made a virtue of Whitehead's concision, observing that the author "prefers a leaner, meaner brand of prose. He may be taking the air out of corporate America's pomposity, but he feels no need to imitate its tendencies to long-windedness. . . . Whitehead has a comic gift that stems in large part from his reluctance to use 20 words where two will serve him just as well." Both of these reviews point towards my conclusion that *Apex Hides the Hurt* is Whitehead's most thorough example of postsoul historiographic metafiction; practically every character and every plot twist contributes to an elaborate allegory about the corrupted nature of the language with which we write our histories, both collective and personal.

Semiotics and Postsoul Historiographic Metafiction

A brief summary of the fundamentals of semiotics is valuable before examining the structure and intentions of *Apex Hides the Hurt*. Arising from the work of Charles Sanders Peirce and Ferdinand de Saussure in the late nineteenth and early twentieth centuries, semiotics is a field of study that places aspects of

traditional linguistics into a broader anthropological context in order to ana-
lyze how and why the meanings of verbal and nonverbal "signs" develop within
a particular culture. Umberto Eco writes in *A Theory of Semiotics* (1976) that
"semiotics is concerned with everything that can be taken as a sign" (7). The
semiotic sign is the smallest unit of communication and is made up of a signifier and a signified, the interaction of which creates meaning that can be communicated between two or more individuals familiar with the sign.

To illustrate this point, one may consider the stop sign. As of the early
twenty-first century, a red octagon bearing a single word printed in white letters
has become a nearly universal traffic signal, indicating that drivers approaching
an intersection marked with such a sign have a legal obligation to bring their
vehicles to a full stop before continuing on through that intersection. The earli-
est versions of stop signs were used in Michigan in the early 1900s and were
yellow and black, but by the 1950s the now-familiar red and white octagon
became the standard in the United States, gradually expanding outward to
the rest of the world. The stop sign's design has become increasingly uniform
throughout the world and has even been formally governed by international law
since 1968, when the red and white octagonal signs were standardized by the
Vienna Convention on Road Signs and Signals.

But how and why did such an abstract sign come to convey this very particular meaning? After all, the word "stop"—as spelled with that particular
arrangement of letters in the Latin alphabet—is not present in the official
languages of many of the countries that have adopted the sign, yet the need
for drivers to obey stop signs is hardly limited to those who can read English.
This problem is not solved by simply translating the written command into the
local languages and alphabets, since doing so in turn makes the sign's message
incomprehensible to anyone unable to read those languages and alphabets. In
the absence of a universal written language, the alphabetical characters (and
the word they spell out) on the sign are themselves only a secondary indicator
of its intended message; the red octagonal shape itself is the most immediate
signifier, but nothing about a red octagon inherently suggests stopping in the
way that fire inherently signifies heat. The efforts to globally standardize traffic
rules are one part of a deliberate meaning-making process designed to quickly
convey the denotative (or most literal) meaning of the red octagon to anyone
driving a vehicle, regardless of their literacy. This conditioning process is intended to make the relationship between signifier (a red octagon emblazoned
with white letters, positioned in close proximity to a road) and signified (you
are expected to bring your vehicle to a complete stop before proceeding) as
universal as possible across cultures. It has been relatively successful, largely
because the perceived need for safe roads is also fairly universal.

But semiotics is not limited either to such literal instances of signs or to denotative meanings. As Daniel Chandler states, "anything which 'stands for' something else . . . words, images, sounds, gestures, and objects" (2) can be a semiotic sign, and meaning is generally far more complex than such simple imperatives as "Stop!" The deeper implications of semiotics appear in the Strivers Row chapter of *John Henry Days,* particularly as Jennifer's mother reacts to hearing her daughter play the "Ballad of John Henry" on the piano. The signifier in this instance is the same for Jennifer and her mother; it consists of a combination of the sounds being produced by the piano and Jennifer's voice, the individual words and phrases in the lyrics, and the physical representation of those sounds and words on the sheets of music that Jennifer has bought. This signifier *denotatively* expresses only the raw plot of John Henry's life and the melody that Jake Rose wrote to accompany it. However, the signified perceived by Jennifer's mother—that the song is "gutter music"—is *connotatively* different from Jennifer's perception of it as a liberating reminder that "you think you push but you are being pushed" (Whitehead, *John Henry* 278). Semioticians would explain that this almost diametrical opposition of signification arises from differences in the "codes" with which the two characters comprehend the world. Fundamentally, semiotic codes are contextual value systems that influence the way an individual will interpret a particular sign. Such value systems can be collective (driver's education courses encode a specific interpretation of the stop sign in all their participants) or highly individualized, as is the case with Jennifer's rebellion against her parents' rigid indoctrination. The ideological rivalry between Empiricists and Intuitionists in *The Intuitionist* can also be framed as a difference in semiotic codes, inasmuch as each group prejudicially values only partial subsets of the full range of possible information available from the elevators they inspect. The more a semiotic code overlaps between individuals largely determines the ease with which they can communicate, as shared codes tend to lead to shared signifieds.

Understanding semiotics is especially relevant to understanding Whitehead because it is an intrinsic element of both historiographic metafiction and postsoul discourse. Hutcheon contends that historians explain the past not only by selecting particular physical and textual signifiers as evidence to support their claims but also by creating and perpetuating particular signifieds (while suppressing or discarding others) that become authoritative cultural codes—i.e., "facts"—over time:

> All documents or artifacts used by historians are not neutral evidence for reconstructing phenomena which are assumed to have some independent existence outside [those documents and artifacts]. All documents possess

information and the very way in which they do so is itself a historical fact that limits the documentary conception of historical knowledge. This is the kind of insight that has led to a semiotics of history, for documents become signs of events which the historian transmutes into facts. The lesson here is that the past once existed, but that our knowledge of it is semiotically transmitted. (Hutcheon 122)

Recognition of this semiotic transmission does not inherently invalidate history, but it does negate the impulse to conceive of historical narratives as "truths" that are exempt from reconsideration. Such blind faith likely contributes to Whitehead's not "find[ing] history very reliable" (Sherman 15).

The postsoul aesthetic likewise consciously seeks to disturb the prevailing semiotic codes regarding blackness both within and outside the African American community. Any aesthetic is a semiotic code that inherently governs the creation and reception of artistic signs deemed beautiful or otherwise valuable by that aesthetic. Thus, Ellis outlines a semiotic code in the New Black Aesthetic that explicitly seeks to alter the signifier–signified relationship for blackness: "Today, there are enough young blacks torn between the two worlds [whiteness and blackness] to finally go out and create our own. The New Black Aesthetic says you just have to *be* natural, you don't necessarily have to *wear* one" (236, italics in original). The intentional "troubling [of] blackness" within Ashe's concept of "blaxploration" defines a process that changes the semiotics of blackness by rejecting any imposed judgments about supposedly "authentic" Black behaviors or beliefs: "Explicit post-soul blaxploration argues that blackness is constantly in flux, and in that way the post-soul aesthetic 'responds' to the 1960's 'call' for a fixed, iron-clad black aesthetic" (615). Finally, museum curator Thelma Golden's concept of "postblack" visual art makes basically the same argument for recoding semiotic associations: "According to Golden . . . the notion of postblack does not entail moving past any connection to race or racialized meanings, but rather traveling beyond past definitions of blackness that delimit creation or that necessitate certain artistic expectations" (H. Elam 381). Cohn suggests that "*Apex Hides the Hurt* can be read as a kind of meditation on . . . the 'post-soul condition'" (20), and I find the semiotic dimension of such a meditation indispensable to understanding the novel.

Again following a pattern established in his first two novels, Whitehead eschews linear chronology in narrating his third: "*Apex Hides the Hurt* alternates between two converging narratives. The dominant story of New York's most successful nomenclature consultant and his emergence from seclusion to take on a large freelance job somewhere in Middle America is interspersed with thematically related scenes depicting his earlier rise to fame and the 'misfortune' that led to his having left his job and become a recluse" (Lukin 125). Although less fantastical than *The Intuitionist* and less sprawling than *John Henry Days*, it still demands that readers reassemble a fragmented narrative that does not always provide information when it is seemingly needed. Whitehead once again tantalizes his reader, with this book's suspense resulting from the protagonist's curious commission to select the new name for a small city hitherto named Winthrop. Whitehead intentionally leaves the parameters of this assignment blurry for much of the novel, revealing the protagonist's reasons for being there at the same slow pace with which he reveals details of his preceding life and unusual career. Artificially separating these two interwoven narratives helps reveal Whitehead's intricate design, so let us turn first to the protagonist's backstory.

The Parable of the Seller: Naming Things, Truly and Falsely

The narrator of *Apex Hides the Hurt* repeats the phrase "They were good times" (3, 5) on three separate occasions in the opening six paragraphs. Validating this claim, the protagonist's professional success is described early on in exalted terms recalling J. Sutter's devotion to prime rib at the buffet in Hinton:

> He gave them the names and he saw the packages flying over the prescription counter, he saw the greedy hands grab them from the candy rack. He saw the names on the packaging printed over and over. Even when the gum wrappers were bunched up into little beetles of foil and scattered in the gutters, he saw the name printed on it and knew it was his. When they were hauled off to the garbage dump, the names blanched in the sun on the top of the heap and remained, even though what they named had been consumed. To have a name imprinted along the bottom of a Styrofoam container: this was immortality. He could see the seagulls swooping around in depressed circles. They could not eat it all. (5)

The ironic association of refuse with immortality and the exultation at the scavenging seagulls' failure to devour all the inedible pollution sets a skeptical tone regarding the ultimate value of a nomenclature consultant's work.

This impression is deepened by the "standard explanation" that the protagonist gives "without thinking" when describing his profession to a bartender: "I name things like new detergents and medicines and stuff like that so that they sound catchy. . . . You have some kind of pill to put people to sleep or make them less depressed so they can accept the world. Well you need a reassuring name that will make them believe in the pill. Or you have a new diaper. Now who would want to buy a brand of diaper called *Barnacle*? No one would buy that. So I think up good names for things" (22). He repeats this speech almost verbatim to a different person a few pages later, bothering only to change the products and names that he uses as examples. His nearly automatic recitation of this formula—itself reminiscent of an advertising "pitch"—testifies to his lack of emotional investment in it, as does his inability to respond to the scoffing reaction it induces in the Winthrop Hotel's crotchety bartender: "People pay you for that shit?" (22).

In fact, people pay him quite handsomely to for it, allowing him to lead a lavish lifestyle—"He was bonused repeatedly. . . . A local magazine picked him as one of the City's 50 Most Eligible Bachelors" (58)—that seemed unlikely at the outset of his strange career: "He had no purpose, he had no vocation. He had a job, which he lost, and so he answered the ad in the paper. The advertisement did not use the words *nomenclature consultant* because the big men upstairs knew that the esoteric is often scary. So the ad promised the chance to get in on the ground floor of an exciting new field and left it at that. With the red pen he had stolen on his last day at his last job, he circled the ad. Here's to new beginnings" (26). The fact that the potentially "scary" reality of his new job's title has to be euphemistically distorted in its own advertisement emphasizes the market demand for his ability to conceive names that are not just "catchy" or "good" but also persuasive to the point of manipulation.

He interviews for the job thinking it "would only be something to tide him over until he got a more permanent gig" and confesses ignorance about what a nomenclature consultant is when asked. He takes an aptitude test that essentially measures his semiotic encoding and recoding abilities: "There were normal everyday things with pretty much fixed names that they asked him to rename. This is an octagon. What would you call it? . . . Then to reverse it, they gave him a list of product names and asked him to think of what they might be attached to" (28). A day later, he is asked to return for an interview with his future boss, Roger Tipple, who glances at the protagonist's aptitude test results but mostly reminisces about their mutual collegiate alma mater, a fictional Harvard-like institution called Quincy: "Their conversation was facilitated by the fact that the same deathless geezers who had been around during Roger's time were still wheezing around during his time. As luck would have it. He was a Quincy man, and it turned out the firm had been founded by Quincy men. The name meant something. He fit right in" (28–29).

His connection to Quincy repeatedly proves even more significant than his almost preternatural gift for naming, one of Whitehead's first intimations that the semiotics of the corporate world are profoundly skewed. The Quincy name does not just mean "something" in denoting a particular institution of higher learning; it also connotes something far more instrumental: "Some names are keys and open doors. Quincy was one . . . . Quincy men formed the steel core of many a powerful elite, in politics, business, wherever there were dark back rooms" (69). Quincy is also described as an incarnate semiotic code that biologically, socially, and politically reproduces itself: "The sons and daughters of the famous attended Quincy and were anointed anew, for now they had two royal titles, one from the circumstance of their birth and the second from the four-year galvanizing process that occurred behind those ivy walls. . . . The presidents of foreign countries sent their sons to be educated at Quincy and they returned double agents, articulating American and Quincian directives in their native tongues" (69). The narrator makes the semiotic nature of Quincy's highly desirable reputation clear by describing it in the context of consumer goods: "On Parents Weekend, the proud relatives swarmed the square and snatched up sweatshirts and mugs with the bright green Q so that everyone would know they were a satellite of the pulsing Q star and somewhere in the Heavens too. It was a strong brand name, as they said in his business" (70).

Whitehead complicates the ethics of the protagonist's adoption of this brand, depicting it as part of a lifelong process of downplaying or entirely negating the significance of his race. His opportunity to become a "Quincy man" began when the college mailed him pamphlets that underscored its "belie[f] in diversity." This sincerity of this language is undercut by the pamphlet's underlying marketing strategy: "He had filled out a form the previous summer at the African American Leaders of Tomorrow conference. . . . The pamphlet that came in the mail was his introduction to the world of mailing lists, target marketing" (70). Stephanie Li notes the superficiality of Quincy's inclusivity:

> Whitehead's protagonist easily enters and succeeds in white-dominated institutions. This difference highlights the success of multicultural reforms of the late twentieth century, but, as the novel repeatedly insists, these changes do not herald a new age of equality. . . . Though it welcomes students from various backgrounds, Quincy does not itself change. Instead it produces students in its own rarefied image. . . . Racial diversity appears to thrive at Quincy, but the "double agents" it produces reveal that any meaningful conception of racial difference has not simply become invisible but has been wholly erased. (*Signifying* 74–75)

Such erasure of difference becomes the novel's primary theme once the product mentioned in the title—an adhesive bandage named Apex—appears.

Even before that, however, the protagonist "erases" aspects of himself at his new job. Lila Mae did something similar by dressing as much as possible like the other inspectors. One of the men ransacking her apartment mocks her behavior as "an attempt to fit in that unavoidably calls attention to itself" and asserts that it marks her unmistakably as being "of the colored persuasion"

(Whitehead, *Intuitionist* 28). Of course, as a "first," Lila Mae's race and sex *are* incredibly significant, but she has learned through a painful history of discrimination how to "make such a sad face hard," hiding the pain that might otherwise make her vulnerable (57). The protagonist of *Apex Hides the Hurt* does not face such open hostility; in fact, upon starting his new job he initially feels superior to his new colleagues: "He believed himself to be of a different caliber than those men. Jocky white guys. He didn't need the same things. The cheap posturing. The signature colognes. The obscure wafting" (34). However, as he comes to understand and to enjoy the work, he begins successfully contributing names to the firm's brainstorming sessions and finds himself undeniably changed: "They looked at him and he said it: *Redempta*. It was the name. It stuck. They got paid. Not long after that he got his own office. He had to admit, it was pretty cool" (36). His sense of being "of a different caliber" dissipates as he begins to enjoy the material benefits of the job whose name he once had not understood. The protagonist's transformation into one of "those men" at the firm echoes the narrator's observation that he "did not come to appreciate the peculiar magnetism of the Quincy name until he graduated, when its invisible waves sorted the world into categories, repelling the lesser alloys, attracting those of kindred ore at job interviews, parties, in bedrooms" (70–71). The protagonist proves eager to "buy into" codes that contradict— or at least depart from—his own values in exchange for material comfort, an ethical transaction that his subsequent "misfortune" hints is damaging and unsustainable.

Before his downfall, Whitehead depicts the protagonist at the literal and figurative apex of his career. The protagonist's firm is hired by Ogilvy and Myrtle, the maker of "the number-six adhesive bandage in the country [which] wanted to re-create itself as the number two adhesive bandage in the country" (87). The narrator recounts the long, unspectacular history of this product, before observing that the company "came to [the protagonist] and he saved them" (79). Prior to becoming Apex, the bandage is notable mostly for being shoddy: "Whatever the reason, poor craftsmanship was the star the company ship steered by, and they tacked expertly. . . . Water or no water, they self-destructed after twelve hours regardless, so that when you reached into your pocket for your wallet, the bandage clung to the rim of your pocket and tore off, the pocket pulled the scab off, and you bled on your clothes and your dollars. A person couldn't win with these things" (77–78). Furthermore, the protagonist considers the bandage's previous name—Dr. Chickie's Adhesive Strips—and marketing strategy to be the creation of "amateur namers of yore [who] were like medieval witch doctors who never saw a patient unless armed with a bucket of leeches" (78). This combination dooms it to obscurity in an

industry dominated by Band-Aid, which is described with a grandiose metaphor borrowed from epic literature: "The name was the thing itself, and that
was Holy Grail territory" (87). His speculations about the likely buyers of Dr.
Chickie's bandages are as uncharitable as J. Sutter's initial thoughts about West
Virginia: "The only people who used the product lived in small hamlets where
everybody believed Truman was still the president; on visiting their homesteads
the mailman shoved in pitches for land deals in Florida and sweepstakes guarantees and little else" (79). In short, the protagonist seems to have his work cut
out for him in achieving this company's goal of "claiming a certain percentage
of future accidents as [their] own" (87).

Before he comes up with the Apex name, though, another unseen and unnamed "whiz kid" (87) radically alters its superficial appearance: "You manu-
facture this thing and call it flesh. It belongs to another race. I have different
ideas about what color flesh is, he told them. We come in colors. And we want
to see ourselves when we look down at ourselves, our arms and legs" (88). This
gimmick relies on a simplistic one-to-one correlation between racial identity
and skin color, promising that "the deep psychic wounds of history and the
more recent gashes ripped by the present . . . could be covered by this wonderful, unnamed multicultural adhesive bandage. It erased" (90). Whitehead's
choice of verbs is immensely important here, as the bandage only pledges to
"cover" and to "erase" the "wounds" and "gashes" caused by centuries of racism. Apex claims to "serve diversity" (89), but as Li points out, "As in Quincy,
diversity is showcased superficially, and integration means conforming to
preexisting values." She adds that "there is a dangerous implication to Apex's
vision of the world that is apparent in its clever slogan. Apex promises to 'hide'
the hurt, not heal it." (*Signifying* 81–82). The bandage's inferior quality is no
more addressed by this rebranding than a crumbling wall is fixed by a fresh
coat of paint. Neither the twenty new colors intended to signify racial diversity
nor the pretentious connotations of the name Apex—"Didn't history rise to a
point? Couldn't they all look down from today and survey all that had come before, all that little stuff we squinted at that was not special and so far away and
pronounce ourselves Apex?" (Whitehead, *Apex* 100)—offset the fact that the
protagonist's ostensible masterwork is merely another euphemism concealing
an undesirable problem. Much as he purges aspects of himself in exchange for
wealth, privilege, and professional success, his signature naming job intentionally distorts reality to sell a product.

Whitehead stated in an interview that Apex is definitely intended to satirize
shallow and/or insincere efforts at pluralism, but that it also targets overly rigid
semiotic codes in general: "Certain forms of multicultural cheerleading are as
susceptible to corruption as capitalist boosterism and frontier idealism, two

other systems I talk about in *Apex*. Every -ism has its weakness. . . . *Apex* isn't
the only Band-Aid in the book" (Selzer, "New" 399). The main problem with
Apex's attempted rebranding is that it actually expands the inferior bandages'
potential to cause harm by offering false hope: "Apex, in superficially fixing one
problem, creates others" (396).

This innate harmfulness reflects back on the protagonist via his "misfortune," which begins with the forgettable act of stubbing his toe: "He couldn't
remember after all that happened what he stubbed his toe on. . . . In all prob-
ability he stumbled over something small and insignificant, as is only appropriate for such a shriveled, gargoyle word like *stub*" (Whitehead, *Apex* 130–31,
italics in original). Despite his toe becoming a "murk of thick blood, cotton
lint, and gashed flesh," he downplays the injury in an echo of Lila Mae's attempts at anonymity in elementary school: "Which toe was it? One of the shy
ones, not the big toe, or the middle, but the one next to the pinky. It sat at the
back of the class and did its homework, not likely to be voted anything. Never
Best this, or Most Likely to that." After applying an appropriately colored
Apex, the protagonist believes this small crisis to be resolved: "The brown
adhesive bandage was such a perfect tone that it looked as if he'd never had a
toenail at all. That he had never stumbled. Did it hide the hurt? Most assuredly
so" (131).

But he *did* stumble and continues to do so, reinjuring and grievously infect-
ing the toe. As he reapplies Apex after Apex, he deludes himself that his "hurt"
is not worsening even though the evidence hidden beneath the substandard
bandages clearly attests otherwise. His decline parallels J. Sutter's choking
episode in *John Henry Days* both in being largely self-inflicted and in warning
about the consequences of carelessness. Both instances depict physical manifestations of an underlying ethical corruption that results from perpetuating
the kind of bad faith that finds fulfillment in free prime rib dinners and immortality in discarded Styrofoam: "The deceptive quality of the product [Apex]
actually aggravates the wound, which, for unstated reasons, must be hidden
from view. . . . Healing wounds will not sell more adhesive bandages; rather,
the consumer must always be left in a state of perpetual injury" (Li, *Signifying*
92). Whitehead implies that a person with even a shred of conscience cannot
maintain such a deceptive process for long.

As his infection worsens, the protagonist becomes more conscious of mis-
using his semiotic talents. While on a mandatory corporate retreat (in which he
refuses to participate, beyond traveling to the country house where it occurs),
his pain triggers a glimmer of enlightenment: "His foot throbbed. . . . He dealt
in lies and promises, distilled them into syllables. They were easier to digest
that way" (Whitehead, *Apex* 153). This insight is pushed aside by a callous

observation about nature's inherent marketability, but his toe seems to send him a corrective message. He loses his balance and steps in foul-smelling mud that soaks both his shoes and his already damaged toe. His mordant observation about this development also conveys an unmistakable satirical commentary on what he has earned for his professional brilliance: "He remembered that the next farm over handled pigs. Look at him, he thought. Top of his field, cock of the walk: up to his ankles in pig shit" (154).

This misstep causes a full-blown medical crisis and by the time the protagonist is slated to attend the Identity Awards, an Oscars-like ceremony exclusively for the nomenclature industry, his toe is a disaster: "Underneath the Apex, the grim narrative continued apace. He peeled off the bandage to moist sounds and released a putrid stench. Twin to the awfulness of the smell was what his eyes told him" (161–62). Ironically his toe is so discolored that "the Apex no longer matched his skin," but he covers it with another bandage anyway, vowing to see a doctor the next day. During the ceremony he hallucinates a semiotically transcendent vision as the presenters and award-winners parade past: "He imagined that all of them had their true names written on their name tags" (170). The protagonist's fever dream momentarily restores a sense that there is a core truth within names that have been reduced to marketing codes: "That would be something. That would be honest, he whispered to himself. LIAR. BED WETTER. . . . If everyone could see everyone's true name, we would cut out all this subterfuge and camouflage. The deception that was their stock in trade, and the whole world's favorite warm teat" (170). He continues identifying people by what he thinks of as their true names until he has to leave, sweat-soaked and near collapse. His name is called, presumably as an award-winner for Apex, but he hears only "fugitive" (171), suggesting that, like Cora in *The Underground Railroad,* he is seeking his freedom from an unjust and harmful environment.

He stumbles into Times Square, the epicenter of his industry's influence: "The names here were magnificent, gigantic, powered by a million volts and blinking in malevolent dynamism. Off the chart. The most powerful of all names lived here and it was all he could do to stare. He had entered the Apex" (181). He stands still, bordering on semiotic overload as all the signs—literal and figurative—around him broadcast their messages. The same nomenclature consultant who previously declared himself "perfect" and "immortal" is suddenly meek and humble: "He saw all the logos and names, and saw himself as some brand of mite lost in the pages of the musty encyclopedia of the world" (181–82). Numbering himself among the "disreputable gods" for "imprison[ing] as *products* . . . these names [that] were the names of heroes who had performed miraculous feats," he recognizes the hubris of his previously unshakeable sense of infallibility: "What he had given to all those things had been the right name, but never the true name. For things had true natures, and they hid behind false names, beneath the skin we gave them" (182, italics in original). From a semiotic perspective, he understands that his industry makes its money by obscuring denotative meanings behind illusory connotative ones; his names construct codes that ensure that his clients' signs—their products and services—communicate only their desirability and nothing else: "A name that got to the heart of the thing—that would be miraculous. But he never got to the heart of the thing, he just slapped a bandage on it to keep the pus in" (183).

When the protagonist collapses from his fever, Whitehead leaves open the possibility that he can metaphorically die and be reborn by embracing this new perspective. However, as he lies in a hospital bed after the amputation of his mangled toe, the empowering potential of his vision is in danger of being drowned out by his consumerist conventional wisdom: "He liked his epiphanies American: brief and illusory. Which is why he felt so disappointed that a week after the operation he still felt such deep disquiet. Pierce the veil, sure, that was one thing. To walk around with the weight of what he had witnessed, quite another" (198). While explaining his toe's decrepitude to his doctor, he illustrates Li's observation about how Apex fosters a "perpetual state of injury" (*Signifying* 92): "He hadn't even known anything was amiss down there, apart from the pain from the constant stubbing, which, truth be told, he had accepted as his lot and gotten used to after a while" (Whitehead, *Apex* 200). Unable to rediscover his zeal for finding the "true names" of things, he also finds it impossible to return to his old life. Like Bobby Figgis in *John Henry Days,* the protagonist withdraws, interrupting his "recluse lifestyle" (201) only when his former boss desperately calls him up for help with an overdue account. A car company needs a name for its "new line of mid-priced hybrid-fuel minivans" and "knew they wanted '100' in the name" in addition to some other "element." Roger Tipple frantically informs the protagonist that the firm's staff is out of ideas; after a brief moment of reflection the protagonist simply says, "Give them a Q," and hangs up (202). Evoking the "Q" on the aforementioned host of Quincy-themed products, the protagonist's curt input earns him a check, but he feels none of his previous satisfaction. In fact, his reaction testifies to the semiotic emptiness of his work: "A Q. It was a name reduced to abstraction. To meaninglessness. It depressed him, the ridiculousness of seeing his whim carved into the culture. How'd you come up with that? Just sitting around and it occurred to me. What curdled in his thoughts was how easy it was, even after his misfortune" (203). He no longer revels in this ease, but Whitehead nevertheless concludes the exposition of the protagonist's life with the blunt assertion that "[n]othing had changed" (203).

Struggling to Decide: Winthrop, New Prospera, or Freedom?

The novel's present-day thread begins three pages into the novel as the self-exiled protagonist receives yet another phone call from his former office, possibly the first since the one regarding the name for the minivan that closes the other timeline: "He hadn't kept up with Roger since his misfortune. . . . He hadn't kept up with anyone from the office and for the most part, they hadn't kept up with him. Who could blame them really, after what happened" (6). Tipple informs him of a "job that wasn't appropriate for the firm because of conflict of interest" (7), adding that he has recommended the protagonist to the client as a qualified freelancer. The narrator indicates that "if Roger had called a week ago he would have said no" (8), but the protagonist accepts the job, although it is unstated whether he does so out of interest in reentering the world, boredom with his endless days of watching television, or some other motivation.

As it turns out, the town of Winthrop's three-person governing council has hired the protagonist to resolve an ongoing dispute about its name. Because of an unusual law dating back to the town's founding, a referendum of Winthrop's residents is not an option, and each of the three council members supports an intractable position based on what and whom they represent. Albie Winthrop is the affable, eccentric heir to a dwindling fortune that his ancestors earned in the old-fashioned business of making barbed wire. The protagonist immediately discerns that seemingly everything of a certain vintage is named for Albie's family, a testament to their longstanding influence: "He was in the Winthrop Suite of the Hotel Winthrop on Winthrop Street in Winthrop Square in the Town of Winthrop in Winthrop County. He didn't have a map of the area, but he told himself that if he ever got lost he should look for the next deeper level of Winthrop" (13–14). Albie unsurprisingly believes in preserving Winthrop's name, since for him it signifies the town's glory days; however, the shambling state of his mansion, his Bentley, and his body all confirm that those days are over.

Standing in contrast to Albie is Lucky Aberdeen, the ambitious head of a software company that bears his name. From the first time the protagonist sees him in "his costume," Lucky exudes the media-saturated, image-conscious celebrity of the electronic age: "His trademark was a fringed leather vest spotted with turquoise sequins on one breast that described the Big Dipper. It was familiar from TV, from the cover of the guy's book, which had been a best-seller a year ago. . . . Lucky had spent some time in the Southwest after he dropped out of a fancy northeast school, and there on his back in the desert, among the cacti and the scorpions, squinting at the night sky, he had formulated his unique corporate philosophy" (16). A visionary, somewhat messianic techno-capitalist in the mold of Bill Gates and Steve Jobs, Lucky is proposing that the town change its name to "New Prospera," which the protagonist associates with "new money, new media, new economy" and "reckoned . . . would look good on maps. Nestled among all those Middletons and Shadyvilles." His initial impression is that "it wasn't that bad a name, certainly no masterpiece" (52).

The council's third member is the town's African American mayor, Regina Goode. Regina favors returning to "Freedom," the name given to the town by the emancipated slaves—one of whom is her direct ancestor—who founded it before being displaced by the Winthrops. Although personally drawn more to Regina than to either Albie or Lucky, the protagonist initially mocks her preference as both outdated and trite: "Freedom. He whistled. If he'd offered up Freedom in a meeting, he'd have been run out of town, his colleagues in full jibber behind him, waving torches. It was like something from the B-GON days, an artifact of the most pained and witless nomenclature" (83).

The protagonist's contract remains unsigned upon his arrival because the council is leery of his unusual stipulation that "they had to let the name [he chose] stand for a minimum of one year" because he "did not want to waste his time" with a group of people unfamiliar with the "rules of the game," unlike his more knowing corporate clients. His policy is designed to circumvent several concerns that might hinder his usual process: "When dealing with such a green group, the chance of encountering that random X factor was considerably higher. The object in question was a town. There was family and clan to think about, and their bickering. There was heritage and history involved, and their inscrutable demands" (31). Just as the bandage's underlying shoddiness requires suppression for Apex's desired connotations of perfection to be conveyed, he treats human relationships as inconvenient obstacles rather than intrinsic realities worthy of consideration.

The omniscient narrator soon exposes that these rigid contractual stipulations are also meant to conceal the protagonist's emotional fragility: "It occurred to him that by forcing such exacting conditions on his clients, he hoped to use their refusal as an excuse. To hide his fear behind the impassive façade of the uncompromising professional. The sad shake of the head that said: I have a list of principles. By removing the possibility of failure, he could return home to his convalescence rooms and continue to sulk, pretending he still possessed his power" (31–32). The contract is still unsigned as of his second night in Winthrop, during which he has a nightmare that symbolically expresses his ongoing anxiety: "Rats bubbled out of the sewers, poured out of gutters and abandoned buildings. Making little rat noises. They were everywhere, and he knew that although they wore the skin of rats, they were in fact phonemes, bits

of words with sharp teeth and tails. Latin roots, syllables to be added or sub-
tracted to achieve an effect, kickers in their excellent variety, odd fricatives, and
they chased him down. They finally cornered him in an old warehouse, and he
woke as they started nibbling on his vanished toe, which had reattached itself
as though it had never been lost" (52–53). Upon awakening he finds an envelope
shoved under his door with a letter inside indicating the council's acceptance of
his terms. Thus, as he starts his work, his mind still resonates with the image of
his toe—a symbol for the "list of principles" (32) he claims to uphold—being
consumed by ravenous fragments of a disingenuous advertising language, much
like Bobby Figgis was "devoured by pop" (Whitehead, *John Henry* 111).

The second section of the novel ramps up its use of postsoul historiographic
metafiction by complicating the protagonist's judgments about the town and
its people. Each of the council members advocates for their desired name by
proffering a highly selective vision of the town's identity. Regina initially presents herself as a savvy politician, able to represent a range of constituencies:
"People look at me and they see what they want to see. Black people see me
as family, because my name goes way back. The white people know what the
Goode name means in this community—tradition, like Winthrop means tradition. And the new people know that I agree with a lot of what Lucky is trying
to do and that he and I have been a team, in terms of trying to bring this place
into the twenty-first century" (Whitehead, *Apex* 114). Nevertheless, she also
tries to appeal to the protagonist's racial solidarity by clarifying why she feels
so strongly that Freedom is the town's "true name" (127): "Sometimes when I
have a hard day and I'm too tired to leave the office . . . I think about how they
got here. In their wagons, all that way from the plantations that had been their
homes. Think about that: those places were their homes. Places of degradation
and death. So I get my ass out of my office because I have a house that is my
own and that's what they fought for, why they came all this way. They didn't
know where they were headed when they started or that they'd end up here,
all they knew was what they had: Freedom" (116). Regina's reverence for the
sacrifices of past generations is literalized by the names of streets in Winthrop's
predominantly African American areas. As she tells the protagonist during a
tour of her neighborhood, "Over here, the streets are people. They're your history, your family. Richards, Nathaniel, Goode. How you know you're home is
when you see yourself on the street" (128).

Coincidental with the protagonist's visit, Lucky hosts a massive conference
that is little more than a sales pitch to lure new investors and new employees to
both Aberdeen Software and what he hopes will soon be New Prospera. The optimistic and forward-looking tone of the entire event affirms the title of Lucky's
autobiography, *Lucky Break: How a Small-Town Boy Took on Corporate*

America—and Won! (93). He also exerts a hidden control over the media by sending a reporter to interview the protagonist for a "puff" piece worthy of the junketeers from *John Henry Days*. The interviewer asks such loaded questions as "What makes New Prospera such a great name?" and reports only those snippets of the protagonist's lengthy answer that reinforce the positive image Lucky wants publicized (104–5). When the protagonist protests that he has not yet decided on the town's name, the ostensible journalist quickly redirects him, basically answering, rather than asking a question: "What I find so interesting is the world of opportunities that a wonderful name like New Prospera will bring to the town. . . . Big business looking for a tax-friendly haven, young people who want a fresh start. To start a family in a positive environment close to the conveniences of a big city" (106). When the resulting article is published with the headline "MAKING THE CASE FOR NEW PROSPERA: CONSULTANT VOWS TO 'KEEP IT REAL'" (155) on the same day that Lucky hosts a massive barbecue for all the conference attendees, the protagonist realizes he has been unwillingly enlisted in Lucky's public relations campaign and reminds himself to explain to Regina and Albie "that, no, he was not in Lucky's pocket as they had suspected from the beginning" (156). Lucky is shown not just as fortunate, but also quite manipulative regarding both the sign of his personal brand and its signified message.

Finally, as befits his role as his family's champion, Albie sends a copy of a "local history written by a town librarian" (12) to the protagonist's hotel room. This book not surprisingly turns out to be little more than a "corporate pamphlet" for Albie's familial legacy: "After a few pages of stuff like 'that famous quality of generosity that distinguishes the Winthrop family' and 'Once again, the Winthrops came to the rescue in a time of need,' he checked the copyright page and confirmed his suspicion. The book had been commissioned by the Winthrop Foundation. Winning over the town librarian for sympathetic press wasn't too much of a task, he figured" (59). The book focuses on the family patriarch, Sterling Winthrop, and is filled with nineteenth-century historical platitudes about the economic benefits of White settlement in the American West: "After winning over the area's main inhabitants—a loose band of colored settlers—Winthrop opened up his factory and started producing his famous W-shaped barb. . . . Grateful for this fresh start, they passed a law and named the town Winthrop, after the man who had the courage to dream" (60–61). Lucky Aberdeen basically proposes to do to Winthrop what Sterling Winthrop did generations earlier to Freedom, linking the two men's perspectives together like peas in a capitalist pod.

The offhand mention of the "colored settlers" (Regina's literal and figurative ancestors) is typical of the version of American history that arises out of

Manifest Destiny, a predominantly nineteenth-century notion that associates civilization and progress exclusively with the arrival of Whites and their ostensible cultural, moral, and technological superiority. Such a mindset is articulated even more directly and heartlessly in *The Underground Railroad* by the slave catcher Arnold Ridgeway. Albie reveals his sympathy with this perspective by insisting that "[i]t was only a settlement really . . . where Regina's family decided to stop one day. They just dropped their bags here" (71). The Winthrops' version of history attributes intent and wisdom only to themselves, effectively erasing the freed slaves' role as founders of the town. The protagonist, no stranger to downplaying racial significance, seems inclined to agree with their viewpoint as he mocks the town's original name: "Freedom. Freedom. Freedom. It made his brain hurt. Must have been a bitch to travel all that way only to realize they forgot to pack the subtlety" (77). His reference to the name's lack of "subtlety" reveals his singular focus on its connotative effectiveness, as though it were an advertising campaign. He later complains that "Freedom was so defiantly unimaginative as to approach a kind of moral weakness" (83) and that "Regina's forebears were the laziest namers he'd ever come across," entirely discounting the fact that recently emancipated slaves might deeply value a forthright denotative declaration of being free. The fact that he calls them "My people, my people" (95) even as he denigrates their self-affirming choice testifies to his lack of real sympathy; he has made it almost impossible for a shared past to register with him.

As Cohn notes, this aspect of the protagonist's characterization again calls back to Whitehead's earlier work (19). Near the end of *John Henry Days,* Whitehead includes a flashback to an orgiastic revel in honor of Godfrey Frank, "the man of the hour . . . [who] shambled through the media like a creature from a science fiction film, a monster whose mutant gigantism he could doubtless locate in nuclear-age anxiety, cold war terror." Seemingly every manifestation of the world of puff is at the party, deeply indulging in its excesses, not the least of which is the superficial erudition of Frank's writing: "He could write about anything it seemed, from baseball to hip-hop to weapons manufacturers, hold forth no historicized interpretations of ladies underwear while sprinkling in obscure double entendres for the Medievalists in the cheap seats" (328). Among the partygoers Sutter "alone was not carefree, this night he was a chap of heavy heart, unswayed by ambient and intrusive cheer." Having recently read about the death of a former black nationalist academic named Toure Nkrumeh, Sutter finds himself somewhat surprised that this news "weighed on him" (323). He remembers taking a course with the elder revolutionary as an undergraduate, enjoying the stories of his exploits with the Black Panthers, and even helping to occupy an administrative office in an effort to gain Nkrumeh's approval (and to meet girls). Sutter also admits to a fellow junketeer nicknamed One Eye that he never spoke to Nkrumeh personally and cannot quite fathom why his death has upset him so. One Eye diagnoses his problem immediately: "You're not upset that the guy's dead. . . . You're upset that you don't care that the guy is dead. That you should be feeling something that good people feel when someone dies" (335). One Eye's next comment, though, is still more disturbing: "Hold on to these days. You still care that you don't care. The time will come when you don't care that you don't care, and on that day you will become a man" (336). In essence, One Eye intimates that Sutter will be fully integrated into the world of puff when signifiers lose all of their emotional power. Such a condition renders impotent any story—whether mythic or historical—reliant on empathic connection. The stories of John Henry and Regina's family are equally imperiled by such a blasé mindset. Although Whitehead's portrayal stops short of venerating Nkrumeh, he acknowledges the detrimental consequences of being completely unmoved by such activism on behalf of African Americans, leading to what Cohn calls Whitehead's sense of "guilty endebtedness to the past" (21).

Like Sutter in the final stages of *John Henry Days,* the protagonist of *Apex Hides the Hurt* haltingly begins working through his own feelings of being "haunted by debts to shadowy cultural fathers and the names they have bequeathed" (Cohn 21). He discovers suppressed information about Winthrop's history that refutes both the romanticized visions of the past and the future that Albie and Lucky, respectively, pitch to him and Regina's oversimplified tale of self-empowerment. He performs some additional research at the town's public library, which he learns is being relocated in order to convert its current location into a trendy clothing store (a fairly blunt satirical comment on contemporary American cultural values). The sole remaining librarian is packing up books for the impending transfer, but she responds eagerly to the protagonist's questions, filling in the massive gaps in the "official" history's two-sentence discussion of Freedom's transformation into Winthrop: "It was basically a business deal, really. . . . Winthrop comes along and falls in love with the area—that river traffic, at any rate—and so they decided to make it all legal. I think it was hard to argue with the kind of access Winthrop'd provide to the outside world—having a white guy up front—so they got together to incorporate the town" (Whitehead, *Apex* 95). She cannot account for why the law empowers only the council to change the name, but she does bring the protagonist an unabridged history that proves considerably more revelatory than the fawning "pamphlet" he had previously read.

Although an initial scan of this expanded version only hints at "a redirecting of the spotlight" rather than a wholesale revelation of hidden details, he encounters numerous references to Regina's ancestor Abraham Goode and his fellow founder William Field, whose opposing personalities earned them the respective nicknames "the Light and the Dark. . . . [Goode] came off as the optimist-prophet type, quick on the draw with a pick-me-up from the Bible and a reminder of their rights as American citizens. [Field] turned out to be a downer-realist figure, handy with a 'this stretch of river is too treacherous to cross' and an 'it is best that we not tarry here past sundown'" (141–42). The volume tells how the group of former slaves were forced to abandon an earlier settlement after a lost White boy accidentally wanders into their camp. The differing reactions of Goode and Field—more accurately, the protagonist's internalized reenactment of it—epitomize their divergent outlooks: "Goode was of the mind that they had a moral duty as Christians and Americans to help him. A modern translation would be something along the lines of 'We shall return this child to the proper authorities.' In response, Field offered . . . 'I think we should point this kid toward the woods and tell his skinny little ass to keep walking,' being of the firm opinion that no amount of explaining was going to keep the Man from bringing his foot down on their collective necks. And just to be safe, the best thing to do would be to pack up and put as much distance between them and him, ASAP" (143). Goode's counsel ultimately wins out, but the settlers are also forced to adopt the second part of Field's recommendation. When asked by his parents about where he has been, the newly returned Lost White Boy responds, "The niggers found me" (145). Instead of being grateful for his safe return, the boy's White community validates Field's prediction, burning down what remains behind after forcing the homesteaders to flee. The narrator ironically remarks that they had once again faced "that kindling problem of being black in America—namely how to avoid becoming it" (145).

Goode's belief that attaining freedom also means gaining full citizenship in American society and respect from "the proper authorities" again echoes a historical discourse within African American culture, namely the "assimilationist" mindset associated—sometimes imprecisely—with Booker T. Washington. Born a slave, Washington became a prominent leader in the Black community at the end of the nineteenth century by advocating a gradual process of compromise with Whites rather than insistence on immediate equality. Although Washington and Du Bois disagreed vehemently in this regard, both were influential in forming the "uplift" philosophy that Whitehead previously scrutinized in *The Intuitionist* and in the Strivers Row section of *John Henry Days*. Field's attitude resembles Washington's perspective far less than that of Marcus Garvey, perhaps the early twentieth century's most ardent promoter of "Back-to-Africa" attitudes. Garvey—and others with similar views going back to the nineteenth century—proposed to end racial strife in the United States by moving the descendants of Africans who had been enslaved and brought to America back to new, independent countries in Africa. The protagonist articulates the philosophical division between Goode and Field—and, by extension, between assimilationism and Black nationalism—as follows: "The Lost White Boy . . . tapped into this key moment where they had to decide if they were going to continue to deal with the white world, or say: You go your way and we'll go ours. Decide what exactly was the shape and character of the freedom they had been given" (144). His thoughts spell out how the unambiguously affirmative connotation of freedom that Regina perceives is not the word's sole possible signified.

Reading further, the protagonist realizes that there "were many lessons to be drawn from that story" and specifies the most salient one: "Listen to the Dark. He was warming up to this Field character. The man had his head on straight" (145). Although Field's nickname initially seems intended to contrast his gloomy realism against Goode's hopefulness, the racial dimension of learning to heed "the Dark" should not be discounted, given that the protagonist has for the most part been denying the significance of his own blackness throughout the book. This personal erasure is paralleled throughout the book by his profession's drive to "hide the hurt" and by the historical suppression of disempowered viewpoints. Thus, what is metaphorically "in the dark" is not necessarily there for valid or just reasons, and "listening to" it requires being open to more critical and less superficial interpretations of signs.

Cora gradually learns a comparable lesson about freedom and darkness in *The Underground Railroad.* Upon boarding the literal subterranean train that takes her away from Georgia, she is advised by a "conductor" named Lumbly to "[l]ook outside as you speed through, and you'll find the true face of America" (69). His words return to her during a later escape from Tennessee, leading her to remark that "[i]t was a joke, then, from the start. There was only darkness outside the windows on her journeys, and only ever would be darkness." (262–63). This pessimism is countered by yet another invocation of Lumbly's advice as she moves—"limping, tripping over crossties"—on foot through the railroad's tunnels near the novel's conclusion. Having recently been disillusioned about yet another source of hope on the country's surface, she now transmutes Lumbly's "joke" into a manner of Intuitionist communion with the darkness below ground: "Her fingers danced over valleys, rivers, the peaks of mountains, the contours of a new nation hidden beneath the old. *Look outside as you speed through, and you'll find the true face of America.* She could not see it but she felt it, moved through its heart. . . . She'd find the terminus or die on the tracks" (304, italics in original).

Such existential significance has already been hinted at in *Apex Hides the Hurt* by the protagonist's epiphany in Times Square about the "true natures [that] hid behind false names" (182). It is reinforced as he drives around Winthrop with Regina, questioning his entire task: "Welcome to Freedom. Welcome to Winthrop. Welcome to New Prospera. Tear down the old signs, put up new ones in their place—it didn't change the character of the place, did it? It didn't cover up history. Not for the last time, he wondered what his clients believed they could achieve. And what exactly he was doing here" (129). Having posed it, Whitehead once again denies the reader the satisfaction of an easy answer to this question. Despite his doubts about the whole renaming process and his stated desire to "listen to the Dark," the protagonist is seduced anew at the barbecue marking the close of Lucky's conference. As he did upon arriving in Winthrop, he initially feels separated from the other attendees, but begins to "fit right in" (173) while filling himself with barbecued meat from Lucky's grill and "half-price margaritas" (171). Moreover, in a parody of advertising's "sex sells" cliché, the librarian who earlier gave him the town's unabridged history now shows up at the party in a "short leather skirt that . . . had become, in the fullness of the evening, a most appropriate addition to the festivities, forward-looking, visionary even, in its erotic promise" (174). Awash in hedonistic comforts, "he had a sudden notion of this last week as socialization boot camp. An artificial environment created to prepare him for his reintroduction to the world." Accepting this drunken euphoria as insight, he decides that "everything around him was Lucky's appeal" and that "these people were already living in New Prospera whether they knew it or not" (174).

He decides that New Prospera is "what they needed. Narcotic. Hypnotizing" (177). Before fully embracing his decision, though, he imagines both Goode and Field in his situation: "Goode announces in preacherly tones, 'We are Americans and the bounty of American promise is our due. It is what we worked for, it is what we died for, and we call it New Prospera.' . . . He pictured Field but the vision was dimmer. He saw a lone figure, withdrawing into the shadow after delivering a grim, pithy 'Where you sit is where you stand.' And really, what the hell were people supposed to extract from that?" (177–78). This rhetorical question is soon answered as the protagonist jumps on a table, prepared to reveal his choice—and thereby renounce his intention to seek deeper meanings from "the Dark": "To be done with his stupid exile. Why had he removed himself so completely from those things that others cherished, with his needless complications and equivocations. It was all very simple, after all. Why did he need to make it so difficult all the time. So dark in outlook all the time, frankly" (179). But before he can slip back into the comfort of easy answers, "something in him gave way, and his bad leg jackknifed with such speed that he was on the floor in an ugly mess before anyone could catch him" (179). Whitehead reinjects the physical manifestation of the protagonist's conscience into the story to remind him (and the reader) of the novel's satirical intentions. New Prospera is *not* the answer, only the same problematic old answer repackaged: "Winthrop the Elder had forced his vision onto this land and his people, and Lucky was no different" (175).

The protagonist avoids a trip to the hospital this time, but he leaves without making his announcement and returns alone to his hotel room, where he again consults the unabridged town history. In another allusion to *The Intuitionist,* he is suddenly struck by the author's word-choices: "Colored, Negro, Afro-American, African American. She was a few iterations behind the times. . . . Every couple of years someone came up with something that got us an inch closer to the truth. Bit by bit we crept along. As if that thing we believed to be approaching actually existed." The protagonist has to this point vacillated between believing that names are innately significant and seeing them merely as surface features that hide true natures. He now perceives a third possibility, more fluid and more ambiguous: "What is the name that will give me the dignity and respect that is my right? The key that will unlock the world. Before colored, slave. Before slave, free. And always somewhere, nigger . . . . What would we call ourselves next, he wondered. If he knew what was next, he'd know who he would be" (192).

Such absolute prescience is ideal but also impossible; therefore, he starts considering an alternative not in the existence of a name but in the absence of one. The more he thinks about the distinction between Goode and Field, the more he realizes that the appeal of Goode's perspective is its convenience: "On paper, in the official history, they were even-stake partners, but when it came to day-to-day matters, you were going to go with one or the other. The Light or the Dark. You had to pick one, he knew. . . . And more often than not, you were going to go with Goode. Sleep came more easily, no doubt, with his words echoing in your head. You understood deep down that what Field had to say was the world's truth, but you were going to pick Goode every time. It was easier that way" (196–97). Like Apex bandages, Goode's view is useful for covering up the immediate hurt without addressing the underlying problem. Searching for an overly tidy solution may be what makes Field's words seem inscrutable or objectionable.

The protagonist becomes aware that Field's telling of inconvenient truths precipitated his literal and figurative insignificance: "Had he seen any signs around town with Field's name? Where were his sons and daughters? He knew more than he wanted about Winthrops, had broken bread with a bona fide Goode? Where was Field's legacy?" (197). He notes afresh a passage in the unabridged town history indicating that illness caused Field to miss the land-mark vote that changed the town's name to Winthrop. The comparable passage in the official version reads as follows: "The motion passed unanimously, and with the stroke of a pen, the town was changed forever. Winthrop was born" (197–98). Field's absence has been stricken from the record and replaced by his implied consent (as part of a unanimous vote) to Winthrop's takeover.

The actual truth differs from both of these written histories. Regina reveals to the protagonist that Field was not only present at the vote, but he actively resisted Winthrop's takeover, only to be betrayed by Goode because "Abraham had a family. . . . Field didn't have anyone" (204–5). Just as the protagonist was prepared to do, Goode sells out to Winthrop for immediate benefit, a story that Regina notes has been suppressed: "I don't know what Winthrop promised him. Property? Money? They definitely didn't talk about that on Easter and Christmas, when we used to sit around and the old folks would tell us the story about how we came here. How proud we all should be that we were related to such strong souls" (205). The protagonist understands the treachery of the town's renaming in terms that are impossible to separate from the country's racist past: "What did a slave know that we didn't? To give yourself a name is power. They will try to give you a name and tell you who you are and try to make you into something else, and that is slavery. And to say, I Am This—that was freedom" (206). In yet another echo of *John Henry Days,* the protagonist asks Regina what name Field had preferred, and Whitehead tantalizingly with-holds her answer from the reader: "It took her a minute before she was able to recall it. Seeing his expression, she shook her head in gentle dismay, her lips pressed together into a thin smile. 'Can you imagine thinking that would be a good name for a place where people live?' she asked" (207).

Four pages later, the narrator reveals that Field's desired name was Struggle, and implies that although it may not be a "good"—or "Goode"—name, it is an honest one: "Freedom was what they sought. Struggle was what they had lived through." The protagonist decides to adopt Field's sober practicality and decrees that Struggle is what Winthrop needs to become for at least a year: "Let lesser men try to tame the world by giving it a name that might cover the wound, or camouflage it. Hide the badness from view" (210). He contextual-izes his decision in terms of his prior success: "Apex was splendid, as far as it went. . . . Was Struggle the highest point of human achievement? No. But it was the point past which we could not progress, and a summit in that way. Exactly the anti-apex, that peak we could never conquer" (211). Although he rightly doubts that his clients will appreciate his choice, he also recognizes that the name possesses a semiotic power missing from the other choices: "He heard the conversations they will have. Ones that will get to the heart of this mess.

The sick swollen heart of this land. They will say: I was born in Struggle. I live in Struggle and come from Struggle. I work in Struggle. We crossed the border into Struggle. Before I came to Struggle. We found ourselves in Struggle. I will never leave Struggle. I will die in Struggle" (211). Struggle is seemingly eternal, but it also works to heal the "sick swollen heart" instead of just distractingly bandaging the surface.

This is by no means a happy ending for the town, the protagonist, or Whitehead's reader. The town's dissatisfaction is easily inferred, and the protagonist's virtuous act does not bring his expected relief: "There had been a moment . . . when he thought he might be cured. Rid of that persistent mind-body problem. That if he did something, took action, the hex might come off. The badness come undone. Plainly speaking, that he'd lose the limp. . . . As the weeks went on and he settled into his new life, he had to admit that actually, his foot hurt more than ever" (212). If the toe has symbolized his repressed conscience throughout, then this continued worsening signifies that he is not exempt from the enduring Struggle that he has imposed on Winthrop. Finally, the reader does not get the conventional literary resolution that any of the other three names would offer and may be asking, as the protagonist once did, "what the hell [am I] supposed to extract from that?" Such a question—the answer to which requires not only considerable interpretive effort but also a deliberate distancing from easy received truths—is precisely the response that Whitehead hopes to stimulate. Having shown innumerable ways in which exclusionary and commercialized constructs of both the past and present have produced a superficially vibrant but intrinsically "sick" society, Whitehead demands that his readers more closely examine *all* the signs through which they receive information, including his books.

CHAPTER 5

Whitehead's "New York Trilogy"

The Colossus of New York, Sag Harbor, and *Zone One*

Although it is the novelist Paul Auster who published a book bearing the title *The New York Trilogy* (1987), three of Whitehead's remaining books constitute a collective commentary on "New York, the city, where it's going, where it's been" (Goble 65). Although there is no indication that Whitehead envisioned formally grouping these works together as a literary trilogy, there are enough thematic overlaps among *The Colossus of New York: A City in Thirteen Parts* (2003), *Sag Harbor* (2009), and *Zone One* (2011) to justify examining them as a unit.

As Phillip Lopate noted in his review of *The Colossus of New York,* Whitehead has "always written about New York" to some extent; although never explicitly named, the Manhattan-like urban setting of *The Intuitionist* is "a mythological, stylized backdrop of power and corruption, similar to Gotham in Tim Burton's *Batman* film." Likewise, New York is "the fallback media-hype center" (Lopate) from which both J. Sutter in *John Henry Days* and the protagonist of *Apex Hides the Hurt* venture outward into a Middle America that they loathe and only barely comprehend. Each of the three books considered in this chapter, however, features Whitehead's native New York (and related outlying places) as a more integral part of both its geographical and cultural settings.

Especially after staging a zombie apocalypse in his hometown in *Zone One,* Whitehead has frequently been asked about his feelings toward New York. Although his affinity for the city is unmistakable—"I'm definitely a New Yorker. . . . I've tried living other places, but I always end up coming back here" (Porter 25)—his answers also indicate a dynamic tension between love and loathing. In discussing *Zone One,* Whitehead wryly noted that "the city has shaped how I see the world, move through the world. I don't think it will come as a surprise that my view of New York after everybody's dead is not too far from how I perceive New York now, when everybody's dead—I mean, trying to make it through the day" (Madrigal). In another interview Whitehead mentioned writing about the simultaneously vibrant and violent New York of the 1970s in which he came of age: "It was so dirty, you were constantly on guard from predators, and it's so cleaned up now that thinking about how it used to be with the danger and the garbage and buildings on fire. . . . That old New York is gone, and that's one thing that's undiscoverable now but I explore in my fiction" (Shukla 103).

These ambivalent feelings shape literary settings that evoke tangible, distinctive aspects of New York while also serving as symbolic microcosms. Even though New York has been his home for all but a few years of his life, Whitehead is adamant that the localized, mildly autobiographical dimensions of the three books he has set there do not supplant broader identifications that his readers—New Yorkers or not—might make with his plots and characters. He made this clear in discussing *The Colossus of New York* with Evette Porter: "I think I identify myself with the metropolis. But America is bigger than the seven-mile strip of Manhattan. So partially, I'm trying to figure out how I fit into America through these different people" (Porter 27). Although *Sag Harbor* is set in the very neighborhood where Whitehead spent his teenage summers, he maintains that it explicitly seeks "to describe a way of being in the world that hopefully overlapped with other people's ways of being in the world" (Chamberlin 61). Even Mark Spitz, the protagonist of *Zone One,* has an idiosyncratic relationship with the city. Like so many other aspirants before him, he has "always wanted to live in New York" (3). Unlike the stereotype of the out-of-towner coming to the city with Frank Sinatra's famed ambition to "wake up in a city that doesn't sleep / and find I'm king of the hill, top of the heap," Mark Spitz is thoroughly unremarkable: "He possessed a strange facility for the mandatory. . . . He nailed milestone after developmental milestone, as if every twitch were coached. Had they been aware of his location, child behaviorists would have cherished him. . . . He was their *typical,* he was their *most,* he was their *average*" (9, italics in original). Even during his childhood visits, his captivation with the city's grandeur and variety leave him feeling like "a mote cycling in the wheels of a giant clock" (4) rather than being spurred to eminence. His utter ordinariness—"He was not made team captain, nor was he the last one picked" (9)—makes him a potential stand-in for any reader, anywhere, despite being "smitten" with the city's uniqueness since boyhood: "It wasn't anyplace else. It was New York City" (6).

Whitehead's "New York Trilogy" is thus nominally precise in its setting, but readers should not infer that just because Whitehead provides them with an annotated—and quite geographically accurate—map of the streets of Sag Harbor, he has also become a diehard enthusiast of factuality. Realism is *not* reality, and these three books serve as telling reminders of the distinction between the two. In an interview about *Sag Harbor,* Whitehead made clear that his intentions in writing about the city—and, in this case, the beach community on the eastern end of Long Island to which a subset of African American city dwellers escape on summer weekends—are neither those of a strictly objective chronicler nor those of a sociologist:

> I'm not sure, outside of two pages, what the story is in a journalistic sense. I mean, they [the original African American residents of Sag Harbor] came in the thirties, started hanging out there, and . . . that's the story. Perhaps there is an interesting story about my grandparents' generation and their ideas of the world and what it means to be American and a black American and what it meant to achieve, to be part of this new emergent black middle class, and to have this place. However, I wouldn't want to spend two years talking to the old timers. . . . Someone else can do that. (Chamberlin 58)

Whitehead has noted that each of his books "has its own way of accommodating my concerns, whether it's about race, America, technology, the city. *Zone One* allowed me to talk about the city in a certain type of way [that was different from], for example, *The Intuitionist*" (Shukla 101). His approach in these three books is encapsulated by another of Mark Spitz's childhood recollections of looking out from his uncle's Lafayette Street apartment: "Millions of people tended to this magnificent contraption, they lived and toiled in it, serving the mechanism of the metropolis and making it bigger and better, story by glorious story and idea by unlikely idea. How small he was, tumbling between the teeth" (Whitehead, *Zone* 4). The "magnificent contraption" of Whitehead's literary New York is "tended to" by the hundreds of disparate, mostly unidentified figures whose fleeting experiences make up *The Colossus of New York,* the family members and friends that surround teenager Benji Cooper during a summer in *Sag Harbor,* and *Zone One*'s motley assortment of survivors trying to fight back the undead hordes in Lower Manhattan.

Building Your Private City: *The Colossus of New York*

As if the literal polyphony in *The Colossus of New York* was not enough, Whitehead goes so far as to personify the city itself. The book's title alludes to the massive statue of the ancient Greek sun-deity Helios that stood on the island of Rhodes, just off the southern coast of modern-day Turkey. On another level, though, it nods toward Emma Lazarus's poem "The New Colossus," which is inscribed on a plaque that was mounted in 1903 inside the Statue of Liberty in New York Harbor. Lazarus's entreaty to "Give me your tired, your poor, / Your huddled masses yearning to breathe free, / The wretched refuse of your teeming shore" helped transform the statue from a French gift commemorating shared national values into an iconic symbol welcoming immigrants to the United States.

This latter allusion strongly influences Whitehead's depiction of New York as a place whose transitory population results in a constantly shifting identity. As Nicholas Howe noted, "Transportation matters in this version of New York because it is a city of mobility. . . . Movement defines Whitehead's New York, the constant searching for the new club in an undiscovered area, the wandering across neighborhoods, the coming from elsewhere, the return to elsewhere" (87). While expressing his affection for the city in an interview, Whitehead emphasized the role that two modes of ubiquitous transportation strongly identified with New York play in managing his anxieties: "I love . . . getting lost but not worrying, just wandering and wandering, knowing that there's always a subway only ten blocks away in any direction. There's always a new neighborhood to discover, a new place to lose your bearings in, and yet however alien it seems you can escape. You can always get a cab. All of life's problems can be solved by hailing a cab" (Shukla 103). Although "getting lost" in the city primarily refers to physical disorientation, it also speaks to a metaphysical sensation that pervades his depiction of New York. Such loss sometimes is productive—as in the case of leaving one's past behind and coming to New York for a fresh start—but it also relates to a regretful sadness that ranges from melancholy to trauma.

The opening paragraph of the book accentuates Whitehead's sense of New York as both a physical reality and an enticing artificial abstraction:

> I'm here because I was born here and thus ruined for anywhere else, but I don't know about you. Maybe you're from here, too, and sooner or later it will come out that we used to live a block away from each other and didn't even know it. Or maybe you moved here a couple of years ago for a job. Maybe you came here for school. Maybe you saw the brochure. The city has spent a considerable amount of time putting the brochure together, what with all the movies, TV shows, and songs—the whole If You Can Make It There business. The city also puts a lot of effort into making your hometown look really drab and tiny, just in case you were wondering why it's such a drag to go back sometimes. (*Colossus* 3)

The reference to the brochure not only anticipates the role that the glossy advertisement celebrating diversity plays in luring the protagonist to Quincy in *Apex Hides the Hurt,* but also resonates with New York's efforts to recover economically and emotionally from the September 11, 2001, terrorist attacks (hereafter, 9/11).

The Colossus of New York developed from an essay entitled "Lost and Found" that Whitehead published in the *New York Times* exactly two months after the attacks. By the time Whitehead published his essay, Mayor Rudy Giuliani had already declared New York "open for business" during the opening monologue of *Saturday Night Live* and President George W. Bush had already linked the coming War on Terror with the protection of American commercial interests and recreational freedom: "When they struck, they wanted to create an atmosphere of fear. And one of the great goals of this Nation's war is to restore public confidence in the airline industry. It's to tell the traveling public: Get on board; do your business around the country; fly and enjoy America's great destination spots; get down to Disney World in Florida; take your families and enjoy life the way we want it to be enjoyed" ("At O'Hare"). Although New York's iconic "I ♥ N.Y." ad campaign has existed since 1977, the campaign to convince both tourists and investors to return to the city before the rubble of the World Trade Center had ceased smoking bears more than a passing resemblance to the diversionary tactic for hiding the hurt that Whitehead would later depict.

Although most of it is not specific to recent events, "Lost and Found" deals with 9/11 explicitly twice. The first instance is a simple expression of grief: "I never got a chance to say goodbye to the twin towers. And they never got a chance to say goodbye to me. I think they would have liked to; I refuse to believe in their indifference" (24). The second reference, though, anticipates the tone of cyclical loss and recovery that pervades Whitehead's quasi-trilogy:

> The twin towers still stand because we saw them, moved in and out of their long shadows, were lucky enough to know them for a time. They are a part of the city we carry around. It is hard to imagine that something will take their place, but at this very moment the people with the right credentials are considering how to fill the crater. The cement trucks will roll up and spin their bellies, the jackhammers will rattle, and after a while the postcards of the new skyline will be available for purchase. Naturally we will cast a wary eye toward those new kids on the block, but let's be patient and not judge too quickly. We were new here, too, once. (25)

Although Whitehead seems sympathetic to the fact that New Yorkers will have a new skyline to carry around as their own, there is also an undertone of cynicism towards this reconstruction's objectives, given the reference to the "postcards [that] will be available for purchase" and Whitehead's penchant for deriding those who ascribe "the right credentials" to themselves.

A version of this essay—with both direct references to the World Trade Center edited out—becomes the prologue to the other twelve essays in *The Colossus of New York*. Retitled "City Limits" and typographically separated from the other chapters in the table of contents, it serves a dual purpose. First, it is something of an invocation that transports the reader into a highly personalized vision of New York: "What follows is my city. Making this a guidebook, with handy color-coded maps and minuscule fine print you should read very closely so you won't be surprised" (Whitehead, *Colossus* 10–11). Second, and perhaps somewhat paradoxically, it is also an instruction to the reader to avoid putting too much stock in Whitehead's vision of the city, given that he repeatedly undermines any impulse to afford authority to *any* such vision: "History books and public television documentaries are always trying to tell you all sorts of 'facts' about New York. That Canal Street used to be a Canal. That Bryant Park used to be a reservoir. It's all hokum. Never believe what people tell you about old New York, because if you didn't witness it, it is not a part of your New York and might as well be Jersey. . . . There are eight million naked cities in this naked city—they dispute and disagree. The New York City you live in is not my New York City; how could it be? This place multiplies when you're not looking" (5–6). Such gestures link *The Colossus of New York* with historiographic metafiction, both in its denial of the impulse "to seek any total vision" and in the way it "blurs the line between fiction and history" (Hutcheon 48, 113). When Whitehead notes that "before you know it, you have your own personal skyline" (*Colossus* 6), he is suggesting that one's personalization of the city even encompasses iconic urban architecture (though no postcards of such an idiosyncratic personal skyline are available).

Whitehead addresses an implied reader throughout much of the book, even telling "you" what "you" have been doing while in New York. This literary technique forces the reader into a degree of close association with Whitehead's narrative, especially if that reader happens to actually have visited the places or done the things Whitehead describes. As Tamar Katz notes, "The book's frequent use of second-person address extends the urban type to include the reader by demanding her identification to establish a kind of community" (823). But what happens to the "you" who has not personally visited New York? In explicitly refusing the kind of authority to dictate someone's experience of the city to him or her, Whitehead embraces what seems like irrationality: "I still call it the Pan Am Building, not out of affectation, but because that's what it is. For that new transplant from Des Moines . . . that titan squatting over Grand Central is the Met Life Building, and for her it always will be. She is wrong, of course—when I look up there, I clearly see the gigantic letters spelling out Pan Am, don't I? And of course I am wrong, in the eyes of the old-timers who maintain the myth that there was a time before Pan Am" (*Colossus* 5). Li stresses that the chronological aspect of "Whitehead's conception of New Yorker identity implies that connection to the city is based not only upon familiarity with its geography, but more importantly, upon the experience of having endured change. Identification with New York requires longevity, the achievement of outliving physical markers, and the subsequent nostalgia produced by an awareness of absence" ("Sometimes" 83). The opening chapter establishes that Whitehead is less concerned with reproducing any one empirical experience of New York than with proposing that "there is no past to the place, and everyone makes the city over in the image he or she wants" (Howe 87).

The subsequent chapters are loosely held together by a "fly-on-the-wall" narrator whose words frame momentary glimpses into other perspectives, those of both native New Yorkers and visitors. Some of the chapters focus on specific places—such as the Port Authority bus terminal, Central Park, Broadway, Coney Island, the Brooklyn Bridge, Times Square, and JFK International Airport—whereas others take place in somewhat more amorphous locations such as "Downtown" or the "Subway." Three chapters—"Morning," "Rain," and "Rush Hour"—lack geographic markers entirely. Katz summarizes the effect of Whitehead's structure as follows: "*The Colossus of New York . . .* envisions New York both as a heterogeneous collection of voices and as a set of common spaces and experiences; we might describe the text's project as creating models of shared community out of dispersed observations. The collection's essays are structured primarily as collages of anonymous but related comments and thoughts" (822). Whitehead has stated that his research for the book consisted of "walk[ing] around and just tak[ing] notes and try[ing] to eavesdrop on the city" (Porter 26–27); the result is a narrative whose fragmented stories vacillate "between the capricious horribleness of the everyday and the absurd beauty of existence" (Chamberlin 60).

Reviewers and critics had mixed reactions to Whitehead's approach. Lopate's review both praised and panned the book, calling it "smooth, dazzling, evocative, but also narrow and monochromatic." His main complaint about evokes those lodged against *John Henry Days* and *Apex Hides the Hurt*. Even as he compared Whitehead favorably with Walt Whitman and James Joyce, Lopate also lamented that "there is the odd shying-away . . . from actual, detailed physical description of these sites. Such descriptions might have balanced the tribal soup of interior monologue and offset its hydra-headed subjectivity with a single narrator's more objective viewpoint." Li similarly takes issue with Whitehead's pastiche, seeing it as an evasion of the pain caused by the 9/11 attacks: "The multiple, intersecting voices of *The Colossus of New York* do not tell stories; they narrate moments, not progressions. . . . By limiting his description of New Yorkers to fleeting encounters, Whitehead further demonstrates an anxiety with confronting the consequences of 9/11. Though we may read his narrative strategy as a clever affirmation of the city's mutability and his representation of destruction as a promise of New York's continuous evolution, the text manipulates absence to avoid a confrontation with actual loss" ("Sometimes" 88). Whitehead's revision of a reference to the "twin towers" ("Lost" 24) into the more generic "old buildings" (*Colossus* 10) perhaps supports Li's contention, although a reader still dealing with the aftereffects of 9/11 can surely interpret that altered sentence—especially its reference to "their long shadows" (10)—to indicate the WTC.

Whereas Lopate and Li find fault with the book's lack of unifying authority, others consider what Lopate dismisses as "tribal soup" to be intrinsic to its author's intent. For example, Robert Butler argues that "instead of providing its inhabitants with a stable place grounded in a shared history, common values, or genuine communal life, [Whitehead's] New York breaks down into the always shifting, subjective perceptions of the countless people who experience it" (72). He also insightfully makes a connection to one of Whitehead's earlier works: "*The Colossus of New York,* like *The Intuitionist,* is premised upon the belief that the postmodern American city is an infinitely complex technological system and, as such, is both extraordinarily powerful and perilously fragile" (78). Given the terrible irony of the vulnerability produced by the World Trade Center's immense height—and the impossibility of using elevators to escape from its upper floors—Butler's observation foregrounds the larger implications of both novels' depictions of fragile power: "Colossal in design and intricate in the way they use a wide variety of interconnected technologies, American cities are vulnerable not only to spectacular terrorist attacks but also . . . to failures brought out by systemic weaknesses deeply rooted in American history and culture" (86).

In a different vein, Katz emphasizes the ways in which Whitehead's fragmented narrative reflects "an intrinsic urban nostalgia . . . [that] figures urban life as formed by loss and thus located in the past" (815). She writes that "the city's constant novelty matters most for the way it generates a perpetually vanishing past. Thus while urban change makes us confront the new, such change still more importantly causes us to inhabit a world by definition gone; it guarantees that we see a city that is no longer there" (811). Like Butler's retrospective correlation with *The Intuitionist,* Katz's comments relate *The Colossus of New York* to Whitehead's larger body of work, given that her observations also pertain to the conflict depicted in *Apex Hides the Hurt.* Both the Freedom that Regina champions and the Winthrop that Albie wishes to preserve exist only tenuously in the era of Lucky Aberdeen's dominance, and the displacement of the town's library by a fast-fashion clothing store indicates that this process is accelerating. Each of the three council members experiences the same geographic location idiosyncratically because of the selective filter through which they perceive/inhabit their town.

Finally, Nicholas Howe reveled in the brevity of Whitehead's individual sketches, seeing them as a democratizing feature: "Reading Whitehead means enjoying the quick take, the telling phrase, the wisecrack that reveals his love of New York City. He does not offer a mindless celebration, a chamber of commerce press release, but instead a catalogue of the treasures he has found by moving through the city" (87). Howe asked a version of the implied question that pervades Lopate's critique—"Is *The Colossus of New York* just a series of clever lines without a narrative or a larger vision of the city?"—but arrived at a very different conclusion. After quoting a lengthy passage from the book in which Broadway is described with two seemingly contradictory words, Howe stated that being able to sustain such a paradox is an integral part of life in New York: "There is, however, a point to all of these individual observations. . . . [They] are bound together in a sense of the place: 'terrible and generous' seem to me as precisely earned as anything ever said about New York. Believe in one at the expense of ignoring the other, and you will be doomed in the city; believe in both in roughly equal measures over a lifetime and you will understand why New York is a colossus" (88). Howe indirectly responded to Lopate's objection that "things like history, physical description, analytical development" are missing from *The Colossus of New York:* "Whitehead's politics are never explicitly ideological and they rarely register the daily facts of elections and governments. But they are powerfully democratic in suggesting that the city is above all else the place that can erase racial, social, and economic distinctions. Whitehead never quite puts the matter as I do here, but his egalitarian embrace of everyone walking down Broadway seems deeply hopeful at a time of power-broker mayors like Rudy Giuliani and Michael Bloomberg" (Howe 88). *Apex Hides the Hurt, Sag Harbor,* and *Zone One* each deal in profoundly different ways with the issue of erasing such distinctions, although their conclusions about whether doing so is necessarily a good thing are, in my view, far more ambiguous than the bright outlook Howe attributed to *The Colossus of New York.*

Black Boys with Beach Houses: *Sag Harbor*

Whitehead's fourth novel, *Sag Harbor,* was also his most accessible to that point. This fact helps explain why it was his first book to make a sustained appearance on best-seller lists. Another contributing factor is surely that the genre it most resembles—the *bildungsroman* or coming-of-age novel—is deeply familiar to many mainstream readers and moviegoers. One reviewer even proposed that readers should "think of it as *Stand by Me* without the corpse, or *A Christmas Story* in the wrong season," insisting that "the only obvious distinction between *Sag Harbor* and those movies is that the characters in *Sag Harbor* are black" (Beck 36). Another reviewer claimed that the novel "isn't about much more than the hilariously trifling intricacies of [the] self-discovery process. . . . [Whitehead] captures the fireflies of teenage summertime in a jar without pretending to have some larger purpose" (Maslin C1). The publisher's marketing of the book certainly fortifies this impression; the front cover of the first U.S. edition features a teenage African American boy standing on a beach in sunglasses, and the plot synopsis on the dust jacket touches upon most of the readily recognizable tropes of the coming-of-age story. As noted previously, Whitehead has warned his readers against deriving presumptions about meaning from the apparent genres of his books. He has stated that he was merely wearing "realist drag" in *Sag Harbor*, thereby again conveying the sense that he wanted readers to have some initial impression of familiarity even as he ultimately delivers "a coming of age novel that doesn't remind me of all the stuff I hate about coming of age novels" (Shukla 100). Although Whitehead narrows his frame of reference drastically in comparison with his earlier works, *Sag Harbor* is still very much postsoul historiographic metafiction. Alongside a recapitulation of what seem like fairly typical summertime adolescent hijinks, the novel critically examines a host of racially coded discourses that profoundly affect the lives of Sag Harbor's Black residents.

At least among its reviewers, *Sag Harbor* may be Whitehead's most misunderstood book. Its apparent simplicity spawned a flurry of critical assertions that grievously neglected its resonance with the rest of Whitehead's writing. For example, Stefan Beck considered it a decadent diversion justified by the complexity and creativity of his earlier work: "Having spent most of his career inventing, at times rather wildly, he's earned the right to indulge in a haze of benign nostalgia. And *Sag Harbor* is, despite a few stabs at adolescent pain, a remarkably and sometimes soporifically benign book" (36). Although Beck asserted that the novel's protagonist Benji Cooper is distinctive because his "upbringing takes place in the interstices between white and black culture," he dismisses the possible relevance of this situation blithely: "Benji isn't interesting because he's straddling the black and white worlds and drawing from both of them. He's interesting because he's interesting, interesting because he's Benji. . . . I don't believe this is because he's an authorial surrogate, lavished with authorial attention. I think it's because many young people, whatever their race, are content to adopt prefabricated personae. It's pretty clear that the young Colson Whitehead was not. No double consciousness, only his own" (37). Given both Whitehead's track record of interrogating racial issues in American culture and the fact that the adult Benji who retrospectively narrates the novel explicitly confirms that "years later in college, I'd read [W. E. B. Du Bois's] most famous essay and been blown away" by its discussion of double consciousness, Beck's "color-blind" assertion becomes fairly indefensible. Whitehead's characterization of Benji is inextricably related to the fact that, "according to the world, we were the definition of paradox: black boys with beach houses" (*Sag* 57). True, he avers that "it never occurred to us that there was anything strange about it" (57), but adult Benji repeatedly undercuts the accuracy of teenage Benji's perceptions about both momentous and trivial matters: "Needless to say, I had no idea how fucked up the haircuts were at the time. To us, they were normal. Just how things were done in our house" (163). The novel is filled with incidents in which Benji is forced to negotiate the complexities and consequences of living, as Janet Maslin put it, "on a 'Cosby Show' racial cusp between white bourgeois comforts and black roots" (C1).

Fifteen-year-old Benji and his fourteen-year-old brother, Reggie, are the offspring of relatively affluent parents residing in Manhattan. They additionally resemble Whitehead in attending overwhelmingly White private schools from September through May of each year. While in the city, they are often treated as outsiders as they walk around in their "gear from the Brooks Brothers Young Men's Department." In particular, Benji recalls "one day in seventh grade when an old white man stopped us on the corner and asked us if we were the sons of a diplomat. Little princes of an African country. The U.N. being half a mile away. Because—why else would black people dress like that?" (Whitehead, *Sag* 4). Also like Whitehead's family, the Coopers own a summer home on eastern Long Island in the beach town of Sag Harbor, parts of which have been inhabited almost entirely by African Americans since the 1940s. The book is set in the summer of 1985, although frequent references to things that happened after that year indicate that the story is being told long thereafter, a point Maslin either missed or overlooked in writing that "Whitehead presents the book's adults the way a 15-year-old might see them" (C1). In fact, Whitehead has explicitly stated that he felt a need to avoid "regressing . . . to his formative years" (Maslin C1) in telling Benji's story:

> Before I started writing, I knew that it had to be an adult looking back on his childhood because I would get bored out of my skull if I had to have a fifteen-year-old's voice for three hundred pages. I know people fudge it by having very precocious narrators who are wise beyond their years, but that feels like a real cheat. I was not a very articulate fifteen-year-old, so why pretend that fifteen-year-olds are incredibly articulate and wise about their world? My narrators generally have a certain kind of critical faculty. They're analyzing what the characters are doing in larger social structures. (Chamberlin 58)

Whereas teenage Benji ends up with a BB in his eye because he succumbs to his friends' peer pressure and participates in a mock shootout, the adult Benji is able (and seemingly compelled) to contextualize this event within subsequent developments both in his own life and in Black masculinity:

> Something happened. Something happened that changed the terms from fighting (I'll knock that grin off your face) to annihilation (I will wipe you from this Earth). How we got from here to there are the key passages in the history of young black men that no one cares to write. We live it instead. You were hard or else you were soft, in the slang drawn from the territory of manhood, the state of your erected self. Word on the street was that we were soft, with our private-school uniforms, in our cozy beach communities, so we learned to walk like hard rocks, like B-boys, the unimpeachably down. (Whitehead, *Sag* 146)

Benji's race is by no means the only thing that makes his story compelling, but it is also not as inconsequential as Beck claims: "the discussion of race is front and center, but, unlikely as it may sound, it often feels forced, even irrelevant" (37). Beck attempts to excise Benji's characterization from its racial context, as though feeling "used to being the only black kid in the room" (Whitehead, *Sag* 7) is a condition utterly devoid of personal or cultural significance: "Once one accepts that Benji is an individual, not beholden to anyone's cultural standards or expectations, what remains is a quiet, gentle tale of growing up in a good and decent place, with good and decent parents, into a good and decent man" (Beck 37).

As George, Neal, Ellis, Taylor, and Ashe each posit in some way, not being "beholden to anyone's cultural standards or expectations" is a fundamental tenet of the postsoul aesthetic; however, as Benji's encounters with both White and Black culture in the book show, actually being accepted as an individual is

not always as simple as "embrac[ing] the contradiction" that others perceive in
him and his friends:

> Black boys with beach houses. It could mess with your head, sometimes, if
> you were the susceptible sort. . . . You could embrace the beach part—revel
> in the luxury, the perception of status, wallow without care in what it meant
> to be born in America with money, or the appearance of money, as the case
> may be. No apologies. You could embrace the black part—take some idea
> you had about what real blackness was, and make theater of it, your 24-7
> one-man show. Folks of this type could pick Bootstrapping Striver or Proud
> Pillar, but the most popular brands were Militant or Street, Militant being
> the opposite of bourgie capitulation to The Man, and Street being the anti-
> dote to Upper Middle Class Emasculation. (Whitehead, *Sag* 58)

Whitehead's association of "real blackness" with a choice of "popular brands"
harks back to *Apex Hides the Hurt,* and the indistinct notion that "some
idea" thereof can form the basis for a full-time identity undercuts any sense of
authenticity that might adhere to such an idea. Nevertheless, much as Jennifer
from *John Henry Days* rebels against the limits imposed by her community
full of "Bootstrapping Strivers," Benji and his friends still very much need such
"typical and well-known remedies" (58) to counteract others' judgments.

For example, the Sag Harbor boys try to be "hard" by buying BB guns and
mimicking pop-culture clichés of toughness that are light years removed from
their economically privileged upbringings: "NP tucked his piece into his belt
like a swaggering cop on the take or the cracker sheriff of a Jim Crow Podunk,
Clive was observed busting a Dirty Harry move when he thought we weren't
looking, and Randy was often found cradling his rifle to his chest, a gruesome
sneer on his face as if he were about to take an East Hampton bistro hostage.
I myself favored a two-handed promising-rookie pose, favored by *Starsky and
Hutch* extras who got clipped before the first commercial and were avenged for
the rest of the hour" (145). Adult Benji interprets this posturing as a sign that
the boys had "learned to change the character of [their] fighting and would
continue to do so for the rest of their lives, readjusting for different provocations, different stakes" (146). Even this constant recalibration, though, does
not suffice: "We heard the voices of the constant damning chorus that told us
we lived false, and we decided to be otherwise. We talked one way in school,
one way in our homes, and another way to each other. We got guns. We got
guns for a few days one summer and then got rid of them. Later some of us
got real guns" (147). When Benji is accidentally shot, resulting in a BB lodging
next to his eye permanently (another trait he shares with Whitehead), the boys
seem chastened, and the reader learns that "the BB guns didn't come out again

that summer" (158). Nevertheless, adult Benji makes it clear that the impulse to present a "hard" exterior did not end that summer and has subsequently exacted a costly toll:

> For some of us, those were our first guns, a rehearsal. I'd like to say, all these years later, now that one of us is dead and another paralyzed from the waist down from actual bullets . . . that the game wasn't so innocent after all. But it's not true. We always fought for real. Only the nature of the fight changed. It always will. As time went on, we learned to arm ourselves in different ways. Some of us with real guns, some of us with more ephemeral weapons, an idea or improbable plan or some sort of formulation about how to best move through the world. An idea that will let us be. Protect us and keep us safe. But a weapon nonetheless. (159)

The comparison of a stable identity—"an idea that will let us be"—to a weapon contradicts any assertion that Benji and his peers feel unthreatened by external expectations about how and why they should act. To be sure, such anxieties are not inherently racial, but Whitehead depicts almost all of the particular pressures that the Sag Harbor boys feel as having some racialized dimension.

As with the compulsion to act "like hard rocks," many of the most confusing and injurious expectations in the novel originate within Sag Harbor's African American community, a realm that Whitehead explicitly calls stiflingly "bourgie" both in the novel and in numerous interviews about it. An omnipresent critical gaze lurks around every corner in this seemingly placid beach town, and it controls behavior without the need for direct confrontation: "This stereotype stuff was hard, no joke, no matter where you came from. Look, we had all kinds in Azurest. We had die-hard bourgies, we had first-generation college strivers, fake WASPs, the odd mellowing Militant, but no matter where you fell on the spectrum of righteousness, down with the cause or up with The Man, there were certain things you did not do. Too many people watching" (87–88). The moderate diversity of types that Benji catalogues in his subdivision at the start of this passage is still clearly constrained by a belief that some behaviors are simply unacceptable in public for African Americans, as Benji explains in a breathtaking run-on sentence: "You didn't, for example, walk down Main Street with a watermelon under your arm. Even if you had a pretty good reason. Like, you were going to a potluck and each person had to bring an item and your item just happened to be a watermelon, luck of the draw, and you drew this on a sign so everyone would understand the context, and as you walked down Main Street you held the sign in one hand and the explained watermelon in the other, all casual, perhaps nodding between the watermelon and the sign for extra emphasis if you made eye contact." Resistance to such pressure is entirely hypothetical in Benji's mind, again recalling Du Bois's notion of double consciousness: "We were stuck whether we wanted to admit it or not." (88)

The tension between such constraints and the desire for unfettered personal expression is at the heart of various takes on the postsoul condition, whether Ellis's "New Black Aesthetic" or Touré's celebration of *Sag Harbor*'s post-Black virtues in his review of the book: "Post-blackness sees blackness not as a dogmatic code worshiping at the altar of the hood and the struggle but as an open-source document, a trope with infinite uses. . . . For so long we were stamped inauthentic and bullied into an inferiority complex by the harder brothers and sisters, but now it's our turn to take center stage. Now Kanye, Questlove, Santigold, Zadie Smith and Colson Whitehead can do blackness their way without fear of being branded pseudo or incognegro" (1). For his part Whitehead has pushed back vehemently in several venues—for example, a satirical essay entitled "The Year of Living Postracially"—about the oft-repeated claim that Barack Obama's election either established or confirmed the existence of a postracial society in the United States. However, the concepts of "postblack" and "postsoul"—often misused synonymously with "postracial" —do not imply that race has become insignificant in the way that Beck's review does. Instead, they resist any authority that would identify "certain things you did not do" because of race. Benji is constantly reminded of his blackness and, much like the narrator of Countee Cullen's 1925 poem "Heritage," he is haltingly redefining what it actually means to him.

Whitehead scatters dozens of episodes throughout the novel that reveal how each of Sag Harbor's two preceding generations places implicit and explicit demands on Benji and his peers. The so-called founding fathers of Sag Harbor's Black community are generally depicted as fairly benevolent eminences whose expectations are communicated passively by example rather than by explicit command. For example, the grandfather of one of Benji's friends is described as "a real gentle guy, always kind to our mangy bunch when we came over." Benji specifies the generational character of this gentleness: "He'd seen a lot of racist shit in his life and was glad that things had turned out better for his children and grandchildren. That cool old breed" (126). This same man later asks Benji whether he has been fishing. Ignoring Benji's answer—"Not this summer, no"—the old man responds that "it's nice to see the young people following in the tradition. I know [your grandfather] would have liked to see you out there, dropping a line like we used to" (199). This uplift-minded generation is commemorated almost entirely in terms of their valiant resistance to racial discrimination: "The first generation came from Harlem, Brownstone Brooklyn, inland Jersey islands of the black community. They were doctors, lawyers, city workers, teachers by the dozen. Undertakers. Respectable professions of need. . . . They had fought to make a good life for themselves, vanquished the primitives and barbarians out to kill them, keep them out, string them up, and they wanted all the spoils of their struggle. A place to go with their families in the summer. To make something new" (51–52). Like in Winthrop's Black neighborhoods in *Apex Hides the Hurt,* many of the streets in Sag Harbor are named for members of this founding generation. They are the sacrosanct, idealized symbols of sacrifice that made their descendants' lives of relative ease possible; therefore, disrespecting one's forebears becomes practically inconceivable.

As is also the case in *Apex Hides the Hurt,* though, the maintenance of such reverence for the past requires a great deal of selective memory, and Whitehead constantly emphasizes the degree to which the community regulates behavior through passive-aggressive shaming. Early on, Benji divulges that "legend had it that DuBois came out to Sag once and ate there," but it is his reaction to this oft-repeated anecdote that is particularly telling: "I nodded in a show of pride whenever my mother told us this story even though I had no idea who DuBois was. I had learned to keep my mouth shut about things I didn't know when I sensed I was expected to know them." Young Benji is unfamiliar with historical figures whose names are spoken "so that they had an emanation or halo," but also notes that "it was too late to ask who they were because I was old enough, by some secret measure, that it was a disgrace that I didn't know who they were, these people who had struggled and suffered for every last comfort I enjoyed. How ungrateful." Upon revealing his ignorance of Marcus Garvey, "the eyes of all the adults in the room slitted for a sad round of tsk-tsking"; when he fails to recognize Haitian revolutionary Toussaint L'Ouverture, his father mocks him by asking, "What do they teach you at that fancy school I bust my ass to send you to?" Benji's sarcastic response—"Not 'Iconic Figures of Black Nationalism,' that's for sure" (13)—is almost surely unspoken, even though it specifies the fundamental conundrum of Benji's dual existence. He is expected to be fully conversant with Black culture, yet he spends nine months of every year in a school notable for both the physical and curricular absence of blackness.

His summers only partially mitigate this dilemma, since his interactions with other African Americans in Sag Harbor tend to be socially, rather than historically, instructive: "Hanging out with NP was to start catching up on nine months of black slang and other sundry soulful artifacts I'd missed out on in my 'predominantly white' private school. Most of the year it was like I'd been blindfolded and thrown down a well, frankly" (29). Benji claims that while in school he does learn "the wide range of diversions our country's white youth had come up with to occupy themselves," such as hacky sacks; however, as he watches his Black friends performing unfamiliar dance moves and exchanging elaborate handshakes, he laments that his knowledge does not include "the assorted field exercises of black boot camp" and again notes that he "couldn't ask what these things were" for fear of being shamed as insufficiently or improperly Black (29–30).

Even his aforementioned friend's nickname speaks to both the stringent expectation of conformity with certain standards of behavior and the perplexing duplicity with which those standards are enforced by Sag Harbor's adults. Benji's friend gets his nickname because of his propensity for stretching the truth: "We called him NP, for Nigger Please, because no matter what came out of his mouth, that was usually the most appropriate response" (30). His nickname is abbreviated because of the thorny history of its initial word: "Shortened to NP because the adults gave us trouble when they heard us using the word *nigger*. For understandable reasons. Like most authority figures, they had a hypocritical streak, as they used the word all the time" (31, italics in original). The adults not only use the word "in its familiar comrade sense" but also in the exclusionary manner of Jennifer's parents on Strivers Row in *John Henry Days*: "They used the word . . . to distinguish themselves from those of our race who possessed a certain temperament and circumstance. The kind of person that made the announcer on the evening news say 'We have an artist's rendering of the suspect,' quickening your heart. There were no street niggers in Sag Harbor. No, no, no" (Whitehead, *Sag* 31). In fact, Benji's father uses the word this way to describe his own son later in the book, not because Benji has committed a crime but simply because of his new haircut: "'Look like one of those corner niggers,' he said. Whenever something went awry in the neighborhood, the corner niggers eagerly stepped up for scapegoat duty" (162). When NP's mother accidentally calls her son by his nickname in a moment of frustration, Benji interprets her usage as a sign that it "had approval at the highest levels" (31). The ethical confusion engendered by this inconsistency is mirrored in many of the adults' attempts to regulate their children's behavior.

Although his father accuses him of being the wrong kind of Black, Benji ironically also struggles with being perceived as not Black enough. He listens to "goth" music, plays Advanced Dungeons and Dragons, and wears black Chuck Taylors, all of which are behaviors so strongly associated with whiteness by his friends' that even adult Benji is still sheepish about revealing them decades later: "Let's just put it out there: I liked the Smiths" (63). His pop-cultural conversations with his friends are described as a "long war over what white culture was acceptable and what was not. We redrew the maps feverishly, throwing out our agreements and concessions. This week surf wear was in, and we claimed

Ocean Pacific T-shirts and Maui shorts as our own. Next year, Lacoste was in enemy territory again, reclaimed by the diligent forces of segregation" (63). In short, Benji's life is marked by a shifting series of codes in which the range of acceptable blackness is extremely narrow, and his seemingly trivial personal choices of what clothes to wear, what music to listen to, or how to wear his hair are all fraught with the implications of being judged by his own friends and family.

Two tense scenes of family strife hint that Benji's father is the principal source for Benji's conflicted sense of identity. They also compellingly illustrate how and why "hiding the hurt" does not solve problems. Andrea Levine's analysis of the violence—emotional and physical—that Benji's father unleashes on those living in what he inaccurately calls "his" house (it is actually an heirloom of Benji's mother's family) undercuts any notion that the novel is, as Beck would have it, a "quiet, gentle tale" about a "good and decent" adolescence: "*Sag Harbor*, then, is as much a novel about the pain of belonging to this family—and living in this house—as it is a clever and poignant exploration of a privileged African American teenager's coming of age" (183–84). Although neither Levine nor Whitehead offers excuses for the domineering behavior that pervades Benji's interaction with his father, Levine also notes that Whitehead at least partially explains it as a response to Mr. Cooper's own struggles with discrimination, both by whites and within his own race. In discussing a scene in which Mr. Cooper expresses his contempt for "these light-skinned pussies they got out here [in Sag Harbor]" (*Sag Harbor*, 163), Levine notes that his "own sense of his marginality as a dark-skinned African American from a working-class background is palpable" (183). Mr. Cooper clearly bristles whenever he feels himself to be an outsider in the frequently snobbish Sag Harbor community into which he married; such intraracial strife is a major theme in many of the "passing" novels mentioned previously in the chapter on *The Intuitionist*. Mr. Cooper's reaction belies one reviewer's assertion that Whitehead is "post-conflicted" in how he depicts Sag Harbor: "Racial prejudice? It's out there. But it's out there like bad weather: It comes and goes and does little damage to the soul" (Alsup). Whitehead uses almost the same meteorological metaphor years later in describing the relationship between racism and the tensions within his own family: "My dad was a bit of a drinker, had a temper. . . . His personality was sort of the weather in the house. . . . He was apocalyptic in his racial view of America" (Jackson 49).

The "damage to the soul" of Mr. Cooper is actually fairly extensive, and he passes it on to his family, as Levine observes: "The extended episode of violence that Benji experiences at the hands of his father stems explicitly from Benji's lack of physical response to a racial slight, a moment in which Mr. Cooper portrays it as his responsibility as an African American parent to 'teach' his son how to respond to such provocations" (181). When Benji's father angrily confronts him one day about getting into a fight at school, Benji is initially puzzled, as the actual incident not only seems thoroughly forgettable but also factually different to him: "The day my father was asking about, we were goofing around during Snack. . . . There was a discussion about tanning while on vacation . . . from which I abstained, and then Tony Reece reached over to my face, dragged a finger down my cheek, and said 'Look—it doesn't come off'" (134–35). As is the case with his lack of knowledge about "Famous Black People" (13), any significance beyond "he was talking about my brownness" is lost on Benji (135); the other children quickly put Tony Reece in his place and Benji largely forgets about the incident, absentmindedly mentioning it to his mother upon returning home. Benji embodies Ellis's claim that the generation of the New Black Aesthetic experiences "racism [as] a hard and little-changing constant that neither surprises nor enrages" (Ellis 239–40). His father, however, belongs to a generation that cannot endure blatantly racist acts so stoically and informs Benji, "He was calling you a nigger" (Whitehead, *Sag*, 135). When Benji fails to respond satisfactorily to his father's questions about why Benji did not punch Tony "like I told you," he strikes his son's face three times, while Benji's brother and sister close their doors "because that's what we always did" (135–36). Mr. Cooper commands Benji not to cry—again obliging him to be falsely "hard"— while explaining his actions as tough love: "Who's going to protect you if you don't do it? Me? Your mother? The world's not going to protect you. That's what I'm trying to teach you." Adult Benji, however, sheds light on how this message changed for him over the years: "The lesson was, Don't be afraid of being hit, but over the years I took it as, No one can hurt you more than I can. The same end result, really" (138).

The later chapter tellingly entitled "To Prevent Flare-ups" divulges that such episodes of corrective violence and willful ignorance were the norm in the Cooper house. The chapter helps explain why Benji's college-aged sister, Elena, no longer comes to Sag Harbor and ardently urges him to "get out when you can" (237) during her one fleeting appearance in the book. The chapter focuses on a day during which Benji's father is barbecuing chicken, a task he performs "every Saturday, every Sunday, in good weather and bad." This dedication has garnered him an almost mythic reputation: "He was known up and down the beach as a master griller, the wind itself in service to his legend, bearing the exquisite smell of caramelizing meat through the developments" (171). The "flare-ups" in the chapter's title literally occur inside the father's meticulously maintained grill, but their figurative meaning becomes achingly clear as Benji relates the various façades beneath which his family hides their hurts. Not only does Benji's father drink heavily throughout the course of the day, but his drinking is described as "fuel" (175) for his volcanic temper, which Benji knows is going to explode from the time he hears a telltale sound: "Before the *poomp* was the *tock* of the liquor-cabinet door sucking away from the magnet. You could hear the *poomp* all over the house; the *tock* was a slighter sound, inauspicious, given that it was the start of things" (172). Those "things" end up being an explosion of domineering petulance that barely stops short of physical violence. It is triggered by a spill involving cheap, faulty paper plates—another allusion to Apex?—that Mr. Cooper had forbidden his wife to purchase.

Whitehead cleverly weaves an intertextual discussion of how television affected perceptions of blackness, especially privileged blackness, into this chapter. In doing so he metafictionally forces his reader to compare the idealized Huxtables of *The Cosby Show* with the Coopers of *Sag Harbor*. The chapter opens by explicitly paralleling the two families, but also immediately undercuts the sense that comforting truths will be derived from doing so: "We were a Cosby family, good on paper, that was the lingo. Father a doctor, mother a lawyer. Three kids, prep-schooled, with clean fingernails and nice manners. No imperial brownstone, but our Prewar Classic 7 wasn't too shabby, squeezing us tight on old elegant bones. Did we squirm? Oh so quietly" (160). Both the television metaphors and the quiet squirming continue throughout the chapter as Benji tries to immerse himself in a beloved dystopian movie, *The Road Warrior,* in order to ignore his father's slow, boozy surge toward fury. This attempt at distracting himself from the unpleasantness fermenting nearby suggests the underlying irony of calling the Coopers a "made-for-TV family": "Every new channel added to our lineup, every magnificent home-entertainment advance increased the possibility that we wouldn't have to talk to one another" (173).

Over the course of the day, Benji and his father repeatedly change the channel between *The Road Warrior* and CNN, though in keeping with family practice neither of them pays much attention to their chosen programs: "The TV was always on in our house, whether people watched it or not. We needed sound, any kind of sound. Watching TV and reading at the same time was standard op" (174). Benji mentions that the family not only compares itself to *The Cosby Show* but also to stereotypical White families on television: "You could only laugh. Sitcom white folk, movie-of-the-week white folk were our coon show. Judge's Daughter Hooked on Pot, Teenage Runaway Sent to Reform School—these earnest cautionary tales played like pure vaudeville, especially in the opening minutes, with the montage sequences establishing the Perfect Home, the Perfect Family. Like, they ate meals together. Come on, now. . . . Things went down differently in our house. These were transmissions from a distant star" (186–87). After subverting the racial implications of a "coon show" by applying that label to a show about White people, Benji again gives way to self-mockery by identifying communal meals as a trait of a "Perfect Family" so far beyond to his experience as to be extraterrestrial.

Awash in empty "noise" from the television, Benji passes his day reading from *The Book of Lists,* which he describes as "that eccentric encyclopedia of the world, boiling down trivia into thick, murky lumps of truth" (174) and whose format he grimly parodies by including two lists of his own—"6 Fake Smiles in Benji's House" and "8 Most Common Silences in Benji's House" (178, 190). Benji's indiscriminate consumption of information is an attempt to block out his father's grilling ritual: "He assembled the pyramid meticulously, perceiving the invisible—the crooked corridors of ventilation between the briquettes, the heat traps and inevitable vectors of released energy, any potential irregularity that might undermine the project. He asserted his order. Built his fire" (176). The extent of Mr. Cooper's imposition of control not only illustrates his pathological need for authority—Benji again uses the language of television in describing him as "our talking head. The only channel we got" (181)—but also metaphorically describes Sag Harbor's rigid value system.

Whitehead's symbolism concerning authority is developed further as Benji remarks that his father's grilling was not a benevolent gesture: "If you told him you weren't hungry, he didn't care. He'd grill anyway. Eventually you'd eat it" (171). Likewise, even though he asks whether Benji would like barbecue sauce on his chicken, Mr. Cooper makes it clear that there is only one correct answer to the question in his mind: "As a concession to the rest of humanity, he'd brush on some barbecue sauce at the end if you asked him for it, but it was obviously beneath him and a betrayal of bedrock values. Slap on some store-bought Heinz crap, to show what he thought of you" (180). This reference to bedrock values is linked to another of Whitehead's frequent topics, the transformation of identity into a commodity. When an old friend of the family shows up to freshen his drink and shoot the breeze with Mr. Cooper, Benji comments on the man's livelihood: "Mr. Turner had his own company, selling package tours to Africa and the Caribbean. See the Motherland, get in touch with your heritage, vacation where everyone looks like you for a change" (177). This last item links Turner's business with Sag Harbor, and Benji's subsequent observation about the superficial connection between Turner's clients and cheap material symbols of African heritage calls Sag Harbor's own cohesion as a community into question: "[Turner] negotiated deals with the trinket outposts hawking authenticity in many forms, bead necklaces and fertility symbols, the omnipresent masks reflecting back the faces of sentimental longing. . . . There were Kenyans driving BMWs up to their mountain villas, big satellite dishes in their backyards, because black Americans needed a little whiff. He provided a service" (177–78).

Mr. Cooper similarly imagines himself to be serving the community and his family, a point he makes clear while angrily shouting at his wife: "You think you'd be sitting down there talking all that horseshit if I wasn't doing what I'm supposed to? All week long slaving for this family. I'm not like all these other pussies out here. I work my ass off. I don't ask for anything except I don't want cheap shit in my house" (191). The irony of this declaration is revealed in the chapter's final lines as Mr. Cooper serves Benji the chicken that is allegedly the envy of the neighborhood: "I took a bite. It was like biting into sand. . . . I looked at the other wings on the plate in my lap. They were charred and shrunken, the lot of them, crumbling into black specks. I chewed up the sand and swallowed." Not only does he eat the unpalatable food that he never requested, but he also lies one more time to keep the peace in the moment: "'It's great,' I said." (194).

The chapter's final pages illustrate the long-term cost of the family's habit of swallowing their tongues: "Something happened to my mother in her life that she never defended or protected herself. That she never defended or protected us, when it was our turn. I don't know what it was. I suppose it was the same thing that prevented me from defending or protecting her, once I was old enough. I kept my mouth shut and watched TV" (190). Moreover, Benji explodes the entire justification behind the pretense of Cosby-like perfection, namely the paranoid belief that others are constantly looking and judging: "For all his fear that people were watching all the time, that people will talk about you unless you're vigilant about what they see, no one was watching at all. No one cares about what goes on in other people's houses. The grubby dramas. It was just us" (193).

The novel ends, as all Sag Harbor summers apparently do, with a big Labor Day celebration on the night before everyone returns to their "normal" lives back in the city. Benji observes that seemingly all of Sag Harbor invokes Mc-Fadden and Whitehead's 1979 disco hit "Ain't No Stoppin' Us Now" as their de facto "black national anthem": "Whether the association was civil rights triumph, busting through glass ceilings in corporate towers, or merely the silly joy of gliding around a roller rink as you chased your friends and occasionally held hands with someone, aloft in a polyurethane heaven, the song addressed the generations. No stoppin'" (259–60). Although the entire book has questioned the lasting efficacy of such uplifting rhetoric, it also echoes the conditionally optimistic endings of each of Whitehead's previous three novels in offering an open-ended motive for facing life's struggles. Although the summer had not transformed him as drastically as he had hoped—for example, only one person started calling him Ben as requested—Benji expresses genuine optimism about the coming year: "It was going to be a great year. I was sure of it."

True to form, though, adult Benji slips in one last qualification to thwart any sense of a fairy-tale ending: "Isn't it funny? The way the mind works?" (273). Ultimately, Whitehead's depiction of the Coopers shows the tenuousness of the postsoul condition, despite—or possibly because of—the relative freedom provided by material comforts. It seems that having beach houses does not solve the problems facing Black boys. As Whitehead noted, "Benji is a bit smarter on Labor Day than he was at the beginning of the summer, and that's the most that the majority of us can hope for as we go through life" (Shukla 102).

Even Angels Are Animals: *Zone One*

At first glance, *Zone One* again seems to be a fairly dramatic change of direction for Whitehead. It certainly fits into the interpretive framework of postsoul historiographic metafiction less readily than most of his previous books, *The Colossus of New York* being the exception. Furthermore, although his adoption of the zombie-apocalypse genre expanded his readership again, it also pushed him further into the realm of popular fiction in many critics' eyes. Whereas detective fiction and the coming-of-age novel are both genres with such respective "literary" exemplars as Edgar Allan Poe's "The Murders in the Rue Morgue" and Jane Austen's *Emma*, stories about zombies have remained within the realm of "trashy" movies, dime novels, and comic books, all of which were largely considered beneath scholarly consideration until very recently. By this point, it should be clear that such judgments do not greatly concern Whitehead, especially given that he considers the genre cinematic rather than literary: "The book takes off from various entries in the zombie apocalypse genre. Which for me is a film genre. I grew up on the first Romero trilogy and various post-apocalyptic films. And those are the main inspirations for the book" (Naimon).

Upon closer inspection, *Zone One* begins to disclose its affinity with Whitehead's previous work. He enumerated some of the commonalities in an interview:

> My first book, *The Intuitionist,* was a take-off on the detective novel. . . . I'm trying to invent my own way of dealing with the conventions, rejecting some, embracing others. I'm doing the same thing in *Zone One.* In *Sag Harbor,* it is sort of an anti-coming of age novel. So I was trying to understand what made that type of story tick and deconstruct it. So I'm always doing my shtick no matter what sort of rhetorical prop I'm using, whether it is teenagers in *Sag Harbor* or flesh-eating monsters in *Zone One.* They really are just rhetorical flourishes that allow me to talk about society, people. (Naimon)

There are structural correspondences between *Zone One* and Whitehead's earlier works that signpost the continuity of this "shtick." As he does in *The Intuitionist* and *Apex Hides the Hurt,* Whitehead once again interweaves two separate storylines that start at different points in time only to approach convergence near the end of the book (the multiple timelines of *John Henry Days* and *Sag Harbor* are more disjointed, as is also the case in *The Underground Railroad* and *The Nickel Boys*).

He also echoes *John Henry Days* and *Apex Hides the Hurt* in featuring a protagonist whose name and identity are only partially revealed to the reader. His nickname is bestowed ironically by a group of his fellow survivors after he chooses to shoot his way out of being cornered by zombies instead of jumping to safety into a river: "Instinct should have plucked Mark Spitz from the bridge and dropped him into the current by now. But he did not move. When he told them later that he couldn't swim, they laughed. It was perfect: from now on he was Mark Spitz" (Whitehead, *Zone* 147). The nonsensicality of naming a nonswimmer—at least on this occasion—after one of the greatest Olympic swimmers in history is one of many oxymoronic dissonances that Whitehead incorporates into a book whose operative premise that the dead are still alive is itself a paradox.

As might be expected, the novel's plot is rather conventional, even if its fragmented presentation is not. Mark Spitz is living a largely unexceptional life in New York when the zombie apocalypse comes. Through a twist of fate, he goes on a gambling junket to Atlantic City and is therefore absent from the city on what he calls "Last Night" (*Zone* 71). Having stayed up all night gambling and drinking in the cocoon of the casino, Mark Spitz and his friend are unaware of the ongoing disaster that has befallen the city and are baffled by the traffic they misperceive only as "end-of-weekend despair, the death of amusement and the winnowing of the reprieve" (67). The significance of what they are witnessing is lost in part because they are listening to music on their iPods rather than to the broadcast news, but like the adult Benji who looks back on his teenage self in *Sag Harbor,* the omniscient third-person narrator offers some retrospective understanding: "perhaps the intensity of that moment, the pressure he felt, was the immensity of the farewell, for this was their goodbye traffic, the last latenesses and their attendant excuses, the final inconveniences of an expiring world" (67–68). The jarring juxtaposition in this final clause sets the tone for the rest of the novel, which focuses on the efforts of the Buffalo-based government and its "American Phoenix" project to restore normalcy. This scheme starts with reclaiming Lower Manhattan, which has been redesignated as "Zone One." The mindset of the so-called "pheenies" (a somewhat mocking name derived from "phoenix") tries to make the horrifying quasi-death of the bulk of the world's population into merely another "inconvenience" that can be cleaned up, allowing everyone to return to their boutique shops and designer coffee.

Making a "mediocre man" whose life was "exceptional only in the magnitude of its unexceptionality" (148) into the hero of a story of against-the-odds survival is provocative gesture in its own right, although it corresponds with the characterization of Ben, the unlikely (and ultimately tragic) hero of George Romero's *Night of the Living Dead* (1968). Whitehead has repeatedly mentioned this film as having struck him from a young age, both for its entertainment value and its racial significance:

> But definitely seeing *Night of the Living Dead* when I was in sixth grade, seeing a really strong black protagonist resonated with me. I'd seen a lot of blaxploitation films. But seeing just a normal Joe who is on the run from a white mob who wants to destroy him seems to be a part of the American chronicle. And George Romero will say in interviews that he cast Duane Jones, the African-American actor, just because he was the best person who auditioned. And he didn't realize until later what sort of resonance it would have in post-civil rights America. (Naimon)

Although race does not at first appear to be a major concern in the novel, Whitehead's comment makes it clear that he is not alone in perceiving a subtle parable of race relations in the Romero's film. Paul Ardoin argues that Whitehead's withholding of explicit mention of Mark Spitz's blackness until the final third of the novel is part of a sly narrative strategy that links zombies with a critique of America's understanding of its racial history:

> [T]he protagonist's race—which readers would usually expect to learn or be able to safely assume very early in the narrative—[is] held back until late and then revealed with little fanfare. Significantly, this revelation is framed by two key elements: one is the potential retroactive revelation about how many times race was actually invisibly narrated right beneath the reader's nose for the first two hundred pages of the novel, and the other is a second apocalyptic turn in the zombie plague. At almost the same narrative moment that the protagonist reveals his race . . . a barricaded section of Manhattan is invaded and overrun by zombies, signaling not only a setback to the reconstruction of human civilization but also a blow to the reestablishment of epistemological order. (171–72)

Whitehead has indicated that his motivation for writing *Zone One* was not to imagine the practical details of apocalypse but rather how zombies reflect the world as it already is. On a psychological level, they are grotesque manifestations of the same spiritual affliction symbolized by the wound festering beneath the bandage in *Apex Hides the Hurt:* "My idea of a zombie is located in a paranoid, misanthropic, orientation to the world, so I see the zombie as your family, your spouse, your mom, your brother, your neighbors down the street, the bus driver, being transformed into the monsters you always suspected they were. So if you have various psychological problems, as I do, the zombie nightmare speaks to them" (Sky). Tellingly, Whitehead temporally locates his apocalypse in the near-present: "I think it's pretty close to how we are now. It's not a radically reimagined future. . . . My take on the ruined world that the survivors find themselves in is not too far from what they experienced before" (Sky). He implies that the pheenies' hell-bent effort to restore a civilization that was figuratively brain dead before the zombie calamity will simply reinstitute the same flaws—including racial discrimination, rampant consumerism, jingoistic politics, and militarism—that doomed it in the first place: "So now that the apocalypse is in abeyance and they're trying to rebuild things, all the people that they used to be, everything that they used to want, all the bad things they used to do are just waiting to be recalled back into existence and play. So even though 98% of the population is dead, and these people have been through incredible trauma, all the sort of terrible stuff of the pre-apocalypse world is just waiting to come back" (Sky). The inevitability of this recurrence is hinted at when the narrator describes the slapdash disposal of corpses in Manhattan: "They belonged to a nation enamored of shortcuts and the impulse persisted" (60). Tim Lanzendörfer articulates the underlying question: "What is worse, the novel seems to ask: the apocalypse or the cheerful hope for a return to how things were before?" (168).

Near the end of the book, Mark Spitz enumerates the "terrible stuff" whose comeback he dreads: "If they could bring back paperwork . . . they could certainly reanimate prejudice, parking tickets, and reruns" (231). The "unexceptionality" of his life explains three of these things, but only his race explains the inclusion of prejudice, the permanence of which the narrator questions: "There was a single Us now, reviling a single Them. Would the old bigotries be reborn as well, when they cleared out this Zone, and the next, and so on, and they were packed together again, tight and suffocating on top of each other? Or was that particular bramble of animosities, fears, and envies impossible to recreate?" (231). That Mark Spitz equally fears the returns of racism and of parking tickets speaks to the emptiness of his life before Last Night made "the world . . . mediocre, rendering him perfect" (148).

His pre-apocalypse job in the "Customer Relationship Management, New Media Department, of a coffee multinational" is yet another regression from J. Sutter and the protagonist of *Apex Hides the Hurt;* the position "doesn't require any skills" at all (149). Basically, he haunts social-media websites, on which "denizens of the void [are] compulsively broadcasting the flimsy minutiae of their day-to-day," and sends users targeted advertising messages. His work is mindlessly automatic, with computer programs causing "references to caffeine, listlessness, overexcitement, lethargy, and all manner of daily combat preparedness [to] ping . . . his workstation, whereupon he dispatched a 'Why don't you try our seasonal Jamaican blend next time you're in the 'hood?' or a 'Sounds like you need a hearty cup of Iced Number Seven!'" (150). Ironically, such seemingly lazy marketing ploys are dependent on "that human touch," since wholly programmed responses failed to sway focus groups because they had "no soul" (151). Mark Spitz's aptitude for this work is a credit neither to him nor to his employer, since his capacity for it is described with multiple words denoting falseness: "He entered into the *artifice* easily, it turned out, a natural at *ersatz* human connection and the postures of *counterfeit* empathy" (150, emphasis added). If machines and zombies are linked by their lack of (a) soul, then Mark Spitz is not far behind.

He is not alone in this condition, though. The book is filled with dark satirical commentaries on survivors' obsessive restoration of a past whose pettiness Whitehead skewers relentlessly. The narrator observes that "New York City in death was very much like New York City in life. It was still hard to get a cab, for example. The main difference was that there were fewer people" (64). The ostensible incentives of the decimated city are repeatedly juxtaposed with a blunt reminder of the underlying reality: "The hottest restaurants always had a prime table waiting, even if they hadn't updated the specials since the winnowing of the human race got under way" (65). In this way Whitehead denies the irrationally hopeful impulse that the "American Phoenix" tries to instill with its jovial—and intentionally vague—news reports about rising birth rates in refugee compounds and restored hydroelectric plants.

One of the novel's most barbed satirical gestures involves a homophonic pun that evokes the etymology of the word nostalgia (literally, the suffering—*algos*, in Ancient Greek—caused by the desire to return home—*nostos*) in associating regret for the lost past directly with illness. During a relatively calm moment in Mark Spitz's job as a "sweeper" (a member of a three-person team that clears buildings in Zone One of any remaining zombies), the narrator observes that "buzzwords had returned, and what greater proof of the rejuvenation of the world, the return to Eden, than a new buzzword emerging from the dirt to tilt its petals to the zeitgeist" (53). The debased language of buzzwords —such as the puff in *John Henry Days* or the advertising lingo in *Apex Hides the Hurt*—is obviously mocked in Whitehead's earlier work, but the idea that buzzwords quickly reflower in *this* shattered world is truly reprehensible.

The "big buzzword of the moment" is "PASD, or Post Apocalyptic Stress Disorder," which is seemingly ubiquitous among the survivors: "Everyone suffered from PASD. Herkimer [the doctor who named the condition] put it at seventy-five percent of the surviving population, with the other twenty-five percent under the sway of pre-existing mental conditions that were, of course, exacerbated by the great calamity" (54). PASD's symptoms include practically every malady that might be imagined to result from the hardships of living in a destroyed society. As Mark Spitz wryly observes, the list is "not so much a criteria for diagnosis but an abstract of existence itself" (55). Its comprehensiveness assures that "one hundred percent of the world was mad," an assessment that "[s]eemed about right" (54) to the narrator. Whitehead makes his pun's intent unmistakable when he depicts a convulsing "teenage soldier whose fresh gear had obviously never been worn before." Mark Spitz inquires whether the man was bitten and hears a comrade's answer as "No, it's his past." Confused, he repeats back what he thinks he has heard, only to be corrected: "His P-A-S-D, man, his P-A-S-D" (55). The narrator points out that the past's pathology even extends to the zombies themselves: "They never came for you when you were vigilant; they came for you when you had one foot in the past, recollecting a dead notion of safety" (86).

The language used by the inhabitants of Whitehead's shattered world reflects the inherent absurdity of the "American Phoenix" project. For example, its policies include antilooting regulations that honor the property rights of companies whose products are haphazardly strewn across the post-apocalyptic wasteland: "Everyone—soldier and civilian and sweeper alike—was prohibited from foraging goods and materials belonging to anyone other than an official sponsor, whether it was Southern whiskey or all-natural depilatories. Food was exempt—juice boxes were still legal tender in some parts of the country—but for the most part, no more stealing, people. There had been laws once; to abide by their faint murmuring, despite the interregnum, was to believe in their return. To believe in the reconstruction" (39). Ostensibly intended to forestall any sense that life has reverted to Darwinist "survival of the fittest," this strategy of enlisting and rewarding the help of largely defunct corporations in recovering from apocalypse becomes the vehicle for Whitehead's most strident satire of unchecked capitalism's depravity:

Buffalo created an entire division dedicated to pursuing official sponsors whenever a representative turned up, in exchange for tax breaks once the reaper laid down his scythe and things were up and running again. (Additional goodies the public would never find out about weeviled the fine print). . . . They generally put a price cap on their goods or specified a

particular product in their brand family, one not too dear, but their sacrifices were appreciated nonetheless. Pledge all your tiny cartons of children's
applesauce, in the nation's far-flung groceries and convenience stores? It
was a no-brainer: they were expired anyway. (39)

Whitehead's pointed use of "no-brainer" here is just one of many instances in
which the living are equated with the mindless walking dead. The slavish devotion to corporate earnings is reminiscent of an American military officer's reluctance to damage a Coca-Cola vending machine to procure the coins needed
to make a phone call that will avert global nuclear catastrophe in Stanley Kubrick's 1964 satirical film *Dr. Strangelove*.

The zombies themselves also contribute to Whitehead's commentary on
what ails contemporary culture. Two kinds of zombies clutter Zone One and
need to be "swept" away as a precursor to reconstruction. The first group,
which Whitehead calls "skels," is like the conventional shambling corpses in
search of fresh meat that are depicted in Romero's films or in the long-running
television series *The Walking Dead*. Whitehead's powers of invention are
unleashed through the smaller faction of zombies called "stragglers," who
seem unaccountably stuck in places that Mark Spitz suspects were somehow
emotionally significant for them: "He wondered if they chose these places or
if the places chose them. . . . Maybe it wasn't what had happened in a specific
place—favorite room or stretch of beach or green and weedy pasture—but the
association permanently fixed to that place. That's where I decided to ask her
to marry me, in this elevator, and now I exist in that moment of possibility
again. . . . Relieved of care and worry, the stragglers lived eternally and undy-
ing in their personal heavens. Where the goblin world and its assaults were
banished and there was nothing but possibility" (159).

Again combining aspects of both the living and the dead, the stragglers'
behaviors resemble those of Mark Spitz and his friend in Atlantic City on Last
Night: "Their brains fogged over as possibility and failure enthralled them in a
perpetual and tantalizing loop" (66). Whitehead explained the different species
of zombies as an attempt to talk about nostalgia and the idea of the self: "In the
same way that the stragglers are completely stuck on who they used to be even
though the situation on the ground has changed, the survivors are also stuck
in the past, trying to bring their former lives into this new world of the disaster. And, of course, it doesn't go as planned. So, in comparing the uninfected
survivors with the infected stragglers and skels, I'm trying to break down the
divisions between the two, to figure out what is dead about the living, and what
is still living in the dead" (Naimon). When a previously docile straggler suddenly attacks one of Mark Spitz's fellow sweepers, it confirms a dictum about

this befouled world that appears, in a different context, early in the book: "Even angels are animals" (11)

Zone One not only refers back to The Colossus of New York, but it also parodies it. Both books are concerned with radical change and how it affects people, but they arrive at very different conclusions about the prospects for adaptation to and recovery from such upheaval. As noted above, The Colossus of New York was part of Whitehead's process to determine "how I could live in this place that I loved so much when it had been changed forever" by 9/11. He indicated that Zone One only tangentially refers to the September 11 attacks "within a larger notion of disaster." Nevertheless, he also noted that Mark Spitz "is using some of the tropes that are in Colossus to describe how he feels about the city" (Naimon). Andrew Hoberek emphasized this point in reviewing Zone One. He commented on a passage in which the young Mark Spitz sits in his uncle's apartment and constructs his personal version of New York out of glimpses of various people he can see in an adjacent building: "This sentence at once captures the romance of the uncle's urban milieu, hints ominously at what will become the all-too-literal dissolution of human beings into body parts following Last Night, and presents New York as an imagistic assemblage of scenes glimpsed through windows: the curator is none other than the author himself" (409). But where The Colossus of New York allowed for some therapeutic restoration of New York after a real trauma, Zone One not only depicts the macabre scenes of the original tragedy—including Mark Spitz walking into his house just in time to see his mother "gnawing away with ecstatic fervor on the flap of his [father's] intestine" (Zone 70)—but then reprises them at the novel's conclusion.

The effort to reclaim Manhattan turns out to be a risky public relations stunt that fails horribly, possibly costing Mark Spitz (among hundreds of others) his life. Another one of Whitehead's protagonists suffers the consequences of "hiding the hurt" rather than dealing with it. Mark Spitz's observation that "there were plenty of things in the world that deserved to stay dead, yet they walked" (231) becomes wistfully ironic given the fact that he seems personally rejuvenated as Zone One collapses around him: "He was smiling because he hadn't felt this alive in months" (250). Nevertheless, Whitehead does not show him being consumed by the zombies in the way that Bobby Figgis is "devoured by pop" (John Henry 111). Although it is a dim hope, the final lines leave a trace of the "utopian side of the zombie story [that] sees the breakdown of our categories of the individual and even the human not as a tragedy but as a form of release" (Hoberek 412). If the world's problem has been a traumatic connection to a corrupted past that no longer works (and probably never really did), the novel's last line may either chronicle Mark Spitz's last living steps or his first steps into a radically different future: "Fuck it, he thought. You have to learn to swim sometime. He opened the door and walked into the sea of the dead" (259). If he learns to swim in this context, the irony of his nickname will disappear, leaving open-ended space that can contain a multitude of new identities.

CHAPTER 6

The Underground Railroad and The Nickel Boys

Writing a decade after "Picking a Genre" was published, Li takes Whitehead to task for *The Underground Railroad*, arguing that it "fulfilled his own satire . . . [by] ultimately adher[ing] to the very protocols that he lampoons" in that earlier essay ("Genre" 19). Describing his methods not only as "compelling and at times majestic" (3) but also as "fantastical and historically irresponsible" (10), Li alleges that Whitehead has abandoned his previous strategy of challenging readers' presumptions: "Whitehead attempts in *The Underground Railroad* to perform history. The folly of what might be understood as a clever literary strategy is that it sacrifices historical and psychological truths for the simplistic desires of readers eager for a tidy resolution to the kind of suffering that endures rather than ends" (11). As noted in the introductory chapter of this book, the turn (or perhaps return) to what appears to be historical fiction in *The Underground Railroad* and *The Nickel Boys* "cemented Whitehead's literary status" (19). Despite her own record of insightful scholarship about Whitehead's work, Li curiously insists that he faced "being remembered as an eccentric African American writer who never quite lived up to his own promise" (19) prior to this acclaim. Moreover, she stops just short of accusing him of selling out: "While I am not suggesting that Whitehead turned to slavery to bolster his reputation, the book's success reflects certain publishing realities. . . . [B]lack artists are celebrated for bringing familiar stories of black suffering to mainstream audiences. They are rewarded for fulfilling the protocols of genre or at least racialized literary expectations. Great black writers write great books about slavery, be they slave narratives, contemporary narratives of slavery, or the peculiar concoction that is *The Underground Railroad*. Whitehead seems to find no trouble in that" (19–20).

Li's perspective runs contrary to both *The Underground Railroad*'s overwhelmingly positive reviews and the extensive body of scholarship that has emerged since its publication. Unlike the handful of unenthusiastic reviewers, Li does not claim that Whitehead "teaches and preaches—like a social-studies teacher, being sure that you recognize America's massive sins" (Nordlinger 38) or that his novel is "marred by a tendency to awkward didacticism" (Cryer). She instead indicts Whitehead's lack of commitment to correcting or augmenting the "historical and psychological truths" of slavery in *The Underground Railroad*: "Although he mines an important truth in noting that no one wants to speak or hear the horrors of slavery, he then runs from this very insight" (Li, "Genre" 13.

Whitehead has stated that despite being "fairly well-educated . . . the true scope of the depravity of slavery was unknown to [him]," adding that researching for the novel "really opened [his] eyes" to the fact that "the truth of slavery" is not taught to students of American history: "In general, we skip to the Civil War and Lincoln and then slavery was done. We don't talk about Reconstruction or Jim Crow. We fast-forward to *Brown v. Board of Education*, which ended segregated schools; we go to Martin Luther King. In schools, we skip to the good parts." At the same time, he acknowledged the urge to avoid this unpleasant history: "Most people are coming from a place of ignorance. But also, who wants to talk about their great-grandparents' culpability? Who wants to talk about how their great-great-grandparents were abused? It's a natural reaction to shy away from the true horror of it. I'm not excusing it, but it is a lot for the mind to handle on top of our ignorance and not wanting to think about the past" (Mochama 145).

Had Whitehead's intentions in *The Underground Railroad* been to rectify the historical record about slavery, then Li's criticisms would be wholly merited. However, his emphasis on the historiography of slavery undermines the premise that "stories about human bondage derive from authentic experiences, real bodies tortured and raped, real battles won and lost, which means that generic considerations of [*The Underground Railroad*] . . . are inextricable from the grounds of history" (Li, "Genre" 1). The removal of that logical pillar in turn destabilizes her objection that he depicts "the historical details and horrific displays of physical and emotional violence" before seemingly "grow[ing] impatient with its limitations, turning instead to other modes of storytelling" (9). It is precisely the "modes of storytelling"—historical, literary, and political—on which Whitehead continues to focus in both *The Underground Railroad* and *The Nickel Boys*. These two novels are as "inextricable from history"—meaning both actual events and the memorialization thereof—as

John Henry Days and *Apex Hides the Hurt*. Whitehead makes this point in an interview with Vicky Mochama:

> VM: Did you write this book to explore how you felt or understood slavery?
> CW: Not so much slavery, but slavery and American history and this character. . . . *The Underground Railroad*, because of its structure, allowed me to talk about different aspects and phases in Black American history. . . . Certain books allow me to discover how I feel about things and then there are other books that allow me to make sense of how the world has come to be what it is. (145)

The Underground Railroad fits far better into the latter category, and Whitehead utters similar views in discussing *The Nickel Boys:* "If we don't think about how we got here, we're going to repeat the same mistakes we've been making for generations and generations" (Arjini).

"But that was not the truth of it": *The Underground Railroad*

Much of the early scholarship on *The Underground Railroad* emphasized its relationship to a complex genre alternately called the "neo-slave narrative" (Bell, Rushdy), "the postmodern slave narrative" (Spaulding), and "contemporary narrative of slavery" (Keizer). Although the definitions of these terms differ slightly, each accounts for the proliferation since the mid-1960s of fictional depictions of the historical institution of slavery in the Americas. Noting their inherently historiographic and metafictional aspects, Ashraf H. A. Rushdy claims that neo-slave narratives "ask questions about and demonstrate the process through which a historical subject constitutes itself by employing or revising a set of ideologically charged textual structures [that is, the conventions of the nineteenth-century slave narrative]" (*Neo-slave* 7). Anticipating Whitehead's comments about "shy[ing] away from the true horror" of slavery, Rushdy elaborates that "the artists who produce neo-slave narratives return to what Leon Forrest calls 'memory-history,' most with an understandable ambivalence toward a force that they, like him, believe 'destroys as it heals.' . . . This is what makes the story of slavery so utterly difficult . . . to tell, what makes it a story one would prefer to pass on rather than to pass on to others" ("The neo-slave" 103). Such works force contemporary readers to forego the privileges and comforts of what Tillet calls "a civic culture that forgets or casts itself in contradiction to the lives and contributions of enslaved African Americans" (6).

The episodic plot of *The Underground Railroad* is simple. A young woman named Cora is urged by a slightly older man named Caesar to accompany him in running away from the Georgia cotton plantation on which they are both enslaved. Soon after their departure, another young slave named Lovey unexpectedly joins them, but she is captured during an ambush by a group of pig hunters, one of whom Cora accidentally kills in the ensuing scuffle. With the help of several sympathetic Whites, they are conveyed to a subterranean train, eventually emerging in technologically advanced and seemingly enlightened South Carolina. Before long, though, this refuge's fraudulence is laid bare, and the escapees are discovered by a terrifying slave catcher named Ridgeway. Cora is forced to flee via the secret train again, but she must do so without Caesar, who she later learns is killed in jail by an angry mob. Cora arrives in North Carolina, which has adopted a genocidal law outlawing blackness. She hides in a reluctant abolitionist couple's attic until their maid betrays them all to the bloodthirsty authorities. Before she can be executed, Ridgeway takes possession of Cora, intending to return her to Georgia after a journey through plague-ridden Tennessee to collect another runaway. While in Tennessee, Cora is rescued by agents of the Underground Railroad and taken to the Valentine Farm, an idyllic community of Black abolitionists and former slaves in Indiana that is modeled on several real-life settlements in that state (Dubey, "Museumizing" 128–29). Cora hesitantly begins imagining a life beyond slavery and even starts having feelings for Royal, one of her rescuers. During a debate about the community's future, a group of White marauders, including Ridgeway, annihilates Valentine Farm, killing Royal and many others in the process; Cora again finds herself in Ridgeway's clutches. To prevent him from infiltrating the Underground Railroad, Cora grievously injures—and possibly kills— Ridgeway and flees through a darkened tunnel, only to surface at an indeterminate location. The novel ends as she joins up with a Black family traveling to California by wagon train.

Setting aside the plot's ahistorical elements, the reader can see that the novel hews closely to numerous conventions of the slave narrative. Of course, Whitehead makes such selective reading almost impossible, thereby rousing consideration of his motives for conspicuously departing from a history that most of his readers would likely presume to know, at least in the "ignorant" fashion that he attributes to himself above. I approach *The Underground Railroad* neither as rationalist counterhistory—a doomed claim, given the novel's indisputable departures from factuality—nor as a psychologically realistic work of fantasy. Instead, my interpretation extends Madhu Dubey's observation that Whitehead's career-spanning technique of "trafficking between literal and figurative" has proven to be the "perfect vehicle for defamiliarizing public narratives about race and national history at the turn of the twenty-first century" ("Museumizing" 1). Matthew Dischinger accentuates a different mixture of discourses, noting that *The Underground Railroad* "uses speculative literary strategies in order to enact political satire of real histories that, of course, stretch into the present. . . . [It] offers a stark, relentless, satiric vision of the US that is itself both true and fantastical. That is, insofar as the novel rearranges history, it engages in the work of speculative fantasy. . . . Whitehead's satire causes readers to first see the work as an obviously fantastical fictionalization that seemingly removes them from its field of vision before slowly reassembling its sharp critique" (85). The novel is a metafictional neo-slave narrative that satirically dismantles a range of both individual and societal narratives that have allowed the White supremacist mindset—and corresponding suppression of African Americans' rights—to outlive legalized slavery by over a century and a half. As Goyal puts it, "The novel clearly does not just relate the story of a fugitive slave's journey to freedom; it meditates on the very state of freedom and possibility" (135), issues that remain as relevant in the early twenty-first century as they were in the more distant past.

Several facets of the novel's storytelling strategy reinforce this interpreta-tion. First, although Cora never achieves a definitive legal freedom, she never-theless develops significantly throughout the book, particularly in her ability to appraise the "stories" that define her world. She even becomes a skilled satirist herself, taking more than one journey down an "avenue of odd humor" (White-head, *Underground* 167) in spurning an attempted imposition of a flawed or unjust view of reality. Such moments illustrate Kevin Young's historiographic and metafictional conception of the traditional slave narrative's productive "counterfeit, the written, textual 'counter fit,' which inverts the white-based construction of authentication. . . . [S]ince even fact-based 'objectively scien-tific truth' has been used to oppress black people and their authors, their au-thors have often sought counterfeit or fictional alternative realities. Such 'troof' also has resonances of 'spoof,' parody, and basic exaggeration" (27).

Unlike the protagonists of most slave narratives, Cora does not tell her own story of escape. Nevertheless, she does not "remain a voiceless observer," as reviewer Dan Cryer lamented. She is the novel's central character, but she also progressively embodies its satirically historiographic perspective through her encounters with numerous forms of storytelling. As she experiences the world beyond Randall plantation, Cora increasingly expresses the novel's "self-awareness of history and fiction as human constructs" that is "the grounds for its rethinking and reworking of the forms and contents of the past" (Hutcheon 5). For example, while describing a slave's forced recitation of the Declaration of Independence, the narrator articulates Cora's growing skepticism of both that text and the nation it signifies: "Now that she had run away and seen a bit of the country, Cora wasn't sure the document described anything real at all. America was a ghost in the darkness, like her" (Whitehead, *Underground* 180).

In addition to Cora's direct subversive commentaries, Whitehead's narrator also actively provokes his readers' consciousness of various cultural narratives that predate the publication of *The Underground Railroad* in 2016. This secondary level of storytelling deliberately lies outside the characters' frame of reference. For example, not only does the novel allude to several literary works and historical events well beyond its antebellum temporal setting but Whitehead also intentionally manipulates the linearity of the book's timeline— a frequent technique in his fiction—to control the precise order in which information that remains unknown to Cora is revealed to the reader. Such moments of narration are integral to the novel's function as historiographic metafiction; Whitehead counts on his twenty-first-century readers to recognize references that his nineteenth-century characters not only do not comprehend but also *cannot* comprehend, thereby forcing the reader to consider the implications of interpreting Cora's story through such retrospective lenses.

Reviewers and scholars have catalogued the novel's numerous literary allusions, including David Walker's *Appeal* (1829), Frederick Douglass's *Narrative* (1845), Harriet Jacobs's *Incidents in the Life of a Slave Girl* (1861), Anne Frank's *The Diary of a Young Girl* (1947), Shirley Jackson's "The Lottery" (1948), Stanley Kubrick's *Spartacus* (1960), James Olney's "'I was born': Slave Narratives, Their Status as Autobiography and as Literature" (1984), and Toni Morrison's *Beloved* (1987). Whitehead also incorporates a series of metafictionally intertextual references to his own books within *The Underground Railroad*. For example, as Cora rides the elevator inside South Carolina's anachronistic skyscraper, her thoughts recall Lila Mae inspecting the Briggs Building in *The Intuitionist*: "[She] never failed to be both delighted and frightened by [the elevator's] magic, bracing herself with the brass rail in case of disaster" (86). Similarly, the residents of Valentine Farm at one point consider a strategy that strongly evokes the migration of the original Black settlers of Freedom/Winthrop in *Apex Hides the Hurt*: "There was frequent talk now of lighting out west, where colored towns sprouted up on the other side of the Arkansas River" (Whitehead, *Underground* 249). Even the depiction of a series of regular children's footraces (23–24) and the mention of "the white tiles" (259) lining the walls of one of the underground railroad's stations nod toward similar scenes in *Sag Harbor* and *The Colossus of New York*, respectively. These linkages affirm the thematic similarities among Whitehead's novels and heighten the metafictional self-consciousness of his most dedicated readers. They make it still harder to forget that one is reading a Colson Whitehead novel from 2016, rather than a story unfolding in the mid-1800s.

Whitehead also inserts subtle intertextual resonances with language intrinsic to "different aspects and phases" (Mochama 145) of postemancipation

American history in which slavery's White-supremacist essence persists. A few of these are mordant jokes, such as when the narrator alludes to Jim Crow–era racial purity laws in noting that the "[o]ne drop" (Whitehead, *Underground* 33) of wine staining the cuff of Terrance Randall's shirt justifies the savage beating of the slave who accidentally bumped him. Similarly, Whitehead gives the horrifying display of Black corpses along a North Carolina highway the same name—"the Freedom Trail" (153)—as Boston's Cold War-era memorialization of the Revolutionary War. This ironic repetition highlights the exclusion of blackness from American patriotic symbols much like Frederick Douglass's "What to the Slave is the Fourth of July?" (1852) speech. Other instances of this allusive technique briefly foreground parallels between past and present, such as the similarity of the behavior of North Carolina's patrollers and the "racial profiling" practices of contemporary police departments: "The patroller required no reason to stop a person apart from color. . . . Before, slave patrollers searched the premises of colored individuals at will, be they free or enslaved. Their expanded powers permitted them to knock on anyone's door to pursue an accusation and for random inspections as well, in the name of public safety" (162, 167). Still others are far more elaborate analogies, such as the novel's noncomic parodies of the infamous "Tuskegee Syphilis Experiment" and of dehumanizingly racist museum exhibits.

Dubey asserts that these various intertextual references cumulatively "constitute [The] *Underground Railroad* as its own museum of previous works, attesting to the capaciousness of the literary archive and emphasizing the heavily mediated nature of the novel's representation of slavery. . . . [This] museum effect in Whitehead's novel promotes a distancing rather than immersive approach to historical understanding" ("Museumizing" 133). Whitehead's historiographic criticism of this figurative "museum of previous works" mimics Cora's experiences at the "Museum of Natural Wonders" (108) in South Carolina. Hired to perform as a silent "type" in three exhibits of ostensibly living history—"Scenes from Darkest Africa," "Life on the Slave Ship," and "Typical Day on the Plantation" (109–10)—Cora subverts not only the curator's claim to be "illuminat[ing] the American experience . . . the truth of the historic encounter" but also his patrons' motivations: "The stuffed coyotes on their stands did not lie, Cora supposed. And the anthills and the rocks told the truth of themselves. But the white exhibits contained as many inaccuracies and contradictions as Cora's three habitats. . . . [N]obody wanted to speak on the true disposition of the world. And no one wanted to hear it. Certainly not the white monsters on the other side of the exhibit at that very moment, pushing their greasy snouts against the window, sneering and hooting. Truth was a changing display in a shop window, manipulated by hands when you weren't looking, alluring and ever out of reach" (116). Cora eventually moves beyond internalized reflections on the museum's flaws and directly confronts her spectators, learning to wield the power of her own subjectivity instead of remaining objectified within a "manipulated" truth akin to a marketing strategy: "She got good at her evil eye. Looking up from the slave wheel or the hut's glass fire to pin a person in place like one of the beetles or mites in the insect exhibits. They always broke, the people, not expecting this weird attack, staggering back or looking at the floor or forcing their companions to pull them away. It was a fine lesson, Cora thought, to learn that the slave, the African in your midst, is looking at you, too" (126). These passages encapsulate the historiographic subversion of constructed "truths" in which Cora, the narrator, and Whitehead each participate on different levels throughout the book.

From the opening chapter, the narrator specifies that multiple voices have been influencing Cora's decision making: "It was her grandmother talking that Sunday evening when Caesar approached Cora about the underground railroad and she said no. Three weeks later she said yes. This time it was her mother talking" (8). That the adolescent Cora derives motivation from the only two relatives she has ever known is hardly surprising. However, Whitehead emphasizes that what Cora believes she knows about each of them is factually unreliable. Although their stories are as much a part of her "inheritance" (42) as the tiny garden-plot—itself described as having "a story, the oldest Cora knew" (12)—amid the slave quarters that passes down from Ajarry to Mabel to Cora, they ultimately both help and hinder Cora's pursuit of freedom.

While recounting the grisly details of Ajarry's enslavement, the narrator makes no effort to correct the wishful "fantasies that gave Ajarry comfort when her burdens were such to splinter her into a thousand pieces" (4). For example, immediately after relating that a ship carrying Ajarry's relatives is burned ten miles off Bermuda after everyone on board had died of an infectious disease, the narrator states one of slavery's tragically axiomatic realities: "Cora's grandmother knew nothing of the ship's fate." By knowing what Ajarry cannot, the reader is already interpreting the novel from a privileged perspective. Ajarry imagines that her relatives survived and "somehow bought their way out of bondage and lived as free men and women in the City of Pennsylvania, a place she had overheard two white men discuss once" (4). Such incomplete and counterfactual inventions can only temporarily plaster over the gaps in her knowledge; the awfulness of her life as a slave requires a far more self-canceling means of perseverance: "Know your value and you know your place in the order. To escape the boundary of the plantation was to escape the fundamental principles of your existence: impossible" (8). In short, Ajarry's story is entirely authored for her by people who perceive debates about her humanity as a non-starter.

While still on the plantation, Cora unconsciously mimics her grandmother's coping mechanisms. Her life is controlled not only by the omnipresent bonds of slavery but also by the spiteful gossip of her fellow slaves. After she is forced to defend her garden from another slave named Blake, she becomes the subject of "tales" whose recognized artifice actually seems to enhance their social utility: "Blake recounted how he woke from a nap behind the stables to find Cora standing over him with her hatchet, blubbering. He was a natural mimic and his gestures sold the story. . . . Young women whispered how they watched her slink away from the cabins on the full moon, to the woods, where she fornicated with donkeys and goats. Those who found this last story less than credible nonetheless recognized the usefulness of keeping the strange girl outside the circle of respectability" (20–21). Much like Ajarry, Cora has plentiful incentive to retreat to her own constructions of reality whenever she can. She even subconsciously gilds the unknowable event of her own birth into a more tolerable tale: "Occasionally Cora's mind tricked her and she'd turn the story into one of her memories, inserting the faces of ghosts, all the slave dead, who looked down at her with love and indulgence. Even people she hated, the ones who kicked her or stole her food once her mother was gone" (12). After being viciously punished for interposing herself between her master and a young slave boy he was beating, Cora realizes the insufficiency of inherited notions of freedom:

> She had not been his and now she was his. Or she had always been his and just now knew it. Cora's attention detached itself. It floated someplace past the burning slave and the great house and the lines that defined the Randall domain. She tried to fill in its details from stories, sifting through the accounts of slaves who had seen it. Each time she caught hold of something—buildings of polished white stone, an ocean so vast there wasn't a tree in sight, the shop of a colored blacksmith who served no master but himself—it wriggled free like a fish and raced away. She would have to see it for herself if she were to keep it. (48)

The grueling slog of escaping from Georgia with Caesar requires her to kill in order to save her own life; nevertheless, because Cora believes that her mother successfully escaped—at the cost of turning Cora into a "stray" (14)—she believes she must adopt a similar self-liberating strategy by formulating a "story" of freedom beyond slavery. Mabel's actual fate (she dies on the same night she left, having decided to return to her daughter) is revealed in the book's

penultimate chapter, but only to the reader, never to Cora. This placement suggests that her story's value lies not in its factual truth, but rather in the impetus
to escape that it offers Cora at an important juncture.

Cora becomes a more discerning interpreter of others' narratives almost
as soon as she departs the plantation. After riding in a rickety boxcar through
the hidden tunnels of the literal Underground Railroad, Cora and Caesar find
themselves in the unexpected safe haven of neighboring South Carolina. Upon
their arrival, a kindly—and somewhat naïve—station agent named Sam hands
them forged identity papers premised on another legal fiction that speaks to the
state's underlying duplicity:

> "It says here we're the property of the United States Government," Caesar
> pointed out.
>
> "That's a technicality," Sam said. . . . Most of the colored folk in the state
> had been bought up by the government. Saved from the block in some cases
> or purchased at estate sales. . . . "They get food, jobs, and housing. Come
> and go as they please, marry who they wish, raise children who will never
> be taken away. Good jobs, too, not slave work. But you'll see soon enough."
> There was a bill of sale in a file in a box somewhere, from what he under-
> stood, but that was it. Nothing that would be held over them. (92–93)

Sam's name conjures up the propagandistic figure of "Uncle Sam" that has
personified American patriotism for better or worse since the early 1800s, and
what he understands as an innocuous "technicality" epitomizes the perils of
South Carolina. Cora and Caesar learn of a disingenuous public health campaign that intends to sterilize the state's black population while also subjecting
them to risky medical research without their consent. Almost simultaneously,
they are informed of the arrival of a group of slave catchers, men who are
previously described as being "of bad character . . . In another country they
would have been criminals but this was America" (75–76). The novel asserts the
absurdity of being subject to—much less being owned by, even as a "technicality"—the government of a country that empowers "criminals" to enforce its
laws, in this case those governing the return of fugitive slaves. Cora manages
to flee just as the slave catchers capture Caesar and burn Sam's house to the
ground. Her physical deliverance is accompanied by another leap in cynicism
toward the stories she is told, including the ones she can now haltingly read
thanks to the limited education she received in South Carolina.

Cora's developing literacy matches her developing ability to see through—
and call out—lies and distortions. This aspect of her characterization places
the novel within a literary lineage that Lesley Larkin describes as follows: "Far
from merely reprising the elements of the slave narrative that have to do with

reading, these [contemporary] literary works reimagine reading and readers themselves. . . . [Some of them] confront or antagonize readers directly, calling attention to problematic interpretive practices" (8–9). Cora both confronts and antagonizes the abolitionist in whose attic she hides in North Carolina as he tries to excuse his wife's seeming coldness. In doing so, she exposes two ironies within his justification:

> Once again, Martin apologized for his wife's behavior. "You understand she's scared to death. We're at the mercy of fate."
> "You feel like a slave?" Cora asked.
> Ethel hadn't chosen this life, Martin said.
> "You were born to it? Like a slave?"
> That put an end to their conversation that night. (169)

Although this response directly ridicules Martin's ham-fisted attempt to elicit sympathy for his comparatively privileged spouse, Cora's choice of words may also indirectly remind Whitehead's reader that the exculpatory phrases Martin uses could appear in any of the hundreds of narratives written by actual slaves prior to abolition.

In a later conversation with Ethel herself, Cora notes several Biblical "contradictions [that] vexed her" in regard to slavery: "I don't get where it says, He that stealeth a man and sells him, shall be put to death . . . [b]ut then later it says, Slaves should be submissive to their masters in everything." Ethel's reply echoes countless European and American defenders of slavery by using the Old Testament story of Ham to justify Africans' bondage: "It means that a Hebrew may not enslave a Hebrew. But the sons of Ham are not of that tribe. They were cursed, with black skin and tails. Where the Scripture condemns slavery, it is not speaking of negro slavery at all." Cora points out the most obvious flaw with this interpretation, while also redirecting the meaning of Ethel's words: "I have black skin, but I don't have a tail. As far as I know—I never thought to look. . . . Slavery is a curse, though, that much is true" (182).

The narrator adds two comments about the manipulation of language by authority. The first reveals the grotesque dehumanizing premises behind Ethel's inherently racist theology: "Slavery is a sin when whites were put to the yoke, but not the African. All men are created equal, unless we decide you are not a man" (182). The second comment amplifies the assertion that "Cora blamed the people who wrote it down" by positing that "[p]eople always got things wrong, on purpose as much as by accident." As is the case after Cora's earlier mild refutation of Martin's viewpoint, Ethel is either unable or unwilling to continue, demurring that "she didn't wake up that morning to get into a theological argument" (182). Her silence foreshadows the revelation—made, once again, to the reader but not to Cora—that Ethel's altruism is nonexistent. In addition to noting that "[s]lavery as a moral issue never interested Ethel" (195), the narrator discloses that she derived her motivation to helping Africans from ostensibly religious narratives that prefigure stereotypes found in the works of Joseph Conrad and H. Rider Haggard:

> Ever since she saw a woodcut of a missionary surrounded by jungle natives, Ethel thought it would be spiritually fulfilling to serve the Lord in dark Africa, delivering savages to the light. She dreamed of the ship that would take her, a magnificent schooner with sails like angel wings, cutting across the violent sea. The perilous journey into the interior, up rivers, wending mountain passes, and the dangers escaped: lions, serpents, man-killing plants, duplicitous guides. And then the village, where the natives receive her as an emissary of the Lord, an instrument of civilization. In gratitude the niggers lift her to the sky, praising her name: Ethel, Ethel. (191)

That the nominally abolitionist Ethel is actually like Ridgeway in believing that "[i]f God had not meant for Africans to be enslaved, they wouldn't be in chains" (195) is hardly surprising after the prefatory subversions voiced by Cora and the narrator.

Cora continues to grow as a subversive historiographer even after being captured by Ridgeway in North Carolina. As they travel through Tennessee on a circuitous journey to return Cora to Randall plantation, she is obliged to listen to his repeated orations on "the American imperative." On one occasion Ridgeway even buys Cora a new dress—replacing the one he impulsively bespattered with the brains of Jasper, another runaway—and treats her to dinner in a saloon. During this meal, he drunkenly torments her with both the details of Caesar's death in South Carolina and his blunt views on the design of American society: "My father liked his Indian talk about the Great Spirit. . . . All these years later, I prefer the American spirit, the one that called us from the Old World to the New, to conquer and build and civilize. And destroy that what needs to be destroyed. To lift up the lesser races. If not lift up, subjugate. And if not subjugate, exterminate" (221–22). Cora's responds to his brutish soliloquy simply by voicing the need to "visit the outhouse," to which he accompanies her while continuing his harangue.

The narrator previously stated that Ridgeway considers the underground railroad to be "a personal slur," making its acts of "subversion" (81) equally applicable to the philosophy he embodies. As Ridgeway continues lecturing Cora through the outhouse door, he turns to an explanation of how his pursuits of both Cora and Mabel blend the personal and the philosophical. Cora furiously believes that her mother betrayed her when she fled: "It had been a whim. Once

Mabel ran, Cora thought of her as little as possible. . . .[S]he realized that she had banished her mother not from sadness but from rage. She hated her. Having tasted freedom's bounty, it was incomprehensible to Cora that Mabel had abandoned her to that hell. A child" (98). Everyone on the plantation assumes that Mabel has successfully escaped because no trace of her has ever been found. After Ridgeway tells Cora that Mabel is "up in Canada, laughing at the Randalls and me," Cora recognizes the irony that Ridgeway "hated her mother as much as she did" (222), albeit for vastly different reasons. Mabel's apparent escape sullies Ridgeway's reputation, intensifying his eventual pursuit of Cora: "For every slave I bring home, twenty others abandon their full-moon schemes. I'm a notion of order. The slave that disappears—it's a notion, too. Of hope. Undoing what I do so that a slave the next plantation over gets an idea that it can run, too. If we allow that, we accept the flaw in the imperative. And I refuse." (223) Mabel's freedom—indeed, that of any slave—contradicts the bigoted and self-serving worldview that governs Ridgeway's life: "If niggers were supposed to have their freedom, they wouldn't be in chains. If the red man was supposed to keep hold of his land, it'd still be his. If the white man wasn't destined to take this new world, he wouldn't own it now. Here was the true Great Spirit, the divine thread connecting all human endeavor—if you can keep it, it is yours. Your property, slave or continent." (80)

Only after the destruction of Valentine Farm—"a community laboring for something lovely and rare" that Cora hoped might represent her own "freedom" (272)—does the narrator provide the actual details of Mabel's escape. This belated disclosure occurs in the last of the six brief biographical interludes—reminiscent of the "flashbacks" in *John Henry Days*—that alternate with the chapters detailing Cora's experiences in particular states; the previous five have focused on Ajarry, Ridgeway, a grave robber named Stevens, Ethel, and Caesar. Having experienced a fleeting, but palpable liberation while resting in the swamp that borders the plantation—"On the bed of damp earth, her breathing slowed and that which separated herself from the swamp disappeared. She was free"—Mabel dies on the same night that she ran away. In a bit of tragic irony, she is bitten by a poisonous snake while acknowledging her obligation to Cora: "She had to go back. The girl was waiting on her. This would have to do for now." (294). Preparing for her ill-fated return to Randall, Mabel expresses the idealism guiding her actions: "The world may be mean, but people don't have to be, not if they refuse" (294). Her ethically inverted repetition of Ridgeway's "refus[al]" of the "notion of hope" (223) represented by a slave's claims to humanity is unmistakable. Mabel demonstrates the very humanity he denies through her own "refus[al]" to accede to the "hopelessness

[that] had gotten the best of her, speaking under her thoughts like a demon" (294). Her words and attendant actions also deliberately echo the wary optimism of Elijah Lander, the abolitionist whose assassination marks the start of the obliteration of Valentine Farm. Lander encourages his listeners not to fear futility: "We can't save everyone. But that doesn't mean we can't try. Sometimes a useful delusion is better than a useless truth. Nothing's going to grow in this mean cold, but we can still have flowers" (285).

Whitehead complicates any readerly inclinations to sentimentalize Mabel's idealism, though. Not only does "the swamp swallow[. . .] her up" (295) before she can show her love to her daughter, but the narrator also makes clear that even though "[t]he first and last things she gave to her daughter were apologies. . . . Cora didn't hear either one" (291). Without the tempering knowledge of Mabel's contrition, Cora can hardly be expected to set aside the contemptuous accusation that she conveys to Royal, her rescuer and prospective lover, while at Valentine Farm: "Cora spoke of her mother, Mabel, who absconded one day and left her to the inconstant mercy of the world" (280). This passage is placed just before the "flashback" to Mabel's demise; moreover, the episode immediately following her death again places Cora in the grave peril of Ridgeway's custody, a fate that presumably would reinforce her grievance against her mother. The significance with which both Cora and Ridgeway invest Mabel's escape evokes the conventions of the slave narrative inasmuch as "Whitehead allows us to believe, perhaps naively, for a time, in the exceptionalism of the single figure who runs" (Farooq 98). However, the fact that Cora and Ridgeway are driven, respectively, by "hate" for Mabel and by "refusal" of her humanity scuttles the usual positive associations of this "exceptionalism," thereby largely nullifying its value to either Cora or the reader.

Entering the book's final chapter, Cora still lacks a story that will help keep her moving instead of restraining her. As Ridgeway forces her to expose the Underground Railroad's station in Indiana—an act she sees as "betraying those who made her escape possible"—Cora wounds and possibly kills him in a manner that grotesquely parodies and inverts the sexual violence done both to Cora personally on Randall plantation and to slaves generally: "Men had put a fear in her, those years ago. Tonight, she told herself. Tonight I will hold him close, as if in a slow dance. . . . She waited until the slave catcher was on the third step. She spun and locked her arms around him like a chain of iron. The candle dropped. He attempted to keep his footing with her weight on him, reaching out for leverage against the wall, but she held him close like a lover and the pair tumbled down the stone steps into the darkness" (302). Both desperate and serendipitous, this act is Cora's clearest display of personal agency. It testifies to her separation from the various external narratives that would influence her, including her anger at Mabel's presumed cruelty, Caesar's and Royal's faith in the Underground Railroad as an institution, Lander's pragmatism, and Ajarry's resigned persistence.

Perhaps most importantly, she also rejects the option to turn Ridgeway's bigoted and bloodthirsty views back against him, an option she only partially declined when given it during her rescue in Tennessee. Despite "want[ing] every bad thing" for him, she contents herself on that earlier occasion with "kick[ing] Ridgeway in the face three times," an act she tells her rescuers is symbolic retribution for the "three murders . . . of Lovey, Caesar, and Jasper." Recalling Weisenburger's assertion that subversive satire is suspicious even of its own formulation of reality (3), Whitehead's narrator states that Cora herself disbelieves this potentially "hokey" (Ramsey 483) moral equivalence: "But that was not the truth of it. It was all for her [i.e., Cora herself]" (Whitehead, *Underground* 228). Ridgeway's reappearance after Cora's act of vengeance and his active role in perhaps the book's most concentrated act of racial violence both indicate her need to replace, not adapt, his story in order to leave him behind.

Only as Cora hurtles down a darkened tunnel away from Ridgeway—who evokes the Puritan writer John Winthrop (and, thus, *Apex Hides the Hurt*) in burbling that the "American imperative is a splendid thing . . . a beacon . . . a shining beacon" even as he is dying—does the narrator describe her perception of a new reality that strongly reverberates with *John Henry Days*: "She discovered a rhythm, pumping her arms, throwing all of herself into movement. Into northness. Was she traveling through the tunnel or digging it? Each time she brought her arms down on the lever, she drove a pickax into the rock, swung a sledge onto a railroad spike. . . . Who are you after you finish something this magnificent—in constructing it you have also journeyed through it, to the other side. On one end there was who you were before you went underground, and on the other end a new person steps out into the light" (303–04). Cora no longer feels bound by either "the counterfeit sanctuaries" or the "endless chains" as she moves toward an indeterminate goal within the tunnel.

After an intensely erotic dream about Royal, the narrative suggests that she leaves even this bittersweet memory behind: "[S]he awoke each time into the void of the tunnel and when she was done weeping over him she stood and walked" (302–03). She emerges from the tunnel into the novel's first unknown geographic location: "She didn't know what Michigan or Illinois or Canada looked like. Perhaps she wasn't in America anymore but had pushed beyond it"

(303). The closing chapter is simply entitled "The North," which here refers not to a geographic or political reality—Indiana, after all, had been a "northern" state in terms of slavery's legal status—but instead to a personal conviction. The only context Cora uses to guide her apprehension of "the northness" in which she stands is devoid of human (and thus narrative) intervention: "The sun told her which way was north" (303). As she joins up with a wagon train headed for California, the past-tense verbs used in both her closing words and her closing thoughts tellingly indicate the blankness of the page on which the rest of her life-story will—and perhaps must—be written:

> "I *was* in Georgia. I *ran* away." She said her name was Cora. She unfolded the blanket at her feet and wrapped herself in it.
> "I go by Ollie," he said. The other two wagons came into view around the bend.
> The blanket was stiff and raspy under her chin but she didn't mind. She wondered where he *escaped* from, how bad it *was,* and how far he *traveled* before he *put it behind him*." (306, emphasis added)

Reading this last line as a scatological double entendre—admittedly, something of a stretch—connects it with Cora's earlier thoughts inside the outhouse. She frames her consideration of Ridgeway's words as a two-sided choice: "Maybe everything the slave catcher said was true, Cora thought, every justification, and the sons of Ham were cursed and the slave master performed the Lord's will. And maybe he was just a man talking to an outhouse door, waiting for someone to wipe her ass." (223). Given that her choice of toilet paper is a "fugitive slave bulletin" (223) like those Whitehead reproduces at the outset of several chapters, her intention to try to "put it [the imposed past of slavery] behind" her seems clear.

Rather than remaining within the novel's figurative "museum of previous works" (Dubey, "Museumizing" 133), she will instead try to contribute to the archive of past and future blackness she encountered briefly in Valentine's now-destroyed library: "She recognized their stories as her own. They were the stories of all the colored people she had ever known, the stories of black people yet to be born, the foundations of their triumphs. People had put all that down on paper in tiny rooms. Some of them even had dark skin like her" (276). Valentine himself expressed the revolutionary potential—and thus the threat to White supremacy—that such an archive represents: "What we built here . . . there are too many white people who don't want us to have it. Even if they didn't suspect our alliance with the railroad. Look around. If they kill a slave for learning his letters, how do you think they feel about a library? We're in a room brimming with ideas. Too many ideas for a colored man. Or woman" (276). Moments before being killed by the invading mob, Lander invoked the innately Black power this collection of stories represents:

> In some ways, the only thing we have in common is the color of our skin. Our ancestors came from all over the African continent. It's quite large. Brother Valentine has the maps of the world in his splendid library, you can look for yourself. They had different ways of subsistence, different customs, spoke a hundred different languages. And that great mixture was brought to America in the holds of slave ships. To the north, the south. . . . The word we. We are not one people but many different people. How can one person speak for this great, beautiful race—which is not one race but many, with a million desires and hopes and wishes for ourselves and our children? (285–86)

Although Lander disavows his own ability to speak for blackness, his words evoke both historiographic metafiction and the postsoul aesthetic in cautioning the reader not to place Cora (or Whitehead) into such a singularly authoritative position, even though "[c]olor must suffice" as a unifying principle (286). Whitehead may even be preemptively subverting his own authority on another level, since Lander employs the same term—"Africans in America" (286)—to categorize his listeners that Whitehead used sarcastically seven years earlier while encouraging the production of "Southern Novel[s] of Black Misery" ("Picking" 23), an exemplar of which Li alleges him to have written.

Whereas Cora previously felt that "[w]hether in the fields or underground or in an attic room, America remained her warden" (172), she ends the novel having learned a means of at least subverting—if not necessarily defeating —the distinctly American narratives that would keep her in chains. Like Lila Mae's reembodiment of the literate slave Fanny Briggs at the end of *The Intuitionist,* Cora has progressed from being the authored object to becoming the authorial subject; Whitehead has written the book of her past, but not (yet) that of her future. Unlike Lila Mae, though, she neither has—nor seemingly wants—guidance of the sort represented by Fulton's notebooks for the second volume of *Theoretical Elevators.* As Nihad M. Farooq puts it, "Cora refuses to be carried along by anyone, whether as Caesar's good luck charm or as a primped token of Ridgeway's victory" (90). Fulton speculates about a vertical corridor that would metaphorically lift those who traveled in it, but Cora has actually moved through an improbably vast network of horizontal tunnels with similarly liberatory intentions. The successes of both the real-life Underground Railroad and Whitehead's literalized fictional version are noble and inspiring, but the novel's retrospective historiography reminds readers that neither one ultimately dismantled systemic racial oppression in the United States any more than South Carolina's superficial magnanimity or the idealistic self-sufficiency of Valentine Farm did. Cora feels the "contours of a new nation hidden beneath the old" (304) as she runs her hands along the darkened tunnel through which she escaped Indiana, but this perception is no more certain to be realized than Lila Mae's prospective third volume of *Theoretical Elevators*. If Cora's "insurrection of one" (172) is to become something more tangible, it must seemingly do so by taking at least a partial cue from Lander's final words. Cora's life and voice must become another singular and original contribution to the collective chorus of Black identity that he, much like Fulton, describes in forward-looking terms as "[s]omething new in the history of the world, without models for what we will become" (286). She still faces a long road in realizing the legally audacious assertion that "SHE WAS NEVER PROPERTY" (298) which appears in the fictionalized runaway slave bulletin that prefaces the final chapter.

"No Visible Terminus": *The Nickel Boys*

Effectively contesting institutionalized racial malice is likewise a central goal for Elwood, one of the two young protagonists of *The Nickel Boys*. Both prior to and during his incarceration, he bases his resistance on principles (e.g., nonviolent resistance, uplift through education) and strategies (e.g., boycotts, sit-ins, strident letter writing) that are familiar from histories of the mainstream civil rights movement. In announcing the novel's selection as the winner of the 2020 Pulitzer Prize in Fiction, the jury used a civil rights–era vocabulary in describing the book as a "spare and devastating exploration of abuse at a reform school in Jim Crow-era Florida that is ultimately a powerful tale of human perseverance, dignity and redemption" (pulitzer.org). Although the first half of this description is certainly accurate, the second portion once again illustrates the tendency to ascribe formulaic intentions to Whitehead's works.

Many of the novel's predominantly favorable reviews similarly interpreted it as an inspirational tale of hard-won survival. For example, Joan Gaylord concluded her review by claiming that Whitehead "infus[es] it with glimpses of hope that reveal how one person's efforts, one person's example can make a difference. And that example needn't be an international figure. It might just be the kid who, thrown into jail, will still hold on to love." In fairness, such comparatively rosy assessments may result partly from a desire not to divulge the book's "secret," as is evident from Constance Grady's cagey declaration that the novel's apparent simplicity is "just part of Whitehead's trick. There's something else going on here, something terrible and heartbreaking."

Although this "something else" is densely concentrated in the novel's final third—most particularly in the epilogue—it is also "invisibly narrated right beneath the reader's nose" (Ardoin 171) before that, much like Mark Spitz's blackness in the early portions of in *Zone One*. Like many of Whitehead's novels, *The Nickel Boys* features multiple narrative threads whose relationship only becomes evident at its conclusion. The prologue and epilogue comprise a frame-story set in 2014 that fictionalizes the fallout from an investigation into the Arthur G. Dozier School for Boys in Marianna, Florida, after its closure in 2011. This framing transforms the entire novel into a work of postsoul historiographic metafiction that "trouble[s]" (Ashe 614) an otherwise "pointedly straightforward and simple" (Grady) historical fiction set in the 1960s. The book's opening line even seems to herald this purpose: "Even in death the boys were trouble" (Whitehead, *Nickel* 3).

In constructing *The Nickel Boys,* Whitehead once again borrows narrative components from a host of literary, historical, and pop-cultural artifacts. He also reprises the self-referential allusiveness found in *The Underground Railroad,* directly linking *The Nickel Boys* with phrases and images from several of Whitehead's previous books. In essence he historiographically "unearths" the various cultural narratives that influence the contemporary reaction to the gruesome evidence of violence uncovered during the "excavati[on of] the school's official cemetery" (4) that serves as the stimulus for the story, both in real life and in Whitehead's fictionalization. Even that cemetery's name at both Dozier and its fictional counterpart speaks to the way in which external voices influence the school's story: "The Nickel Boys called the official cemetery Boot Hill, from the Saturday matinees they had enjoyed before they were sent to the school and exiled from such pastimes" (5).

The prologue fictionally depicts the process by which Whitehead originally learned of the Dozier School. While helping clear a cemetery on the site of a recently closed reform school, a college student unintentionally discovers evidence of another hidden graveyard, triggering both police and media inquiries. The narrator makes clear that neither truth nor justice were the objective of the months-long dig during which this exhumation takes place: "The state couldn't dispose of the property until the remains were properly resettled, and the archaeology students needed field credits" (4). The narrator's wry comment that the "secret graveyard redeemed" the student who "found it while wandering the grounds in search of a cell signal" (5) likely does not refer to the kind of redemption the Pulitzer jury had in mind.

The scene echoes the "flashback" chapter in *The Underground Railroad* about Stevens, a medical student in Boston who robs graves to procure Black corpses for medical research. Stevens justifies his actions by insisting that "when his classmates put their blades to a colored cadaver, they did more for the cause of colored advancement than the most high-minded abolitionist. In death the negro became a human being. Only then was he the white man's equal" (White-head, *Underground* 139). Similarly, neither the testimonies of living Nickel Boys nor the bodies of murdered ones have any significance until the student's unwitting intervention: "All the boys knew about that rotten spot. It took a student from the University of South Florida to bring it to the rest of the world, decades after the first boy was tied up in a potato sack and dumped there" (4). Although the contemporary student seemingly lacks either Stevens's need for or interest in self-justification, both scenes testify to the complete absence of an opportunity for living African Americans to have their claims to fundamental human rights heard; Black lives are shown unambiguously not to matter in these contexts and even Black deaths are unimportant until somehow "[brought] to the rest of the world" by another (presumably White) person. Whitehead drives this point home by recasting the distinctive image of dancers-for-hire that he also used in *The Intuitionist* (213) and *Sag Harbor* (233): "Nickel Boys were cheaper than a dime-a-dance and you got more for your money, or so they used to say" (6). The narrator makes a similar point more bluntly later in noting that they "were fucked before, during, and after their time at the school, if one were to characterize the general trajectory" (144).

Watching news coverage in New York about the investigation at the school, one of its former residents recalls his prior disinterest in the various communal activities—including informational websites, petitions for legal action, annual reunions—of other Nickel Boys. Although not particularly noteworthy at first glance, the narrator's precise word choice in stating that the man "went by the name of Elwood Curtis" (7) foreshadows the book's surprising ending. The prologue ends with the narrator's declaration that the nominal Elwood "knew he'd have to return" (8) in light of the hidden graveyard's discovery.

The book's first chapter is set in 1963, when Elwood is a high-school student in the predominantly Black Frenchtown section of segregated Tallahassee. He lives with his strict but loving grandmother, his parents having abandoned him when he was six. From the age of twelve, he earns a reputation as an industrious employee at multiple jobs, and his curiosity and diligence impress his history teacher. Mr. Hill is also a civil rights activist and embodies the philosophy that Elwood encounters on a record of Dr. Martin Luther King Jr.'s speeches that his grandmother fretfully bought for him: "[I]t was the damnedest ten cents she'd ever handed over. That record was nothing but ideas" (34).

Much as Cora must reckon with conflicting influences, Elwood feels torn between Hill's political engagement and his grandmother's leery practicality. Elwood is equally intrigued by Hill's scar from "where a white man had slugged him with a tire iron" and by his strident elucidation of American history: "at every opportunity Mr. Hill guided them to the present, linking what had

happened a hundred years ago to their current lives" (30). The figurative scars
of resistance have made Elwood's grandmother more circumspect: "Act above
your station, and you will pay. Whether it was God angry at her for taking more
than her portion or the white man teaching her not to ask for more crumbs
than he wanted to give, Harriet would pay. Her father had paid for not step-
ping out of the way of a white lady on Tennessee Avenue. Her husband, Monty,
paid when he stepped up. Elwood's father, Percy, got too many ideas when he
joined the army so that when he came back there was no room in Tallahassee
for everything in his head" (33–34). In language reminiscent of Troy Maxson
lecturing his son in August Wilson's play, *Fences,* Harriet tries to use a sense
of obligation to spare Elwood the pain that racism inflicted upon her: "Hard
work was a fundamental virtue, for hard work didn't allow time for marches or
sit-ins. . . . Duty might protect him, as it had protected her" (34). Elwood dis-
obeys his grandmother and participates in a protest against a segregated movie
theatre, experiencing a fleeting elation much like Mabel's flash of freedom in
the swamp: "At the demonstration, he had felt somehow *closer* to himself. For a
moment. Out there in the sun. It was enough to feed his dreams." (37, italics in
original). Despite his grandmother's disapproval, Elwood devours the copy of
James Baldwin's *Notes of a Native Son* that Mr. Hill gives him, writes a soar-
ing (if also naïve) pseudonymous letter to the *Chicago Defender,* and dreams of
going off to college to "[f]ind his place in the busy line of young dreamers who
dedicated themselves to Negro uplift" (37).

Elwood's life seems to be following this plan when Mr. Hill apprises him
of an opportunity to take preparatory courses at a nearby historically Black
college. While hitchhiking to this school, though, Elwood is picked up by a
stranger who turns out to be driving a stolen car. After the man gets pulled over,
Elwood is charged as an accessory to the theft and is sentenced to a term at the
Nickel Academy; that Whitehead does not depict Elwood's trial implies that
his obvious innocence is irrelevant to the prejudicial system. Elwood initially
intends to endure his sentence by doing what he is told, but it soon becomes
clear that the institution's rules are both skewed against its Black students and
capriciously enforced by the staff. Elwood befriends several fellow students,
most notably a somewhat jaded youth named Turner. He also meets a boy
named Jaimie whose indeterminate ethnic background confounds the school's
racial segregation:

> He bounced around Nickel a lot—his mother was Mexican, so they didn't
> know what to do with him. On his arrival, he was put in with the white kids,
> but his first day working in the lime fields he got so dark that Spencer had
> him reassigned to the colored half. Jaimie spent a month in Cleveland, but

then Director Hardee toured one day, took a look at that light face among the dark faces, and had him sent back to the white camp. Spencer bided his time and tossed him back a few weeks later. "I go back and forth . . . One day they'll make up their minds, I suppose." (61)

Though darkly comical in the moment, this scene also exposes the insubstantial and arbitrary construction of race. Jaimie's racial classification is, of course, massively significant in Jim Crow Florida, but he seemingly cannot shape the decision.

Elwood's earnest request to continue his education provokes both other students and several of the school's administrators, particularly its director, Hardee, and a superintendent named Spencer. In a callback to Cora's protection of a young slave from Terrance Randall's fury, Elwood intervenes as two older students bully a younger one. Rather than being praised for peacemaking, he is beaten alongside the victim and the tormentors. Their punishment takes place in a terrifying outbuilding whose brutality is euphemized differently according to race: "The white boys bruised differently than the black boys and called it the Ice Cream Factory because you came out with bruises of every color. The black boys called it the White House because that was its official name and it fit and didn't need to be embellished. The White House delivered the law and everybody obeyed" (66). This latter name's symbolic linkage of local and national power intimates that their shared purpose is not law enforcement but rather force enlawment; might makes right in both White Houses.

While Elwood recovers in the school's infirmary, he hears the theme to *The Andy Griffith Show* on the radio, leading the narrator to assert that "[t]he song was a tiny, quiet piece of America carved out of the rest. No fire hoses, no need for the National Guard. It occurred to Elwood that he'd never seen a Negro in the small town of Mayberry, where the show took place" (80). The contrast between this iconic pop-culture fragment and Elwood's reality is even more jarring than that separating *The Cosby Show* from the Coopers' lives in *Sag Harbor*. Elwood's mood is similarly dissonant as he wavers between remaining acquiescent and exposing the school's injustices to external authorities: "Elwood told Turner about his grandmother and the lawyer, Mr. Andrews. They'd report Spencer and Earl and anybody else up to no good. . . . Mr. Hill knew people who'd want to know about a place like Nickel, once they got ahold of him. 'It's not like the old days . . . We can stand up for ourselves'" (82). Turner mocks his idealism, arguing that avoidance is the only means of survival: "[Y]ou got to see how people act, and then you got to figure out how to get around them like an obstacle course" (82). The middle portion of the novel essentially becomes a debate between Elwood's optimism and Turner's resignation: "You can change the law but you can't change people and how they treat each other. Nickel was racist as hell . . . but the way Turner saw it, wickedness went deeper than skin color. It was Spencer. It was Spencer and it was Griff and it was all the parents who let their children wind up here. It was people" (105).

Elwood and Turner are eventually chosen for a bogus "Community Service" detail that involves helping a school employee resell supplies stolen from the school's pantry and doing unpaid odd jobs such as painting and yard work for prominent White residents of the nearby town of Eleanor. The boys also witness a boxing match between the respective champions of the Black and White campuses of the school. Strongly reminiscent of the "Battle Royal" section of Ellison's *Invisible Man,* this event is largely a gladiatorial spectacle designed to extract illicit gambling income for the school's administrators from a crowd of White visitors. When Griff, the Black students' champion, fails to throw the fight as instructed by Hardee, his murder reiterates the penalties for contradicting White authority. Moreover, the other boys' memorialization of him evokes both Ajarry's "fantasies" and the slaves' speculations about Mabel's fate in *The Underground Railroad:* "He was all of them in one black body that night in the ring, and all of them when the white men took him out back to those two iron rings. . . . The story spread that he was too proud to take a dive. That he refused to kneel. And if it made the boys feel better to believe that Griff escaped, broke away and ran off into the free world, no one told them otherwise, although some noted that it was odd the school never sounded the alarm or sent out the dogs." (114).

These episodes—and others—make the school's depravity unmistakable to Elwood, who nevertheless still believes that it can be transformed by an appeal for justice to a higher authority. At the same time, he begins questioning whether he can answer Dr. King's entreaty to his followers to "cultivate that pure love for their oppressors. . . . The beatings, the rapes, the unrelenting winnowing of themselves. They endured. But to love those who would have destroyed them? To make that leap? Elwood shook his head. What a thing to ask. What an impossible thing" (172–73). After Turner grudgingly helps Elwood pass a letter documenting the school's corruption and abuse to a visiting inspector, Elwood is beaten and then placed into a lengthy solitary confinement. The psychological strain of the latter destroys his last shred of belief in reformative resistance: "He thought long on Dr. Martin Luther King Jr.'s letter from the Birmingham jail, and the powerful appeal the man composed from inside. . . . Elwood had no paper, no pen, just walls, and he was all out of fine thoughts, let alone the wisdom and the way with words. . . . No, he could not make that leap to love. He understood neither the impulse of the proposition nor the will to execute it" (195). These disavowals directly contradict Gaylord's interpretation of the novel while also foretelling the "terrible and heartbreaking" additional meaning at which Grady hints.

Like Caesar in *The Underground Railroad*, Turner proposes an escape, and Elwood agrees readily. The boys sneak out of their dormitory and are bicycling toward Tallahassee when they are spotted by armed officials of the school. Both the circumstances and Whitehead's use of language during this escape allude again to his earlier works: "Turner zagged and put his head down as if he could duck buckshot. *Can't catch me, I'm the Gingerbread Man.* He looked back again as Harper pulled the trigger" (201). Turner's recollection of this folktale harks back to an earlier episode. Turner finds a card with the Gingerbread Man on it as he helps decorate the school for its Christmas Fair, which is "the pride of the administration, a fund-raising bounty that proved reform was no mere lofty notion but a workable proposition." Turner smiles as he "remember[s] the folk hero's rallying cry: 'You can't catch me, you can't catch me.' A good way to be. He didn't remember how the story ended" (118). Most versions of the tale end with the Gingerbread Man being eaten by the fox who pursues him, an outcome that mirrors Elwood's demise. However, Turner's incomplete memory of it allows him to derive idiosyncratic inspiration from an otherwise tragic story, much as Whitehead repurposed John Henry's legend for his own ends.

Turner's eventual assumption of Elwood's identity seems intended both as a strategy for evading capture and as a means for extending Elwood's life beyond the moment in which Elwood's "arms went wide, hands out, as if testing the solidity of the walls of a long corridor, one he had traveled through for a long time and which possessed no visible terminus. He stumbled forward two steps and fell into the grass" (201). The strong echo of Cora's final moments in the tunnel leading away from Indiana—"Her fingers danced over valleys, rivers, the peaks of mountains, the contours of a new nation hidden beneath the old. . . . She'd find the terminus or die on the tracks" (Whitehead, *Underground* 304)—and the repetition of the uncommon word "terminus" in describing an as-yet undiscovered endpoint both suggest that Elwood's physical death also represents a moment of indeterminate narrative rebirth for both boys. Like Cora, "Turner kept running" (201), in part by figuring out a new story to tell about himself that still allows him "to honor his friend. To live for [Elwood]" (202).

In addition to continuing where the prologue left off, the epilogue completes a narrative thread that only begins late in the book. Whereas the first ten chapters follow the 1960s timeline in linear fashion, the final six alternate between what appear to be significant moments from Elwood's post-Nickel life in New York and the resolution of the earlier timeline. Importantly, the narrator refers to the central character of these post-Nickel chapters exclusively through pronouns; he is specifically identified as Elwood only twice, once in dialogue by another character (Whitehead, *Nickel* 135) and once on a business card (167). Chapter Eleven depicts him newly residing in the city during the infamous 1968 sanitation workers' strike. Chapter Thirteen is set in 1988, and the man now owns his own moving company, fulfilling a goal he had expressed in Chapter Eleven. Most of this chapter deals with his accidental—and unwanted—encounter with a fellow "Nickel Boy" named Chickie Pete. He does not contradict Pete's recollection that Elwood was released in 1964, but he also laments that he has not become a "Nickel legend" like Griff: "The students passing his story around as if he were a folk hero, a Stagger Lee figure scaled down to teenage size. But it hadn't happened. Chickie Pete didn't even recall how he got out. If he wanted to be remembered, he should have carved his name into a pew like everyone else" (165). His comment reaffirms the trouble that Nickel Boys' stories have in finding an audience, apparently even among themselves. Tangential details such as the "petition against that new mosque opening up" (185) situate Chapter Fifteen in 2010, as the man reflects on his winding path to both professional success and marriage. Each of these three chapters solidifies the impression—established in the prologue—that Elwood has survived. Therefore, the depiction of his death in Chapter Sixteen purposefully robs the reader of a previously foundational interpretive presumption just a few pages before the end of the book. Like Turner fleeing from his pursuers in 1964, the reader must adapt on the fly to a radically different story.

The epilogue begins as the man prepares for his return to Florida as foretold in the prologue. He is explicitly identified by the narrator as Turner while using Elwood's name to check in for his flight (202). He has been calling himself Elwood since "two weeks out of Nickel," when it was the "[f]irst thing that popped into his head" upon being asked his name at a diner (202). Turner eventually forges official documents that legalize this deception. Although Elwood's identity has been Turner's for fifty years at that point, he still seems unsure about this strategy's results: "It was not enough to survive, you have to live—he heard Elwood's voice as he walked down Broadway in the sunlight or at the end of a long night hunched over the books. . . . In Elwood's name, he tried to find another way. Now here he was. Where had it taken him?" (204–5). His adult life has been a necessary "counterfeit," as Kevin Young would put it, but Turner still doubts whether it has told—or can yet tell—a useful alternate "troof" (Young 27).

As he waits for his plane to depart, Turner thinks back to the night before, when he revealed his true identity to his wife, Millie. Though understandably shocked—like the reader—Millie nevertheless accepts his explanation: "His name didn't matter. The lie was big but she understood it, given how the world had crumpled him up, the more she took in his story. To come out of that place and make something of himself, to become a man capable of loving her the way he did, to become the man she loved—his deception was nothing compared to what he had done with his life." She asks him for his actual first name, learning it at the same time as the reader: "'I'll try it on,' she said. 'Jack, Jack, Jack.' It sounded okay to him. More true each time it came out of her mouth" (Whitehead, *Nickel* 206). Millie further fosters truth-telling by supporting his plans for Florida: "He'll find Elwood's grave and tell his friend of his life after he was cut down in that pasture. How that moment grew in Turner and changed his life's course. Tell the sheriff who he was, share Elwood's story and what they did to him when he tried to put a stop to their crimes. Tell the White House boys that he was one of them, and he survived, like them. Tell anyone who cared that he used to live there" (209). The book ends with Turner in his Tallahassee hotel on the night before the press conference at which he intends to answer his own internalized call: "Who spoke for the black boys? It was time someone did" (209).

Several of Whitehead's narrative choices in these final two pages convey his suspicions that the nation is—like Martin and Ethel when confronted by Cora in *The Underground Railroad*—unwilling or unable to respond meaningfully to the reality of racialized injustice. It is perhaps worth remembering that his novel is set in the same state in which Trayvon Martin was killed in 2012 and was being written while professional athletes protesting anti-Black police violence by kneeling during the national anthem were openly denigrated as "sons of bitches" by the chief resident of the White House. Whitehead explicitly stated in a July 2020 interview that his idea for the novel germinated during the summer of 2014 "when Michael Brown was killed and Eric Garner was killed in Staten Island. The reason the story of Dozier stayed with me was because it was the summer of people getting away with murder, literally, and no one being held accountable, whether it's a security guard at Dozier or a policeman in Missouri. Six years later, obviously, those inequities remain" (Canfield).

Turner remembers that Elwood's "fine moral imperatives and his very fine ideas about the capacity of human beings to improve" were at best greeted with silence, including his own (207). Given that Turner's plans rely on similar faith that speaking truth to power matters, Whitehead offers the reader ample reasons to doubt that things have changed significantly. For starters, Turner recognizes "his own pitiable state" and is "revolted [by . . .]how scared he got seeing the name of the place and the pictures. . . . He'd been scared all the time. He was scared still" (208). Channeling Turner's anxiety, the narrator states that the school's closing means that "[i]t couldn't hurt them now, snatch them up at midnight and brutalize them. It could only hurt them in the old familiar ways" (209). Millie's sympathy with a trauma that is both suppressed and "familiar"—like the "stray-cat notch in his ear . . . [that Millie] never noticed but was right in front of her" (206)—explains her imperturbability in light of Turner's imposture. Like him, she suffers because "[t]hey treat us like subhumans in our own country. Always have. Maybe always will" (206). Turner worries with good reason that instead of being shamed by his testimony, the authorities will simply arrest him as a fugitive: "Was he a wanted man? Turner didn't know the law but he had never underestimated the crookedness of the system. Not then, not now" (209). None of these justifiable fears instill a sense that Turner's stories will stimulate restorative justice for himself, Elwood, and the other Nickel Boys.

Whitehead goes one step further in seeding these misgivings by having Turner stay in the same hotel in which Elwood worked as a dishwasher while it was off-limits to Black patrons. On a superficial level, the renovation of the old Richmond Hotel into the gleaming new Radisson might imply meaningful progress, symbolized most obviously by Turner's very presence there as a guest. On the other hand, the narrator's description of the refurbishment recalls two of Whitehead's earlier books in questioning the substance of advancement between 1964 and 2014:

> The dark modern windows and brown metal siding of the new parts clashed with the red brick of the bottom three stories, but it was better than demolishing the place and starting anew. . . . The chain had redone the dining room in contemporary hotel style, with a lot of wipeable green plastic. Three tilted television sets nattered the same cable news station at different angles, the news was bad and ever was, and a pop song from the '80s blipped from hidden speakers, an instrumental version with the synthesizers out front. Formerly the Richmond Hotel, it was a Tallahassee landmark and great care, they said, had gone into preserving the spirit of the grand old establishment. The shop by reception sold postcards. (210)

The final reference summons up the somewhat cynical mention in *The Colossus of New York* of selling postcards featuring the rebuilt Manhattan skyline after 9/11. The renovated architecture, décor, and soundscape of the restaurant all hint at an effort to "wipe" away the perpetually bad news blaring from the television screens, replacing it with a "synthesized" and uncomplicated nostalgia in a manner reminiscent of *Apex Hides the Hurt*.

The book's final two sentences imply that the Richmond's transformation has effaced the significance of its past even for a person whose life has been intricately bound up with it for a half-century: "If he had been less tired he might have recognized the name from a story he heard once when he was young, about a boy who liked to read adventure stories in the kitchen, but it eluded him. He was hungry and they served all day, and that was enough" (210). Just as the Richmond "made for a good foundation" (209) for the modern-day hotel built atop it, Turner's desire to emulate Elwood in order to "honor" his life and death seems contigent on fully recognizing Elwood's past, including his troubling formative experiences at the Richmond. Perhaps a good night's sleep will help Turner recover this knowledge, but Whitehead remains characteristically silent about any of the ramifications of Turner's inevitable return; the "terminus" of his story, too, remains invisible.

Conclusion

Whitehead's books help us see more clearly the sometimes crooked—and often artificially straightened—paths by which we have arrived at the present, but they also resist claiming to contain a blueprint for a better future. The conclusions of most of his books to date imply that positive change definitely requires more substantive engagement with our surroundings and reconsideration of how the voices of the past have shaped the present. Whitehead continually warns that neither of these offers an ironclad guarantee of betterment, even though they are preferable to the senseless, uncritical familiarity he endeavors to avoid in his writing.

It remains unclear at the end of *The Underground Railroad* whether Cora ever arrives in California or whether that journey will afford her any real freedom from the ostensible "destiny by divine prescription" (Whitehead, *Underground* 222) that Ridgeway embodies. Similarly, the ramifications of the revelation that Turner, not Elwood, escaped the Nickel Academy alive, are still unwritten. Although Turner believes that he "had been telling Elwood's story ever since his friend died, through years and years of revision, of getting it right, as he stopped being the desperate alley cat of his youth and turned into a man he thought Elwood would have been proud of" (204), Whitehead never confirms that such assertions are not simply a strategy for coping with the anxiety and guilt that Turner still feels fifty years later. Despite achieving some measure of escape, both Cora and Turner are still not far removed, respectively, from a "destiny" and a "story" deeply rooted in White supremacy and lethal violence.

Since *The Intuitionist,* Whitehead has left it to his readers to connect the historical dots. Like Oedipa Maas awaiting the start of the stamp auction at the conclusion of Pynchon's *The Crying of Lot 49,* Lila Mae, J. Sutter, the nomenclature consultant, Benjy Cooper, Mark Spitz, Cora, and Turner all sit perched on existential frontiers at the close of the novels in which they appear. Despite their travails and development, none of them possess concrete answers to the questions that loom over their respective futures. Whitehead indicated in a June 2020 interview that *The Nickel Boys* intentionally shifts in its final third from exposing the conjoined realities that "[t]he guilty escape punishment. The innocent suffer" to "all the other stuff that is not in those two lines: what do you do with that? How do you live with that knowledge? And, how do you make a life?" (O'Hagan). The nationwide upheaval in the wake of the killings of Ahmaud Arbery, Breonna Taylor, George Floyd, Rayshard Brooks, and numerous others in the late spring and summer of 2020 suggests that American society still urgently needs both parts of this difficult reckoning.

BIBLIOGRAPHY

Books by Colson Whitehead
Apex Hides the Hurt. Doubleday, 2006.
The Colossus of New York: A City in Thirteen Parts. Doubleday, 2003.
Harlem Shuffle. Doubleday, 2021 (announced).
The Intuitionist. Doubleday, 1999.
John Henry Days. Doubleday, 2001.
The Nickel Boys. New York: Doubleday, 2019.
The Noble Hustle: Poker, Beef Jerky, and Death. Doubleday, 2014.
Sag Harbor. Doubleday, 2009.
The Underground Railroad. Doubleday, 2016.
Zone One. Doubleday, 2011.

Uncollected Writings by Colson Whitehead
"Better Than Renting Out a Windowless Room: The Blessed Distraction of Technology."
   Publishers Weekly, 25 April 2011: 140.
"Don't You Be My Neighbor." *New York,* 3 May 2004, p. A33.
"Down in Front." *Granta,* 1 July 2004: 237–42.
"The End of the Affair." *New York Times Book Review,* 3 March 2002, p. 8.
"Finally, a Thin President." *New York Times,* 6 November 2008, p. 33.
"Flava of the Month." *New York,* 28 April 2008, pp. 68–70.
"The Gangsters." *New Yorker,* 22 December 2008: 90–103.
"The Great Reboot." *The Harper's Monthly* June 2009: 38–39.
"Hard Times in the Uncanny Valley." *Grantland,* 24 August 2012, www.grantland.com
   /story/_/id/8300060/colson-whitehead-olympics. Accessed 30 May 2013.
"How to Write." *New York Times Book Review,* 29 July 2012: p. 8.
"I Scream." *New York Times Magazine* 16 July 2006: 57–58.
"I Worked at an Ill-Conceived Internet Start-Up and All I Got Was This Lousy Idea for
   a Novel." *Bold Type* vol. 5, no. 1 (May 2001), web.archive.org/web/20140618041521
   /www.randomhouse.com/boldtype/0501/whitehead/essay.html. Accessed 13 Oct. 2020.
"I Write in Brooklyn. Get Over It." *New York Times Book Review,* 2 March 2008: p. 31.
"Lost and Found." *New York Times Magazine* 11 November 2001: 23–25.
"Occasional Dispatches from the Republic of Anhedonia." *Grantland,* 10 July 2011, www
   .grantland.com/story/_/id/6754551/. Accessed 30 May 2013.
"Picking a Genre." *New York Times Book Review,* 1 November 2009: p. 23.

"A Psychotronic Childhood." *New Yorker* 4 June 2012: 98–105.

"Swept Away." *New York Times Magazine* 3 November 2002: 15–16.

"Visible Man." *New York Times,* 24 April 2008: p. A25.

"When Zombies Attack!" (With Alex Pappademas). *Grantland,* 7 October 2011, www
.grantland.com/story/_/id/7113150/when-zombies-attack. Accessed 30 May 2013.

"Wow, Fiction Works!" *Harper's* February 09: 29–31.

"The Year of Living Postracially." *New York Times,* 4 November 2009: p. A31.

Secondary Sources

Ardoin, Paul. "'Have You to This Point Assumed That I Am White?': Narrative Withholding since *Playing in the Dark.*" *MELUS: Multi-Ethnic Literature of the United
States* vol. 44, no. 1, 2019, pp. 160–180.

Arjini, Nawal. "Colson Whitehead Opens Up." *The Nation,* 19 July 2019, www.the
nation.com/article/archive/colson-whitehead-interview-nickel-boys-novel/.

Ashe, Bertram D. "Theorizing the Post-Soul Aesthetic: An Introduction." *African
American Review* vol. 41, no. 4, 2007, pp. 609–23.

"At O'Hare, President Says 'Get On Board.'" *George W. Bush White House Archives*
27 September 2001. georgewbush-whitehouse.archives.gov/news/releases/2001/09
/20010927–1.html. Accessed 11 July 2020.

Austerlitz, Saul. "Identity Crisis." Review of *Apex Hides the Hurt,* by Colson Whitehead. *Boston Globe,* 19 March 2006, www.boston.com/ae/books/articles/2006/03/19
/identity_crisis/.

Beck, Stefan. "Caveat Emptor." *New Criterion* vol. 27, no. 9, 2009, pp. 33–38.

Bell, Bernard W. *The Afro-American Novel and Its Tradition.* University of Massachusetts Press, 1987.

Berlant, Lauren. "Intuitionists: History and the Affective Event." *American Literary
History* vol. 20, no. 4, 2008, pp. 845–60.

Bernstein, Sanders I. "Colson Whitehead '91: One of Harvard's Recent Authors Keeps
It Real." *Harvard Crimson,* 16 April 2009, www.thecrimson.com/article/2009/4/16
/colson-whitehead-91-the-work-of/.

Bérubé, Michael. "Race and Modernity in Colson Whitehead's *The Intuitionist.*" *The
Holodeck in the Garden: Science and Technology in Contemporary American Fiction,*
edited by Peter Freese and Charles B. Harris. Harris, Dalkey Archive Press, 2004, pp.
163–78.

Butler, Robert. "The Postmodern City in Colson Whitehead's *The Colossus of New
York* and Jeffrey Renard Allen's *Rails under My Back.*" *CLA Journal* vol. 48, no. 1,
2004, pp. 71–87.

Canfield, David. "Colson Whitehead is now the most decorated writer of his generation.
He's not slowing down." *Entertainment Weekly,* 15 July 2020, ew.com/books/author
-interviews/colson-whitehead-nickel-boys-pulitzer-prize-quarantine/.

Chamberlin, Jeremiah. "Who We Are Now: A Conversation with Colson Whitehead."
Fiction Writers Review, 30 May 2009. Rept. in *Conversations with Colson Whitehead,*
edited by Derek C. Maus, University Press of Mississippi, 2019, pp. 56–62.

Chandler, Daniel. *Semiotics: The Basics,* 2nd ed. Routledge, 2007.

Cohn, Jesse S. "Old Afflictions: Colson Whitehead's *Apex Hides the Hurt* and the 'Post-
Soul Condition.'" *Journal of the Midwest Modern Language Association* vol. 42,
no. 1, 2009, pp. 15–24.

Cryer, Dan. Review of *The Underground Railroad*, by Colson Whitehead. *San Francisco Chronicle* 18 August 2016. Accessed 11 July 2020. www.sfchronicle.com/books/ article /The-Underground-Railroad-by-Colson-9171269.php.

de Caro, Frank. "'Authentic Local Culture': *John Henry Days* and the Open Textuality of a Folk Tradition." *Folklore Historian* vol. 23, 2006, pp. 3–18.

Dickson-Carr, Darryl. *African American Satire: The Sacredly Profane Novel*. University of Missouri Press, 2001.

Dubey, Madhu. "Museumizing Slavery: Living History in Colson Whitehead's *The Underground Railroad*." *American Literary History* vol. 32, no. 1, 2020, pp. 111–139.

———. *Signs and Cities: Black Literary Postmodernism*. University of Chicago Press, 2007.

Du Bois, W. E. B. "The Talented Tenth." *The Social Theory of W. E. B. Du Bois*, edited by Phil Zuckerman, Sage, 2004, pp. 185–95.

"Eavesdropping: Conversation with Walter Mosley and Colson Whitehead." *Book*, 2001, pp. 44–46. Rept. in *Conversations with Colson Whitehead*, edited by Derek C. Maus, University Press of Mississippi, 2019, pp. 3–11.

Eco, Umberto. *A Theory of Semiotics*. Indiana University Press, 1976.

Elam, Harry J., Jr. "Change Clothes and Go: A Postscript to Postblackness." *Black Cultural Traffic: Crossroads in Global Performance and Popular Culture*, edited by Harry J. Elam Jr. and Kennell Jackson, University of Michigan Press, 2005, pp. 379–89.

Elam, Michele. "Passing in the Post-Race Era: Danzy Senna, Philip Roth, and Colson Whitehead." *African American Review* vol. 41, no. 4, 2007, pp. 749–68.

Ellis, Trey. "The New Black Aesthetic." *Callaloo* vol. 12, no. 1, 1989, pp. 233–43.

Ellison, Ralph. *Invisible Man*. Random House, 1952.

Farooq, Nihad M. "'A Useful Delusion': Valentine Farm and the Flight for Freedom." *Utopian Studies* vol. 30, no. 1, 2019, pp. 87–110.

Fassler, Joe. "Colson Whitehead on Zombies, 'Zone One,' and His Love of the VCR." *Atlantic* 18 October 2011, www.theatlantic.com/entertainment/archive/2011/10/colson -whitehead-on-zombies-zone-one-and-his-love-of-the-vcr/246855/.

Franzen, Jonathan. "Freeloading Man." Review of *John Henry Days*, by Colson Whitehead. *New York Times Book Review*, 13 May 2001: pp. 8–9.

Garner, Dwight. "A Poker-Faced Nihilist, Stoically Slumming." Review of *The Noble Hustle*, by Colson Whitehead. *New York Times*, 9 May 2014: p. C23.

Garunay, Melanie. "The President's Summer Reading List." *Obama White House Archives*, 12 August 2016. obamawhitehouse.archives.gov/blog/ 2016/08/12/presidents -summer-reading-list. Accessed 11 July 2020.

Gates, David. "You Are Now Entering ———." Review of *Apex Hides the Hurt*, by Colson Whitehead. *New York Times Book Review*, 2 April 2006: p. 12.

Gaylord, Joan. "'The Nickel Boys' reckons with a legacy of racism and abuse." *Christian Science Monitor* 16 July 2019, https://www.csmonitor.com/Books/Book-Reviews /2019/0716/The-Nickel-Boys-reckons-with-a-legacy-of-racism-and-abuse. Accessed 11 July 2020.

George, Nelson. *Buppies, B-Boys, Baps and Bohos: Notes on Post-Soul Black Culture*. HarperCollins, 1992.

Goble, Corban. "Colson Whitehead Interview." *Epilogue* 6 June 2009. Rept. in *Conversations with Colson Whitehead*, edited by Derek C. Maus, University Press of Mississippi, 2019, pp. 63–66.

Goyal, Yogita. *Runaway Genres: Global Afterlives of Slavery.* New York University Press, 2019.

Grady, Constance. Review of *The Nickel Boys,* by Colson Whitehead. *Vox* 18 July 2019, www.vox.com/culture/2019/7/18/20696706/nickel-boys-colson-whitehead-review. Accessed 11 July 2020.

Grausam, Daniel. "After the Post(al)." *American Literary History* vol. 23, no. 3, 2011, pp. 625–42.

Harrison, Stephenie. "Colson Whitehead: Oprah, American History, and the Power of a Female Protagonist." *BookPage* 12 August 2016. bookpage.com/interviews/20269 -colson-whitehead-fiction#.Xwnp8JNKhos. Rept. in *Conversations with Colson Whitehead,* edited by Derek C. Maus, University Press of Mississippi, 2019, pp. 108–15.

Hoberek, Andrew. "Living with PASD." Review of *Zone One,* by Colson Whitehead. *Contemporary Literature* vol. 53, no. 2, 2012, pp. 406–13.

Hodge, Daniel White. *The Soul of Hip Hop: Rims, Timbs and a Cultural Theology.* InterVarsity Press, 2010.

Holt, Elliott. "The Rumpus Original Combo: Colson Whitehead." *Rumpus* 17 July 2012. therumpus.net/2012/07/the-rumpus-interview-with-colson-whitehead/. Accessed 4 July 2013.

Howe, Nicholas. "Bi-coastal Myths." Review of *The Colossus of New York,* by Colson Whitehead. *Dissent* vol. 51, no. 2, 2004, pp. 86–90.

Hutcheon, Linda. *A Poetics of Postmodernism: History, Theory, Function.* Routledge, 1988.

Inscoe, John C. "Race and Remembrance in West Virginia: John Henry for a Post-Modern Age." *Journal of Appalachian Studies* vol. 10, no. 1/2, 2004, pp. 85–94.

Jablon, Madelyn. *Black Metafiction: Self-Consciousness in African American Literature.* University of Iowa Press, 1997.

Jackson, Mitchell S. "Author Colson Whitehead Reminds Us to See Ourselves." *TIME,* 8 July 2019, pp. 46–51.

Kachka, Boris. "Off the Shelf: Colson Whitehead." *New York* 27 March 2006. nymag .com/arts/books/features/16457/. Accessed 4 July 2013.

Katz, Tamar. "City Memory, City History: Urban Nostalgia, *The Colossus of New York,* and Late-Twentieth-Century Historical Fiction." *Contemporary Literature* vol. 51, no. 4, 2010, pp. 810–51.

Keizer, Arlene R. *Black Subjects: Identity Formation in the Contemporary Narrative of Slavery.* Cornell University Press, 2004.

Kirkus Reviews. Review of *Apex Hides the Hurt,* by Colson Whitehead. *Kirkus Reviews* 1 January 2006, pp. 15–16.

Lanzendörfer, Tim. *Books of the Dead: Reading the Zombie in Contemporary Literature.* University Press of Mississippi, 2018.

Larkin, Lesley. *Race and the Literary Encounter: Black Literature from James Weldon Johnson to Percival Everett.* Indiana University Press, 2015.

Lavender, Isiah, III. "Ethnoscapes: Environment and Language in Ishmael Reed's *Mumbo Jumbo,* Colson Whitehead's *The Intuitionist,* and Samuel R. Delany's *Babel-17.*" *Science Fiction Studies* vol. 34, no. 102, 2007, pp. 187–200.

Levine, Andrea. "'In His Own Home': Gendering the African American Domestic Sphere in Contemporary Culture." *WSQ: Women's Studies Quarterly* vol. 39, no. 1/2, 2011, pp. 170–87.

Li, Stephanie. "Genre Trouble and History's Miseries in Colson Whitehead's *The Underground Railroad*." *MELUS: Multi-Ethnic Literature of the U.S.* vol. 44, no. 2, 2019, pp. 1–23.

———. *Signifying without Specifying: Racial Discourse in the Age of Obama*. Rutgers University Press, 2011.

———. "'Sometimes Things Disappear': Absence and Mutability in Colson Whitehead's *The Colossus of New York*." *Literature after 9/11*, edited by Ann Keniston and Jeanne Follansbee Quinn, Routledge, 2008, pp. 82–98.

Liggins, Saundra. "The Urban Gothic Vision of Colson Whitehead's *The Intuitionist*." *African American Review* vol. 40, no. 2, 2006, pp. 359–69.

Lopate, Phillip. "New York State of Mind." Review of *The Colossus of New York,* by Colson Whitehead. *Nation* 1 December 2003. www.thenation.com/article/new-york -state-mind#axzz2XYxoGPJl. Accessed 4 July 2013.

Lukin, Josh. "The Resistant Body: Disability, History, and Classical Heroism in Colson Whitehead's *Apex Hides the Hurt*." *Engaging Tradition, Making It New: Essays on Teaching Recent African American Literature,* edited by Stephanie Brown and Eva Tettenborn, Cambridge Scholars, 2008, pp. 123–42.

Madrigal, Alexis. "Bookforum Talks with Colson Whitehead." *Bookforum* 17 October 2011, www.bookforum.com/index.php?pn=interview&id=8491.

Maslin, Janet. "Black Teenage Memories, Under the Hamptons Sun." Review of *Sag Harbor,* by Colson Whitehead. *New York Times,* 27 April 2009: p. C1.

Maus, Derek C., ed. *Conversations with Colson Whitehead*. University Press of Mississippi, 2019.

Mazurek, Raymond A. "Metafiction, the Historical Novel, and Coover's *The Public Burning*." *Critique* vol. 23, no. 2, 1982, pp. 29–42.

Mendelson, Edward. "Encyclopedic Narrative: From Dante to Pynchon." *Modern Language Notes* vol. 91, 1976, pp. 1267–75.

Mochama, Vicky. "'If You Don't Have Hope, Then Why Go On?': An Interview with Colson Whitehead." *Hazlitt* 12 September 2016. hazlitt.net/feature/if-you-dont-have -hope-then-why-go-interview-colson-whitehead. Rept. in *Conversations with Colson Whitehead,* edited by Derek C. Maus, University Press of Mississippi, 2019, pp. 142–47.

Naimon, David. "Q & A: Colson Whitehead." *Tin House* 12 September 2012, tinhouse .com/q-and-a-colson-whitehead/. Accessed 11 July 2020.

Neal, Mark Anthony. *Soul Babies: Black Popular Culture and the Post-Soul Aesthetic*. Routledge, 2002.

Nordlinger, Jay. "Freedom Trails." Review of *The Underground Railroad,* by Colson Whitehead. *National Review* 10 October 2016, pp. 38–39.

"Obituaries March 19, 2009." *Sag Harbor Express,* 20 March 2009, sagharboronline .com/sagharborexpress/obituaries/obituaries-march-19-2009-2541. Accessed 4 July 2013.

O'Hagan, Sean. "Colson Whitehead: 'We invent all sorts of different reasons to hate people.'" *The Guardian,* 21 June 2020, www.theguardian.com/books/2020/jun/21 /colson-whitehead-we-invent-all-sorts-of-different-reasons-to-hate-people.

Porter, Evette. "Writing Home." *Black Issues Book Review* vol. 4, no. 3, 2002, pp. 36–37. Rept. in *Conversations with Colson Whitehead,* edited by Derek C. Maus, University Press of Mississippi, 2019, pp. 25–27.

"Post Office to Unveil Colson Whitehead Stamp." *PowellsBooks.Blog* 10 October 2006. Rept. in *Conversations with Colson Whitehead,* edited by Derek C. Maus, University Press of Mississippi, 2019, pp. 34–43.

Publishers Weekly. Review of *Apex Hides the Hurt,* by Colson Whitehead. *Publishers Weekly* 30 January 2006. www.publishersweekly.com/978-0-385-50795-0. Accessed 4 July 2013.

Rambsy, Howard. *Bad Men: Creative Touchstones of Black Writers.* University of Virginia Press, 2020.

———. "Four Contemporary Black Male Writers & Their Fathers." *Cultural Front* (personal blog) 20 May 2011. www.culturalfront.org/2011/05/four-contemporary -black-male-writers.html. Accessed 13 May 2020.

Ramsey, William. "An End of Southern History: The Down-Home Quests of Toni Morrison and Colson Whitehead." *African American Review* vol. 41, no. 4, 2007, pp. 769–85.

Rose, Margaret A. *Parody: Ancient, Modern, and Post-modern.* Cambridge University Press, 1993.

Rushdy, Ashraf H. A. "The Neo-slave narrative." *The Cambridge Companion to the African American Novel,* edited by Maryemma Graham, Cambridge University Press, 2004, pp. 87–105.

———. *Neo-slave Narratives: Studies in the Social Logic of a Literary Form.* Oxford University Press, 1999.

Russell, Allison. "Recalibrating the Past: Colson Whitehead's *The Intuitionist.*" *Critique* vol. 49, no. 1, 2007, pp. 46–60.

Saldívar, Ramón. "The Second Elevation of the Novel: Race, Form, and the Postrace Aesthetic in Contemporary Narrative." *Narrative* vol. 21, no. 1, 2013, pp. 1–18.

Schulman, Martha. "PW Talks with Colson Whitehead: My Horrible '70s Apocalypse." *Publishers Weekly* 18 July 2011, p. 131.

Seaman, Donna. Review of *The Intuitionist,* by Colson Whitehead. *Booklist* 1 December 1998, p. 651.

Selzer, Linda. "Instruments More Perfect than Bodies: Romancing Uplift in Colson Whitehead's *The Intuitionist.*" *African American Review* vol. 43, no. 4, 2009, pp. 681–98.

———. "New Eclecticism: An Interview with Colson Whitehead." *Callaloo* vol. 31, no. 2, 2008, pp. 393–401.

Shapiro, Anna. "Whitehead Does Nomenclature—A Cool, Zero-Affect Satire." *New York Observer,* 27 March 2006, observer.com/2006/03/whitehead-does-nomenclature -a-cool-zeroaffect-satire-2/. Accessed 11 July 2020.

Sherman, Suzan. "Colson Whitehead." *BOMB* vol. 76, 2001. Rept. in *Conversations with Colson Whitehead,* edited by Derek C. Maus, University Press of Mississippi, 2019, pp. 12–24.

Shukla, Nikesh. "Colson Whitehead: Each Book an Antidote." *Guernica* 24 April 2013. Rept. in *Conversations with Colson Whitehead,* edited by Derek C. Maus, University Press of Mississippi, 2019, pp. 98–103.

Sky, Jennifer. "Colson Whitehead's Brains." *Interview,* 28 October 2011, www.interview magazine.com/culture/colson-whitehead-zone-one.

Spaulding, Timothy A. *Re-forming the Past: History, the Fantastic, and the Postmodern Slave Narrative.* Ohio State University Press, 2005.

Steinberg, Sybil. Review of *The Intuitionist*, by Colson Whitehead. *Publishers Weekly*, 16 November 1998, p. 56.

Taylor, Paul C. "Post Black, Old Black." *African American Review* vol. 41, no. 4, 2007, pp. 625–40.

Tillet, Salamishah. *Sites of Slavery: Citizenship and Racial Democracy in the Post-Civil Rights Imagination*. Duke University Press, 2012.

Touré. "Visible Young Man." Review of *Sag Harbor*, by Colson Whitehead. *New York Times Book Review*, 3 May 2009: p. 1.

Treisman, Deborah. "Fiction Q. and A.: Colson Whitehead" *New Yorker* 15 December 2008, www.newyorker.com/online/blogs/tny/2008/12/q-a-colson-whitehead.html. Accessed 11 July 2020.

Tucker, Jeffrey Allen. "'Verticality Is Such a Risky Enterprise': The Literary and Paraliterary Antecedents of Colson Whitehead's *The Intuitionist*." *Novel: A Forum on Fiction* vol. 43, no. 1, 2010, pp. 148–56.

Weisenburger, Steven. *Fables of Subversion: Satire and the American Novel, 1930–1980*. University of Georgia Press, 1995.

Wixon, Christopher. "Vertical Bearings: Dashiell Hammett's *The Maltese Falcon* and Colson Whitehead's *The Intuitionist*." *Notes on Contemporary Literature* vol. 42, no. 3, 2012, n.p.

Wood, James. "Virtual Prose." Review of John Henry Days, by Colson Whitehead. *New Republic* 6 August 2001, p. 30.

Young, Kevin. *The Grey Album: On the Blackness of Blackness*. Graywolf, 2012.

Zalewski, Daniel. "Tunnel Vision: An Interview with Colson Whitehead." *New York Times Book Review*, 13 May 2001: p. 8, p. 15.

INDEX